The Ice Maiden Cometh Not

The 9th Gil Yates
Private Investigator Novel

Alistair Boyle

ALLEN A. KNOLL, PUBLISHERS
Santa Barbara, CA

Allen A. Knoll, Publishers, 200 West Victoria Street,
Santa Barbara, CA 93101-3627
© 2012 by Allen A. Knoll, Publishers
All rights reserved. Published in 2012
Printed in the United States of America

First Edition

17 16 15 14 13 12   5 4 3 2 1

Library of Congress Cataloging-in-Publication Data

Boyle, Alistair.
The ice maiden cometh not : the 9th Gil Yates private investigator novel / Alistair Bc
-- 1st ed.
    p. cm.
ISBN 978-1-888310-09-2
1.   Yates, Gil (Fictitious character)--Fiction. 2.   Murder--Investigation--Fiction
Mystery fiction. I. Title.
PS3552.O917I27 2012
813'.54--dc23

2012033637

Also by Alistair Boyle

They Fall Hard
The Unholy Ghost
What Now, King Lear?
Ship Shapely
Bluebeard's Last Stand
The Unlucky Seven
The Con
The Missing Link

text typeface is ITC Galliard, 12 point
printed and bound by Sheridan Books, Michigan

Good can take care of itself. Evil is the problem.

—*William Golding*

The Iceman Cometh

—*Eugene O'Neill*

The Ice Maiden Cometh Not

—*Alistair Boyle*

1

Handsome? You haven't seen handsome until you've seen the Kulps of Muhlenheim, Pennsylvania: father, mother, and daughter.

His greeting should have been a tip-off. He left his message on my voicemail. I didn't have any telephone or answering machine in my "office"—a three and a half inch space between two sheets of drywall and a mail slot. There was also a dummy door that went nowhere—the other side of the wall being someone else's office. In case anyone happened by, or worse, came looking for me, they could see my name on the door:

GIL YATES

PRIVATE INVESTIGATOR

"Gil, this is Dr. Kulp. Give me a call at _____."

Well, peaches and milk, he's "doctor" and I'm plain old "Gil." No "please" or "*would* you call me"— more an imperial command.

When I heard the voice, I realized one of the main reasons why I hadn't taken a case in eight years: some clients can be a pain where it can't be reached. I had made a lot of money, which coupled with the pittance I got from my father-in-law, that world-class gasbag, Elbert Wemple, saw me through those winters.

Funny, he had gotten into his forehead where his brain was supposed to be, that I was silver-bricking with some other livelihood that rendered him second fiddle— a position in the orchestra he was constitutionally unable to stomach. He would never settle for less than being the big baloney—or one of those food items—I was never big on clichés.

What did I do in those eight years? You may well ask—or not as the case may very well be. I watched my cycads grow a couple inches (they do about seven feet a century, so eight years worth). Little less than seven inches may not seem that big a deal to you land lubbers, but those cycad afficionados among us know that's almost enough to get lathered up about.

Since my operation is decidedly low key word-of-mouth sort, I was bound to have spells of dryness among my most active years. My most satisfied mouths were either staying shut or not opening to anyone who needed my services as an extravagantly expensive, highly effective, very private detective.

For, popular opinion to the contrary, everyone wasn't possessed of illegal tendencies or the subject of predation.

There are some things in life we are better off facing. One is that eight years of an undiverted life with the glass blower and the gasbag strained my sanity. I was ready to go back to work. Itching you might say, or I might never have returned the "Doctor's" phone call.

Under these circumstances I figured I didn't have anything to lose. I could always hang up if he got unbearable. The trick to that was to break the connection while *I* was speaking, so he would think it was an accident, then leave the phone off the hook so he couldn't call back.

Though some may call me hen-pecked at home, I held out for one financial, practical victory. I didn't underwrite my wife, Tyranny Rex's glass blowing losses which were considerable. She could blow like no other mortal and the house and garage were gorged with her ridiculous creations—the defecating cow, the urinating elf—but she was the only scion of Daddybucks Wemple, King of chintz finance, CEO of Elbert Wemple Ass. Realtors and the fruit of his loins doesn't fall far from the rest of him.

I put in a call from my "business" phone at home—it was a telephone without a ring tone—so as not to fluster Tyranny Rex.

Tyranny was in the garage blowing glass with her world-class lungs and hard-core lips. I took the opportunity to use my phone (no extensions) to call his imperial majesty, Dr. Kulp, in Pennsylvania.

Was it a receptionist who answered his phone? Or a nurse? An operator? Whoever it was, she was not overburdened with personality.

"Are you a patient?" she inquired, with that voice of suspicion only one at the very pinnacle of her profession can manage.

"No," I said, not wanting to venture more than that, lest I hoped for a shred of privacy from this ghoul.

"May I tell him what this is in regard to?"

"I'm returning his call," I said, draining the last vestige of human warmth from my voice.

There was an electric silence while that sank in. She broke it reluctantly. "Doctor is with a patient," she said, relishing her control. "May I have him call you?" she asked, switching to automatic pilot.

"You may," I said, "but I don't answer the phone either, so if you don't want us to play telephone hostage to kingdom come, I suggest you tell him I'm on the phone."

If you've ever heard a "Harumph!" as only seen in the comics, you'll understand what I experienced in the silence that followed that *bon mot*, of which, let us admit, I am inordinately proud.

"Hold, please," she said at length. At least I think she said please, but just now I couldn't swear to it.

I drummed my fingers on the desk that held the phone, expecting to be cut off at any second and resolving not to call him again, when the voice of Prince Charming came on the line.

"Look here, Yates, I'm very busy here. I'll call you back when I get a breather."

"I don't answer the phone," I said, and I'm embarrassed to confess the retort was power-driven. I wonder what Confucius would say about working for someone you wanted to overpower.

"You what?" He was incredulous, being a man in a profession for which power was second nature.

"I don't answer the phone. I call out, I don't take calls."

"Is there a reason for that?"

"I suppose there is," I said.

"Hmm, then may I ask you to call back in an hour and a half? I'll be able to talk to you then."

Okay, he won that round. I agreed to make another call. But, cognizant of doctors being late for patients, I added twenty minutes.

His secretary/receptionist, Miss Congeniality, must have gone home, because he answered the phone himself.

"Dr. Kulp, " is all I heard.

"Yes, doctor, this is Gil Yates calling you back."

"Okay, yes, good. You've been highly recommended as a detective of astounding powers, impressive results and absolute discretion."

That's very nice, I thought. "By whom?"

"My wife went to college with the ex-wife of Harold Mattlock. Claims you kept his head from being blown off. Speaks highly of you and your skills. Of course, she was several wives back."

Indeed I had. It had been touch and go, but Harold Mattlock had been a stand-up client, paying my considerable fee promptly without flinching. Though that fee was a pitifully small percentage of his wealth. I suspected whatever the fee in this case, it would put a larger, if not insurmountable, dent in the doctor's bottom line.

"So what do you want me to accomplish?" I asked.

He laid out his story for me. His daughter was grieving over the loss of her husband. "She is convinced there was foul play involved."

"How did he die?"

"He was pushed off the roof of his Straus and Sons department store."

5

"How do you know he was pushed?"

"As I say—she is convinced."

"You?"

"I am too. Nothing in this world is as important to me as my daughter. Her well-being and happiness are paramount."

"Only child?"

"Yes," he said. "How did you know?"

I didn't answer.

"So...what would you charge me to come here and talk it over with me?"

"Five thousand dollars," I said, almost without thinking.

"What? Just to talk to me?"

"No. I'll talk to you for nothing. On the phone—or you can come out here. No charge."

"That's out of the question." When people were really important things often became out of the question. Especially if it would put him out. "B...b...you don't expect me to hire you for a sensitive job like this without meeting you?"

"I don't *expect* anything. I'm not asking you for a job—the situation is reversed."

"But surely you need to work?" When I didn't answer he must have sensed a presumptive faux pas. "Like all the rest of us," he added, I suppose so I wouldn't think him a trust fund baby.

"Granted," I said, "my fees are high. I'm selective about the cases I take, and it may do me no credit, but ability to pay tops my list. That, and a certain bearable congeniality."

I'll be damned if he didn't start turning on the congeniality. I mean, you wouldn't mistake him for a contestant in a Mr. Congeniality contest who had a snowball's chance in the furnace room of placing anywhere in the running, but he was trying and I was touched. Not far from my thoughts was the idea he thought he could substitute congeniality for bucks.

"You came so highly recommended," he said so congenially. "I suppose I should try to get someone closer."

"And cheaper," I offered.

"Well, I won't pretend it's not a consideration."

"Well, make some calls. If it doesn't satisfy you, you have my number."

"No," he said, "your distance is an advantage. Your absolute discretion is a must, and I'm told you have it in spades."

Oh, I thought, that's how that one goes. I'd have said clubs—you have it in clubs. Well, they're both black cards.

"This is a very sensitive matter," he said. "My daughter is beside herself with grief. It's almost as if she wants to be personally responsible if it was a suicide. That's foolish, of course, but she is convinced there was foul play involved."

"What do the police say?"

"Pff—the police. This is a small town. Our police force has—how shall I say it? nice enough officers, but they are wont to take the easy way out. In this case, rule it a suicide and close the case. It is as though anything beyond that could tax their constitutions to a fare-thee-well."

"Do you have any evidence of foul play?"

"Suppositions only. No hard evidence. That's where I want you to come in," he said. "But look here, can we do something about a fee?"

"Nothing I can think of," I said, "besides paying it."

"That's a lot of money."

"I'm going to shoot three days. If there's no money at the end of the rainbow, I'd just as soon spend those days with my cycads."

"Your what?"

"Cycads—plants—fossil plants. The dinosaurs used to feed on them."

"And you still have them?"

"Still," I said, "well, they aren't the *same* plants, but directly related."

"So what can I do to get you to lower your fee?"

"Come out here."

"Out of the question." There it was again.

"Look, I don't fudge fees. I pick up all the expenses—and that can be quite a nut. But if five grand is giving you ulcers, you'll never pay my fee for the case."

"What will that be?"

"Depends on the case. Have to get all the particulars and know exactly what you want done—then I'll tell you."

"How about an average?"

"One hundred thousand and up."

"Up? How high?"

"The sky—millions."

"Ouch."

"You asked."

He was thinking—unless you can have a silence that long without thinking.

"Tell you what," he said, "you may be a little rich

for my blood. I'll sleep on it and get back to you."

When he hung up I figured I'd never hear from him.

I was wrong.

2

There are people, I'm told, who get a kick out of flying. I'm not one of them. "Flying high in the sky is my idea of nothing to do…" or something like that.

And all those people in airports? Why can't they stay put? This is my preference—stay put.

The Chicago airport was an animal farm. (Something like that; as I have noted, I'm not swift with clichés.) I was obliged to stop there on my way to Muhlenheim—where hung out the redoubtable Dr. Chester Kulp, to be sure—just don't forget the "Doctor".

Troublesome as airport terminals were, they couldn't hold a flashlight to the dreaded act of flying itself. For me there was nothing more reassuring than having my feet touch the ground. Man was not made to leave this earth—climbing trees was as high as we were meant to go. Once you sacrificed your moorings it was anyone's guess what might become of you.

Of course, once in the plane I put up a brave, almost cavalier, front. No one should ever guess I wasn't as comfy as I was in my own living room. Well, okay,

Tyranny's living room. And my comfort level there could be calibrated by whether or not Tyranny was in residence.

I was always the last one on the plane. Why put myself in harm's way before I had to? The flight was announced over the speaker system by someone whose inflections told us she couldn't care less about our fate.

I watched my fellow passengers coalesce at the door to hand in their tickets, all seeming to put on a brave front. I was looking for attractive young women, in the hope of getting one for a seatmate, rather than the sumo wrestlers or unemployed Santa Clauses which have heretofore been my fate. Armrest-hogging guys whose self-esteem was wrapped up in how much of your space they could claim. Chicago to Muhlenheim was a smaller plane than the behemoth from L.A. to Chicago, so mathematically I had a better chance at a young woman—there seemed to be three of them queuing for doom. No rare beauties with bee sting lips and hauteur befitting a movie star, but not so large I would make the trip with an elbow in my lap. When I couldn't escape flying, I always asked for an aisle seat in the back of the plane. This was where they put the crying babies, which was no picnic, but in a head-on collision, the front would act as a shock absorber—a hypothesis only valid if the collision were on the ground.

The aisle seat was necessary for a crash landing and an easier escape than being trapped between a metal wall and the aforementioned wrestler.

And it was good to have crying babies close to the bathroom so it would be handy to dispose of the diapers. Sometimes you might wish the disposal was effected with the baby still in the diaper.

I made my way up the aisle as the last to board, pausing intermittently so some of my fellow passengers could try to cram their entire household into the overhead bins which were already groaning from others with similar designs.

At last I arrived at my seat to see a young woman smiling at me as though her fondest dream had come true.

I quickly sat as though to bar her from seeking a more desirable seat.

Poor girl, I thought, with her whole life before her being trapped in a window seat.

"Hi there," she said interrupting my gloomy thoughts. It was a musical rendition. The "hi," naturally enough, hit the high notes, the "there" a little lower. "I'm Jessamyn."

"Hi, Jessamyn," I said, startled, "I'm—" and I almost said Malvin Stark, but I thought Gil Yates would serve better since I was going to Muhlenheim shrouded in this pretension, "—Gil Yates."

Her next question startled me, for I assure you, I was Mr. Cool personified. The brave front, as though I had invented and patented it.

"Are you afraid of flying?" she asked, with an engaging tilt to her slight body.

"No," I lied, for you don't impress your girls by being a wimp about flying. "Are you?"

"Nah," she said. "I was flying before I realized I was. One of those crying babies." She smiled. And a *nice* smile it was.

"Why did you ask?"

"I don't know, you just seemed…well, a little nervous."

Reality took hold of me. I quickly realized Jessamyn was not going to elope with me, wimp or no. "Well, you are perceptive," I said. "I have been known from time to time to harbor some...*apprehension* about flying. It's not that I'm afraid to fly or anything," I said, calling on my brave front, "no—my fear isn't flying, it's falling."

She, God bless her, giggled and launched into an impressive array of statistics about flying being the safest form of travel (one death in forty-seven million travelers), with the possible exception of the steamship. The most dangerous part about flying is the car trip to and from the airport. All very interesting if you were hung up on logic.

The small talk machine in high gear, it turned out Jessamyn was a senior at Pinecrest, a Muhlenheim college.

Remembering my college days, I popped the proverbial question, "What's your major?"

"Journalism."

My reaction would have been embodied in a frown, though I tried to suppress it with as much success as I did with my macho gung ho flyer act.

"I see you frowning," she said. "Afraid the journalism biz is on the skids? Layoffs, papers closing, magazines folding—isn't that what you're thinking?"

"Well, I...I suppose you have thought about it?"

"Sure. But it's what I love. Should I take environmental studies instead?"

"No, no, you should always do what you love," I said, thinking of my unbeloved career as a property manager under the thumb of my father-in-law, the insufferable Elbert Wemple.

"I think so too. I work part-time at the paper and I love it."

"Good for you."

"I'm an intern—no pay—so it isn't as red hot as it sounds."

"What do you do there?"

"Pretty low-level stuff," she said, with a shake of a disappointed head. "Gofer, writing shorts, delivering messages."

"Didn't work on the story about the department store heir who jumped off the roof—or was pushed, as his wife would like to have it—did you?"

"No, but I sort of remember the story."

"What was the gist?"

"Police said he jumped," she said. "Wife said he didn't. Suspected foul play."

"Who do you believe?"

"I don't know much about it. I guess at the time I went with the police, but—" she stopped.

"But what?"

"My father used to work at the store. He knew the place inside and out. He doesn't go with the intruder pushing him scenario."

"Why not?"

She shrugged.

"You know anything about the people involved?"

"Nah. A socially prominent family is all. Prominent doctor—and the police—I haven't had anything to do with the cops, thank goodness. Got the impression everyone was tiptoeing around the story. Lot of punches pulled in the writing."

I nodded. "Say, do you think you could get me the articles from the paper about it?"

"I suppose I could. But why would you want them?"

"I'm a—" I stopped. "Let's just say I may have an interest."

"You live in town?"

"California," I said.

"Oh, that's exciting. How is it there?"

"Well, depends where you are and what you're doing. It isn't always *exciting*. What's it like in Muhlenheim? Exciting?"

"Hardly. Kinda dull, actually."

"Like school?"

"It's okay. I'm graduating this year and it won't break my heart."

"What will you do?"

"Try to find a job."

"Where?"

"*Anywhere*. Beggars can't be choosers."

How well I knew that, marrying into my job with the blowhard Wemple, all for the hand of his daughter Dorcas. The hand was bad enough, but I was obliged to take the rest of her too.

"Would you consider doing some work for me?" I asked.

"What kind of work?"

"Remains to be seen. Legwork—media liaison," I said, making it sound important.

"Would you pay?"

"Of course."

"That sounds good," she said. "How much?"

"Oh, you can decide that, if it goes that far."

"Mystery?" she muttered.

"Yes," I said. "Very. You been to the department

stores in town?"

"I adore Ness's—incredible store, world-famous. The other one, Straus was kinda dull by comparison."

"Why?"

"Dowdy is the word. Ness is entertainment—big time. That Manny Ness is a genius."

"Maybe you should go work for him."

"I *wish*," she said, tilting her pert body, "he is so good to his employees. People work there fifty years. Runs a full-page ad every year with small pictures of employees who have been there five years and more. There are hundreds of them."

I'll say this for Jessamyn, she kept my mind off the danger of falling out of the sky. I didn't even notice we were landing until I felt the liver-jarring thud of the touchdown.

Jessamyn gave me her cell phone number and I gave her mine. I also gave her my landline in California. The one that didn't ring anywhere, but went straight to voicemail, or whatever it was that took messages.

I got off the plane with Jessamyn. She had this cute way of walking, as though her knees were made of rubber, and each step threw her upper body to the opposite side.

Zimmy Zimmerman was awaiting me as promised. I introduced Jessamyn to him as my traveling companion.

Zimmy was impressed.

3

Zimmy offered Jessamyn a ride, but she had a friend meeting her. I don't know why I was relieved to see it was a girl. "Have a good one," she said, as we parted like two canoes in the night.

Zimmy, I was to discover, was a Pennsylvania Dutchman to the core, fried potatoes up to here. He lumbered not unlike a grizzly bear. Dutch, I learned, was not Holland Dutch, but a local corruption of the German word for German: Deutsch. They were Pennsylvania German, or Pennsylvania Deutsch, corrupted to Dutch. He greeted me with a disarming smile, and together with my carry-on bag, he led me to his shiny black Cadillac that would not have been out of place in any upmarket funeral procession.

"Nice car," I said.

"It's the doctor's," he said.

I nodded. It made sense.

Attempting to read my mind, he said, "I drive my own car when it's required. It's just cheaper for the client for me to drive their car."

Zimmy came around to open the door for me. He opened the front door. I didn't fight it.

"The doc's kind of...cheap, is he?"

"Oh, he treats me all right. His checks clear."

"Get any tips?"

"Tips?" he said, as though that were a foreign concept. "I got a few in my time."

"From the aforementioned customer?"

"Well...that may not be one of the doctor's virtues."

"Little tightfisted, is he?"

"You might say that," he said, driving off. "Course, I'd never say it." His confirmation of my feelings made me glad I had insisted on my five-thousand dollar fee in advance.

A light snow was falling and the ground was blanketed in white.

"Pretty," I said.

"What?"

"The snow."

"Oh, that. I suppose if you're from California it's pretty. Those of us who live with it get it up to here."

"You drive exclusively for Doctor Kulp?"

"Oh, no, I'll drive for anyone—who pays me."

"Like it, do you?"

"Oh, I love to drive," he said, nodding. "I've logged over three million miles in my time."

"Wow. I'll bet you know all the secrets of the upper crust."

"It's true. I drive for most of our prominent folk—and they like to talk, most of 'em."

"Drive for these department store people?"

"Now, Mr. Ness, why he has his own private chauffeur. I drive the Strauses now and then."

"What kind of people?"

"Salt of the earth. You won't find much finer. Treat me real good, yes, sir."

"Ever drive Edward, the one who...died?"

"Sandy? Sure did."

"What kind of guy?"

"Same," he said. "Salt of the earth. You won't find anyone in these parts to say a bad word about Sandy. Everyone called him Sandy. Prince among men, that one."

"And his wife?"

"Ginger. You bet. I drive her still."

"Salt of the earth?"

He seemed to stiffen beside me. A fringe benefit of sitting in the front seat, I got a good sense of body language.

"I can tell you this," he said, "you won't find a more beautiful girl, not anywhere."

I thought I had my answer. When you talk about beauty and nothing else, it is often because there is nothing else.

"You know what I'm doing here?"

"Not really," he said. "The doctor doesn't share everything with me. What line of work are you in?"

"Private investigation," I said, and let it go at that.

"Oh, I see. Well that would figure," he said. "They—the Kulps—never were satisfied with the police investigation. Strong suspicion of foul play."

"What do *you* think? Foul play...or suicide?"

"Well, I wouldn't know," he said. "You aren't going to find me contradicting my clients."

No, I thought, but you have a perfect opportunity to weigh in with strong support, and I don't hear you doing it.

"Now, Zimmy," I said, like an old buddy, "I have a feeling you're holding out on me."

"Holding out? What?"

"You could fill me in on the incident—the untimely demise of the department store heir."

"Really don't know much. Upset the Kulps, that's no secret."

"What *are* the secrets?"

He curled his upper lip. "Don't know any."

"Well, what's the talk around town?" I asked.

When he didn't answer, I said, "Come on, now, you strike me as a man who never lets his ear get far from the ground."

"Oh, I hear things, sure."

"What kind of things?"

"Scuttlebutt mostly. Can't put a nickel's worth of credence in any of it."

"Well...what kind of things?"

"Nah," he said, "I'm working for Doctor Kulp. He wouldn't approve of me gossiping about the...tragedy. And it *was* that—a tragedy. A fine young man—a terrible loss for the community," he said, then added, "and for mankind."

"Well, what was so great about him?"

"I don't know, just a fine person. Not an enemy in the world."

"So it's hard to believe someone would push him off the roof?"

Zimmy said nothing. I realized he was telling the story by omission.

"And how is *Mrs.* Kulp?"

"They're *all* aces with me," Zimmy said. "You

won't get me to say any different."

Zimmy had been instructed to take me to my hotel and I was to call Dr. Kulp at precisely eight in the morning—that was Eastern time—like five a.m. where I came from. I had the feeling Dr. Kulp was a man bent on getting his money's worth.

"How close are these department stores to my hotel?"

"Close. One's just across the street, the other's a couple blocks up Adams Boulevard—that's the main street."

"Could we drive by the scene of the crime, or the accident, as the case may be?"

"Sure thing. I always say I aim to please—keep the customers happy and they'll come back for more."

We turned off Adams Boulevard onto an alleyway that seemed to cut the Straus Department Store in two. It was dark—the store was closed and minimum lighting illuminated the parking lot.

"Not much light," I said.

"No. The other side—out back there—is houses, and the Strauses minimized the lights in consideration of the neighbors. In appreciation, the neighbors watch out for any hanky-panky at the store in the nighttime.

"Now, up there," Zimmy said, gesturing to a rooftop on the building across the alley from the parking lot, "that's where it happened."

"When did it happen?"

"Oh, I expect it was a year or so now."

"Day or night?"

"Night, if I recollect rightly. He ended up in that courtyard kind of place in there."

"Who found him?"

"Teddy Straus, I believe."

"Who is he?"

"He's the parking attendant."

"And a *Straus*?"

"Well, yeah, that's what he goes by anyhow. He's not playing with the full deck, if you know what I mean."

I did.

"Illegitimate son of one of the founders, is the scuttlebutt."

"Nice of them to give him some work."

"Yeah, he's the spitting image of Uncle Jonathan. I can't hardly tell them apart."

"So when was Sandy found?"

"Next morning, I believe. Doctor Kulp can give you better answers," Zimmy said.

I looked up at the roof. "How did Sandy get out there?"

"There's a window facing the roof. That side of the store is the offices. This bigger building over here is the store itself."

"Is that a wall around that roof over there? The one he…fell off?'

"A low wall—yes."

"How low?"

"Can't say. A couple feet anyway, as I recall."

"Think we could get up there?"

"Not now," he said. "I expect we could in the morning, when the store's open."

"Is this side connected to the store part?"

"Yes, sir. See that overhead walkway?"

I looked up and there it was spanning the alley. But the roof was only two stories off the ground. I wondered, if he had suicide in mind, might he not have found a surer thing? He could have made this jump without breaking a bone, unless he had the guts to swan dive it. I couldn't understand how anyone could choose such a fate.

"Zimmy," I said, "how do you suppose the department store business is these days, in Muhlenheim?"

"I don't expect it's very good. Not for Straus; Ness is always booming."

Back on Adams Boulevard I checked out the facade and the window displays. Jessamyn was right: dowdy.

Zimmy dropped me off at the Hotel Muhlenheim across the street from the big—perhaps a bit garish—blinking Ness sign. He offered to take me inside, but I assured him I could handle checking in.

He gave me his card and told me to call him anytime, as he would be only too happy to be of service any time of the day or night.

I checked in and asked for a room where I could see the Ness sign. The clerk seemed surprised but he obliged me. I thought it might give me inspiration.

Since it was eleven-thirty at night, Eastern time, but only eight-thirty or so where I came from, I ventured out on the street to check out Ness' window displays.

They were a knockwurst—animated figures, music, low-key displays of merchandise amidst the more prominent, entertaining display.

This guy, Ness, I thought, wouldn't be jumping off any roofs.

4

My eight a.m. (on the spot) call to Dr. Kulp was perfunctory. He was sending Zimmy for me in fifteen minutes.

After all, what good is breakfast?

Before I knew it, the phone rang announcing Zimmy's presence downstairs.

He greeted me in his black funeral suit, the color doubtless selected to signify his trade. If the idea was black was slimming, it missed. It was snowing outside.

"Well, California, welcome to the frozen north," Zimmy said. "How do you like our weather?"

"Cold," I said.

"Come back in July," he said, nodding, "then we'll be able to complain about the heat."

Zimmy opened the door of a different car. "This is my car," he explained. "I took the doctor's back to him last night."

Severe. That was the word for Dr. Chester Kulp. He was severe. You had to speculate on his facial expressions, so narrow was the range: from severe to more severe.

If you could gauge the range of human emotions expressed in a person's face on a scale of zero to one hundred, Dr. Kulp's range weighed in from about zero to six.

He met me about midrange. My telephone impression was verified. The doctor was not a chap who got a lot of laughs out of life.

He dismissed Zimmy with, "You can go, Zimmy, I'll take him back."

Zimmy bowed as any good humble servant might and took his leave.

While I sat across the desk from Dr. Kulp he said, "The office is closed today so we need not worry about unwelcome auditors."

Unwelcome auditors? I thought. I'm not worried.

Between us, on his desk, was a plastic model of a human heart. Dr. Kulp noted me looking at it.

"Tools of the trade," he said.

"You're a heart surgeon?"

"Yes. The chambers open up," he said, and demonstrated like pulling out dresser drawers.

"Impressive," I muttered.

"Large responsibility," he said with his face hovering on a severe expression.

"Good business?" I asked.

"Profession," he muttered.

"Oh, yes, of course it is. Sorry."

"Yes," he said. "I can't complain."

It was an admission that seemed to make him uncomfortable.

There comes a time in some doctor's lives when they decide they are just people—or that's the way they should play it, at any rate. Others feel it serves them better to be thought godlike—it keeps the infirm from getting too chummy.

The doctors who are in the "Call me Al" category are those in the more modest specialties: general practitioners, dermatologists, or those who work with your feet. The hardliners who hold the balance between life and death in their hands are liable to feel—perhaps justifiably—more godlike. Dr. Chester Kulp was firmly in the latter category.

Was there a medical man more exalted than a heart surgeon? If brain surgeon comes to mind, consider what good the best brain would do without a functioning heart. I'm sure Dr. Kulp took all this into careful consideration when he selected his specialty.

"Yes, life has treated me well, until this...tragedy," he said, choosing his words carefully. "And that's why I am talking to you. I'm told you can help. Do you think you can?"

"Can what? What kind of help are you looking for?"

"Simple," he said, his lips frozen tightly. "I want you to investigate this terrible tragedy until you can establish foul play and wipe out, once and for all, the ridiculous notion that it could have been suicide."

"Why, I may ask, is that so important? Suicide happens—any stigma is on the perpetrator, not the survivors."

"Yes, easy to say," he said, "and in some circumstances, I'm sure you are right."

"How do you think it happened?"

"Don't know," he said. "I just know he did *not* jump."

"I went out to the scene last night," I said. "Apparently there is a two foot wall around the roof. So if someone pushed him, first he had to get him to climb up the wall, or carry him up..." I shook my head. "It's a tall order."

"Unless he had a gun pointed at him."

"Why?"

"Robbery? Except for the night watchman he was alone in the store."

"Lot of cash lying around?"

"I suppose a robber might think so."

"How would he have gotten in the store?"

"I don't know."

"Any sign of forced entry?"

"The police," he shrugged, "they know nothing. It could have been an employee who had access."

I was beginning to think I was robbing the good doctor myself, taking his five grand ones to talk about such thin oatmeal.

"You look troubled," Dr. Kulp said.

"Yes," I said.

"What's the matter?"

"You've spoken to other private detectives?"

He nodded. "I even hired one."

"What happened?"

"He didn't do anything, as far as I can see, besides talk to the police."

"How long did he work for you?"

"I don't know, nine or ten months, I suppose— off and on—and from the results, it was more off than on."

"And what makes you think I can please you if he couldn't?"

"Your references for one," he said. "You're in another league entirely."

"That's very flattering," I said. "I am good; thorough, incisive—have an analytical mind—and have had much success. I don't give up. But I realize I don't do miracles. One of my success formulas is I don't take hopeless cases."

"And you think this is hopeless?"

"I'm afraid pleasing you—that is, getting the result you want—proving foul play may not be in the dominoes."

"Dominoes? What are you talking about?"

"Not in the dominoes—it's a saying, you know, meaning pretty impossible. You have a row of dominoes and what you want isn't in them."

"Oh," he nodded. "Yes," he said, "not in the *cards* is the way that goes."

"Well, okay," I said. "I don't see how that's much different, but okay."

"Or how about this? Sandy was working late and he saw, or thought he saw, a man, or men, with guns, and he took what he thought was his best escape—through the window and over the wall—an easy jump—he was an athletic guy. But something went wrong. Instead of landing on his feet, he landed on his head. When the robbers saw what happened, they left."

"Why is this so important to you?" I asked.

"My daughter is beside herself. I must have told you that?"

"Well, it's normal to suffer if you lose a loved one."

"Not just a loved one," he corrected me. "They were the ideal couple—had a perfect marriage."

"Is that possible?"

He gave no ground. "Was with *them*. But this is not just the ordinary heartbreak. She wants to take the blame if it was suicide—and we all know it wasn't—but the stupid police have decreed it, and that's that in this town."

"I must say my experience with the police is different than yours. Sure, I've met a few whose IQs aren't going anywhere, but I imagine you know a few doctors who aren't geniuses."

"Perhaps, but I wouldn't want to equate the police academy with medical school."

"Okay, but it may be self-defeating to ignore the police opinion. Most of the cops I know understand their trade, have a better insight into the criminal mind, maybe even understand human nature better than the rest of us. And are conscientious about proving the truth."

He stared at me. "Well," he said, "do you want the job?"

"I don't know. I'm still a ways from knowing. When can I meet your wife and daughter?"

"Oh, no, I'd rather keep them out of it. If you get results, it will be a pleasant surprise. If I build them up for another fiasco, it will be doubly devastating."

I let that sink in, hoping he'd realize the folly of that approach. He didn't. He just gave me his severest look.

I thought of a bunch of arguments, but decided, why argue? I wouldn't take the case without meeting the star. Perhaps I could tell if she was way out there and the entire enterprise would be a farce.

We sat in silence as though each were waiting for the other to blink. No one did, so I rose from my chair and said, "Well, I guess this is it then. It was nice to meet you, and I'm glad we were able to clear the water without a lot of investment."

The doctor looked stricken. Could that simply be the basic variation on severe? "Investment? What about my five thousand dollars?"

"Oh, that, I'll give it back if it's that important to you," I said, looking around his grandiose office.

That stunned him.

Would I have done it? Okay, I expect I'd have deducted my expenses first. I was thinking this was not a guy I'd want to work for. I couldn't see the slightest possibility of 1) Pleasing him. 2) Making a financial arrangement to my benefit. 3) Getting any laughs. So I decided to escape.

As soon as I turned my back on him he said, "No, wait. Don't be hasty."

I looked at him.

"Sit down," he commanded me.

I sat, but I was bemused.

5

The doctor saw the wisdom of listening to my conditions if he wanted me to work for him.

Meeting his wife and daughter made some sense to him, he conceded that. When we agreed on all the silly stuff we got down to the nitty-nitty, my fee.

"You were, as I told you, highly recommended," the severe doctor said, looking just a tad over my shoulder—for surely he had weightier things on his mind. "One of the most appealing aspects of the recommendation was your *modus operandi*, to wit," (honest to the deity, he said "to wit" as though he were a hotshot lawyer or something), "*contingency.*" This he gave special emphasis. He let it lay there like an egg fallen from a very important ostrich. I let it lie. His gaze shifted from over my shoulder to my actual face. That great sacrifice on his part seemed to beg a response.

"Yes," I said, throwing an aura of gravitas into my casual posture. "I have always worked on contingency. They were cases that lend themselves to it— solving murders, keeping the client alive until his predator was caught—cases where the object was clear."

"Is my object not clear?" he said. "I want you to

find out who killed my daughter's husband."

"And so I would be happy to do," I said, "if it were clear that he had been killed. The weight of the evidence along with the judgment of the police is that he *jumped* off the roof. I would agree to investigate to see if there might have been some evidence of foul play, but I couldn't base my fee on getting the result you want."

"Well, how about a nice bonus if you do?"

I shook my head. "Wouldn't be ethical," I said. "Do you ask for a bonus if your patient lives?"

"Well, that's not the same," he said. "I'm a *doctor.*"

Oh, my, yes, I thought, and a *professional* man, and that makes all the difference.

"Here's what I can offer. I will investigate for foul play or, failing that, for a reason for him to jump off the roof. But my fee will not be contingent on giving you the answer you want. In other words, if I discover he jumped because he couldn't stand his father-in-law, and I have the evidence to back it up, I will have earned my fee."

Did he blanch at that father-in-law stuff? Or did I imagine it? There was at least a flicker on that severe face.

"And what exactly would your fee be?"

"Ten thousand dollars a day, including expenses—five day minimum in advance." I was watching him—his narrow range of facial expressions was expanding. "If I solve the case in those five days, I will expect a fifty thousand dollar bonus." Now I really had him.

"Why, man, that's a hundred thousand dollars!"

"Yes, your arithmetic is solid. Shall I go on?"

"On? There's more?"

"Yes. I will agree to cut it off if you are not satisfied with my progress after five days."

"But, man," he said, "that's a lot of money."

"I hope so," I said. "May I ask what you charge for a heart operation?"

"Well, it depends on the type of operation."

"Sure. What's the range?"

"Oh," he said, waving a hand, "that's not relevant."

"Would a hundred thousand dollars be in the right neighborhood?"

"There's a lot more to it," he said.

"You mean, two hundred thousand dollars?"

"I mean, putting a price on saving someone's life—that's…well, it doesn't lend itself to, or correlate to, dollars and cents."

Cents? I thought, there aren't *any* cents—we're talking about dollars—big dollars.

"And how long does the hundred thousand dollar job take you? A couple hours?"

"Not the same," he said. "Not that simple."

"My information is you can do two hundred thousand to three hundred thousand dollars in one day—the pittance I am asking is an embarrassment by comparison. I don't have a great interest in working as a volunteer. If I did, I expect I would turn to the Red Cross rather than someone like you."

I realized I was talking myself out of a job but *c'est la guerre.*

"Look here, Yates," he said. "I'm not asking you to work for nothing. But that's ten times what I paid the other detective."

"And what results did you get?"

"Nothing."

"I rest my case."

"But…but there's no guarantee I'll get any more from you."

"Do you guarantee the results of your surgery?"

"Well, how can I do that?"

"And if the patient dies, do you still expect your fee?"

"Look here, Yates, I won't have the practice of medicine compared to *gumshoe* work."

"Fair enough," I said. "But work is work, time is time. My fees are a small fraction of yours. Whether or not they are worth it is your decision, and it is a matter of some indifference to me. I have always had plenty of work, and therefore plenty of money." This could be construed as a stretch after eight years away from the trough.

"Look here," he said. "Let's be reasonable. I'd like you to tackle this, and apparently you have *some* interest or you wouldn't have come across the continent to talk to me. But how much time is this taking you?"

"Three days."

"Exactly!" He clapped his hands in celebration of his victory. "And I am paying you—what?"

"Five thousand."

"Exactly!" Another round of applause from the self-congratulating doctor. "So, by my calculation, that's some thirteen hundred a day—eminently reasonable. I'll pay you that."

I couldn't help smiling and, I'll admit it, if I'd have had a mirror I'd have seen it as the sappy smile it was.

"How clever you are, Doctor. If I might try to steer us back to the context here. I am here not in the performance of my investigating trade, but to schmooze about the possibility of a job—saw out the details, so to speak."

"Hammer," he corrected me.

"Good enough. I imagine, and *do* correct me if I am wrong, you are compensated somewhat more for actually operating on a patient than for any discussion you have before the operation?"

"All part of it," he said.

"Well, okay, but if you will recall, I offered this schmoozing gratis if you had come to California."

"Out of the question."

"And here I am," I said, sinking back in my chair. "The actual work comes higher."

He was silent. To me it indicated I had won a round.

Sensing a turn in the tide, I seized the initiative. "So if I can meet your women today, I'll be on my way tomorrow, and we can both ponder the imponderables and decide if we want to do business."

He took in some air, as though to stimulate his brain cells. He nodded (severely). "I'll take you back to your hotel. You can visit the Straus store if you like—or do whatever you want. I'll have Zimmy pick you up for dinner at six. We'll go to the club."

Sounded good to me. I always aspired to have a "club."

6

The doctor dropped me at my hotel without having to suffer a surfeit of small talk. I inquired at the desk for the location of the police station. It was just a few blocks away. I took a stroll in that direction.

It was another brick bulwark—these bricks were red.

One of the advantages of a small town was the police are more accessible. Not everyone who shows up at the front desk is treated like a criminal.

Sergeant Laudenslager was a friendly sort who preferred eating to exercising. I told him my story in what passed for his department's detective room: desks and chairs mostly—indestructible, so if some con came shooting the damage to the furniture would be minimal.

The sergeant was a plainclothesman with the emphasis on the *plain*. His face indicated he was not acquainted with sunscreen. He had a pair of spectacles, which hung precariously on the end of his nose. I never saw him look through the lenses.

"I'm here from California," I said, by way of introduction. "Testing the ice, so to speak."

He frowned. "Testing the ice? Is that like testing the waters?"

"Well, ice is water, isn't it? So I suppose—I'm thinking of taking this case—or not—the Kulps—the Straus case—a suicide, was it?"

"You better believe it. I expect the doctor wants you to prove it was murder." He didn't phrase it as a question, or wait for me to answer, just shook his head. "Good luck. Not a shred of evidence, physical or otherwise."

"So I should stay home?"

"I was you, you couldn't get me to leave sunny California for this ice bucket, for all the tea in China. Of course we all have to make a living."

"Yeah, one way or the other."

"If you have another, take it."

I didn't tell him my "other" was Daddybucks Wemple, a more insufferable excuse for a human being you couldn't hope to meet.

"What's your take on the family?"

He peered suspiciously over the top of his glasses. "You meet them?"

"Just the doctor."

"Piece of work—richer'n God. The girl, I forget her name, most beautiful woman I ever saw, but I don't get out much."

"She has that reputation."

"Deserved," he said. "Mom is nice enough, a little mousy around her godlike husband. But the girl—what's her name?"

"Ginger."

"Yeah, I can't get a fix on her. I mean, that's not a surprise—that kind of beauty has got to be a burden.

Can you imagine being stared at wherever you go?"

"I don't have that problem."

"Neither do I."

I accepted his understatement without flinching. "So I guess I can't imagine it," I said.

"Truth be known, neither can I. But there's something funny there. All my time with them, I could never put my finger on it."

"What kind of funny?" I asked.

"Well, peculiar. Not ha-ha. I don't get the feeling there is a lot of levity in that household."

"He did seem pretty serious."

"That's a safe bet," he said. "And my take was the doctor set the tone for the whole operation."

"Make it a little tough, did it?"

He nodded, his flexible face set in grim mode. "You have heart trouble, go to Dr. Kulp. You got a criminal investigation, he may not be your man. But he doesn't know it. The Kulps are well-meaning people. *Important* people. But there is something wrong there."

"But what?" I asked.

"They seem—how do I say it?—unusually fixated on the method of death. They just can't accept the suicide. Everyone else has—his brothers, his mother. The doctor bugged the bejesus out of us to turn in *his* findings. When we didn't oblige, he hired a private detective."

"Did he do a report?"

"Don't know. Never saw it, if he did."

"So what kind of town do you have here?" I asked.

"What kind? What kind of kind?"

"Crime under control?"

"Never, or I'd be on the dole."

"What crimes predominate?"

"Smaller stuff, some theft, lots of drugs, domestics."

"Maids?"

"No—man–woman violence, threats, relationships," he shrugged.

"How many murders?"

"One or two a year. But mostly acquaintances or relatives, fairly easy to solve."

"Suicides?"

"'Bout the same. There you hit on an illegal act where the successful perpetrator always gets away with murder."

"Satisfied Mr. Straus was the perpetrator of his own death?"

He didn't answer right away. I asked him why not.

"Oh, I'm convinced all right. But you being here from the other side of the country reminds me the good Dr. Kulp is not. So I don't want to answer too fast."

"Okay, here's another question. You don't have to answer quickly. Do you think there is any point in me taking the case further?"

"Point? Money's the point, isn't it?"

"Okay, but beyond that?"

"Beyond that?" he said. "What is beyond that? You think I'd be working if I wasn't making money?"

"Okay, but let me shock you. I've made a lot of money in this trade. A large part of it came with no little grief. This has grief written all over the page."

He nodded. "I'll give you that. Kulp is grief. So if you do it—and believe me, I wouldn't advise it—get plenty of moola because you'll earn whatever you get."

"Thanks for the tip," I said.

"So, are you going to take the case?"

"Don't know. I'm still pondering. Doctor Kulp said there was another private guy who tackled it."

He nodded, a solemn nod you might have experienced down at the funeral home.

"Anything come of it?"

"Not so's I could tell."

"What happened?'

"Don't know," he said. "I was well free of it by then."

"Think there's any point in talking to him?"

"Don't see how it could hurt. Give you some insight working for the doctor."

"A problem, eh?"

"Don't get me wrong," he said. "I know a lot of doctors that are aces with me."

"Dr. Kulp?"

He shook his head, "Not one of them."

"If I did take the case, could I look at your files on it?"

"Be my guest. No secrets here."

"What would I find there?"

"Nothing. Lot of dead ends. We ruled it a suicide and closed the case."

"How about this…private detective. What's his name again?"

"Wessner. See for yourself. He lives just down the street."

"You think he'd be home now?"

He smiled one of those maddeningly knowing smiles. Maddening because you didn't know why it was knowing, or what it knew about.

"I daresay," he said. "He doesn't get out much."

"Works from home?"

"You could say that. When he works. You might find different, but Wessner is not what is known around here as a live wire."

He gave me Wessner's address and directions to his house. I thanked him for his help.

I started out the door on my way to Wessner's house, and wondered if I'd ever see Sergeant Laudenslager again. Perhaps Wessner and the Kulps that night would have a clue. Dr. Kulp thought cops were a bit lazy and closed cases before they were completely sure they were doing the right thing. I was not yet convinced I should rule out all his opinions completely.

7

Wessner was at home. Tyranny Rex would say, "Oh, joy, oh, rapture."

He was a nice enough guy, a little heavy on the fat cells, but I was beginning to think that went with the territory here. Something in the air, or the fried potatoes.

Wessner lived in one of those ubiquitous brick row houses with the loveseat–sized swing hanging on chains from the ceiling of the front porch. If you sat and swung on the swing your view would have been of the identical brick row houses across the street.

Wessner moved like a man who should have long since retired, but he still dyed his hair to keep up with the young'uns. He had a Pennsylvania Dutch accent that I found intriguing. We for Willie and gee for Glarance, and stuff like that there.

He invited me to sit in his living room, which opened cold chicken to the outside. In the corner was a modest desk, the surface of which was devoid of any intrusion.

He was friendly enough, but he seemed to frown perpetually, as though he were preoccupied with pressing, weighty matters.

I told him my story and asked his advice. "Should I take the case?"

"Yes, well, we all have to live, I suppose."

Not exactly an answer.

"Do you think it is possible to get some other result?"

"Well, of course I don't. But you might have better luck. Where you from?"

"California."

"And you came all this way for Dr. Kulp's case?"

"Investigating it."

"Why would he go all the way to California to get a dick?"

"There's no accounting for taste, I guess."

He opened his mouth to say something but quickly closed it and substituted a curt nod instead.

"Can you tell me why you stopped working on the case?"

"Yes, well," he said, after a healthy pause. "You might say there were philosophical differences between the good doctor and myself."

"What sort of...?"

Wessner held his hand up. "I don't go into that—there's such a thing as privilege, you know. I'm not violating the ethics of my profession."

"Fair enough," I said, though I didn't think it was very fair. We were in the same line of work, both theoretically searching for some result. Any help he could give me should not harm him or the doctor. But then, I thought, if I succeed where he had failed, that might not, in Wessner's estimation, make him look too good.

"Are you glad you took the case?" I asked him. "Would you do it again?"

"That's two questions," he cracked his face again in a tortured smile.

Well, yes, I thought, so give me two answers and we'll be rectangles.

"I suppose," he said, reflecting, "in retrospect, that is, the answer to both questions is no."

"Why so?"

"Let's just say working with the good doctor was no piece of cake. So knowing what I do about him—having experienced him close up—" he stopped short.

I tried to encourage him with looks to go on.

He shook his head. "Nah," he said. "I've said too much already. We had a privileged relationship. You can understand that, being in the same line of work."

"Well, but you no longer work for him," I said. "I'm thinking about jumping into the same tank. Is it sharks?"

He nodded.

"So you could help a fellow detective out by forewarning him of any...problems he could encounter."

"Don't know. Yours could be different, could be smooth sailing for you."

"Believe that, do you?"

"Not really."

"So what should I look out for?"

"I expect you'll have your own experiences."

"Look," I made one last plea. "I've come across the continent to find out if I want to take this case. First of all, that's a long way from Muhlenheim, Pennsylvania. The chance of me breaking a confidence in Pennsylvania is remote. Second, privilege ends with the case."

"Oh, no," he said. "You're mistaken about that. It only ends with the death of the client. Dr. Kulp is alive and well."

"Is that a good thing or a bad thing?"

"For you, or for me?"

"Either."

He broke that frown again. "That's for you to find out. Who's to say your experience with him will be the same as mine?"

"Oh, millennia of human nature."

He shook his head. He wasn't budging.

"Okay," I said. "So I can assume if it was a happy experience, you wouldn't mind talking about it. And if it was good, you'd still be on the case."

He stone-faced that.

"So you did some kind of report?"

His lips tightened before a curt nod.

"May I see it?"

"I did it for Kulp. He wants to show it to you, it's no skin off my nose. You're not getting it from me."

"Whose idea was it to end the relationship?"

"You're going to see Dr. Kulp again?"

I nodded.

"Ask him," he said.

"Okay," I said. "I get it. Just one more question."

He didn't look happy with that.

"If I take the case, would you help me out?" Seeing no sign of life from Detective Wessner, I added, "If I paid you?"

That breathed some life into that big body. Then he seemed to deflate as he thought it over. "Privileged information is not for sale around here."

"Fair enough. But would you help in any other way—that didn't sacrifice your very high principles?"

"Well," he said, with a dubious cast to his big head, "come back if you get the job. It'll depend, I suppose, on what you want."

8

Zimmy picked me up at the hotel in his car. The doctor took his family in his Caddy. Though there would have been room for me, it was a touch out of his way and there was no sense contaminating the atmosphere with a potential hired hand.

We left the hurly-burly section of the downtown area of Muhlenheim and drove through the rural environs until we reached a woodsy area, where we turned off the main road. There we traversed the golf course until we got to the clubhouse. A pleasant country-clubbish building looking a little southern plantationish—Tara, without the pillars.

"Ever eaten here?" I asked Zimmy.

"Never have," he said. "I'm just the driver."

"Well, come on in with me," I said.

"Oh, the doctor wouldn't like that," he said.

"We won't ask him."

He chuckled, then shook his head. "I don't need that," he said. "I'm a simple guy—don't have high falutin' aspirations."

"Neither do I," I said, "and I'm doing it. Come

on Zimmy, you're no better than the rest of us."

He just shook his head, the chuckle wound down.

"Have a nice dinner," he said. "I'll be back to get you."

"The doctor doesn't want to take me back?"

"Wants to be with his family."

"Big family man, is he?"

Zimmy shrugged. "See for yourself," he said. "Have a nice dinner."

"Thanks," I said, and got out of the car.

As though to mimic the long driveway to the clubhouse, the long corridor to the dining room was a good hike from the cloakroom where I deposited my overcoat. It gave me time to think—what exactly did I want? Working for the doctor wasn't going to be a piece of cheesecake, that much I had grasped. But if he met my price, a hundred grand might come in handy. I was in no position to deny that.

The club looked like it had been a movie set dressed by an MGM set decorator: crystal chandeliers, crystal goblets, white table clothes, flowers amidships on each table, heavy silver and dramatic china to make you think you were at a presidential dinner, plush carpet underfoot and an army of servers, mostly female, in severe black, no-nonsense dresses with cutesy white aprons in front. Penguins came to mind.

The dining room was neither large nor full. The Kulps were easy to spot—mom, dad and kid. Mom looked like she had dressed for a spread with one of those fashion magazines that catered to the big bucks classes. The kid was as beautiful as advertised—perhaps a touch more so—and dad was dad.

It was really a model family. You could have seen them in any number of magazines that catered to the envy classes. The caption would simply state: Dr. and Mrs. Chester Kulp dining at their country club with their beautiful daughter, Ginger.

Attendance was sparse this night, but when someone stopped by the table to nose around at the stranger in their midst (yours sincerely), Mrs. Kulp would effuse over a dress or a hairdo and the doctor would proffer a tight smile that said, "So nice to see you, but don't linger." It was the price of celebrity. Ginger strived to maintain the air of the aggrieved widow without making her dishrag too damp. In her peachy cashmere dress, Ginger was one of those women you wanted to touch, but was, underneath, untouchable.

Mom, too, had been such in her heyday. Now she had the look of a bow to botox, or another of those eternal youth elixirs, but as those rejuvenating jobs go, hers was a good one.

How many of the resident well-wishers were curiosity seekers who'd heard so much about Ginger's sorrow they wanted to get a closer look? They would barely suppress a morbid glee and mutter how sorry they were, keeping their eyes on Ginger's face for her reaction, which was a dutiful lowering of her eyelids and a low breath of thanks.

Apparently there were multiple levels to this opera.

The doctor looked up at me and without sacrificing his seated position at the table waved at the empty chair across from him at the round table.

I sat between the missus and Ginger. I liked that.

Of course, everything has a downside. Here I was

looking directly across the table into the inimitable eyes of the great Dr. Chester Kulp. Under the circumstances, I think it would have been more profitable to be able to look into the eyes of Ginger—she was the keyhole to this operation—but perhaps I would die of asphyxiation as a result of her sapping my breath.

Dr. Kulp made the introductions right out of the etiquette book—wife first, daughter second—I was presented as though to royalty.

"I'm so *pleased* to meet you," Mrs. Priscilla Kulp said. Ginger said simply, "Hello," but she accompanied it with a smile that could have leveled Al Qaeda. But then, as quickly, it was gone and the lips turned anemic.

"How do you like our snow, Mr. Yates?" Mother Kulp asked—and when I thought "Mother," I thought the chief of some austere religious order, not too far from the Vatican.

"I kind of like it," I said. "I think it's beautiful. Zimmy says it's because I don't have to live in it." That elicited a chuckle from Mrs. Kulp, a grim smile from the doctor, and a deadpan from Ginger—almost as though I had caused a faux pas in the conversation by introducing the word "live." Probably my imagination.

A penguin arrived with a basket of bread, which she set in the center of the table. There was something odd looking in the middle of the napkin-lined basket.

"Oh, good," Mother Kulp said. "Sticky buns. I just *love* the club's sticky buns, don't you, Dear?"

Without much enthusiasm, the good doctor allowed as, yes, he too, loved the club's sticky buns.

The cinnamon rolls were with gooey brown caramel coating and looked more like a dessert to me, though I did take one when the basket was proffered in my direction.

We made some small talk—the adults mostly—Ginger seemed to be licking some unseen wounds and sat silently for the most part. The talk was *so* small, I forgot what it was.

The penguin showed tableside with her notepad; we ordered. I had the prime rib, rare, which Mother Kulp assured me was the club's signature dish. I saw by the frown on the doctor's face he might have preferred if I'd had something cheaper.

Ginger had some fish, trout perhaps, but steamed, not pan-fried—no butter. The *pater familias* had steamed veggies and Mother Kulp joined me for the prime rib. As Dr. Kulp noted, *she* had never seen an artery clogged with globules of fat.

I decided it was time to bring Ginger into the conversation and further the investigation at the same time.

"Did you like your husband?" I asked Ginger.

"*Like* him?" she said, the indignation shooting through her head. "I *loved* Sandy." Then, as though that weren't strong enough, she added, "We were *married!*"

Doctor Kulp got in on the action. "Watch your tongue, Yates."

I was surprised, perhaps I shouldn't have been. I shrugged, "I meant no offense. Where I come from, marriage is no testament to lifelong love, as the divorce rate of over fifty percent attests. People who start out head over heels in love wind up hating each other."

"Well," Ginger said, "that's because they started the wrong way."

"Oh? What is the *wrong* way?"

"Emphasizing the physical," she said, "rather than the spiritual. First, you should be soul mates."

Soul mates? How sweet, I thought. Since I suspect it was a cliché I had to realize I probably would have mangled it—matcs of the spirits perhaps, but I couldn't deny I liked the ring of "soul mates." I wondered if Tyranny Rex and I were soul mates? Were we *ever*?

A couple, on in years, came to the table under their own steam and all smiles. The doctor didn't stand for them either, so I took his cue and stayed put.

"I see you have company," the man said. I didn't pay a lot of attention to his name, Bortz or Stortz or something local. The doctor kept his chilly demeanor when he introduced us.

"Oh, nice," Bortz or Stortz or maybe Brobst, said. "What brings you to our fair city? Mr. Bates, is it?"

"Yates," the doctor said, saving me the trouble. I had opened my mouth to respond when the doctor said, "He's a colleague."

"Oh, really? Nice," said Pabst or whatever his name was. "Where from?"

I let Dr. Kulp do the honors.

"California," he said.

"Oh, wow, sunny California. How do you like our snow?" Kulp let me field that one.

"It's very beautiful," I said.

"If you don't have to live in it." And believe it or not, I laughed as though I'd never heard that, when I was laughing because of how *often* I'd heard it.

I don't remember how Dr. Kulp dispatched this pest, but he managed.

"Snoops," he said succinctly, when the couple retreated. "People are so insufferably nosey."

"People are curious, dear," Mother Kulp said,

"You know that."

"I call it nosey," he remained firm.

"I do hope you can help us with this," Mother Kulp said. "Ginger's been so depressed ever since…" she looked at Ginger who was gazing straight ahead at her mother, but it was obvious she was not on her radar. It was as though she had heard her cue to act depressed. "We all are convinced Sandy would *never* commit suicide. He was a happy-go-lucky guy."

"How was your marriage?" I asked Ginger.

Her father answered. "Idyllic. Wasn't a better marriage in the county."

I looked to Ginger for verification. "I was hoping for a response from one of the principals."

"It was fine," Ginger said.

Fine? Well, okay, I thought. Doesn't quite rise to the idyllic standard, but fine is better than lousy.

The doctor caught my doubt. "Ginger is depressed, you have to understand. She will not give you any superlatives on any subject as she certainly would have—before this tragedy."

"It wasn't my fault," Ginger said.

"We know, dear," the doc said, reaching over to pat her hand under the table. "That's why we have Mr. Yates here, to help us solve this once and for all."

"I don't know if I want to dredge it all up again," she said.

"But," I said, "Why do you say it wasn't your fault? Has anyone suggested it was?"

"Oh, I know what they say behind my back."

Her father frowned and shook his head. "I fear she is imagining the worst. And it really is only imagination."

"May I see your last private detective's report?" I asked.

"Report? What do you know of a report?"

"I went to see him. He said he had written a report. He wouldn't show it to me. Said it was confidential."

"And so it was," the doctor frowned. "Why are you out stirring things up? You haven't been hired yet."

"Just trying to see if I want the job. While I'm here, I thought I could get some objective background."

"Oh? And what did he tell you?"

"Nothing, really."

"Well, he apparently told you about the report."

"But not what was in it."

"That's because there *was* nothing in it."

"So you shouldn't mind showing it to me?"

Kulp frowned. "I hadn't thought to make it public."

"It won't be public. Only I will see it."

That seemed to be okay with him. "Only if we make the deal," he allowed.

"Of course," I said. "Why would I make work for myself if there was no rainbow at the end of the pot?"

Before we wrapped up dinner with calorie dripping desserts—Mother Kulp and I; and fresh fruit—Ginger and Kulp; I asked Ginger, "Is this something you want to do? Have me pursue this case?"

Her instant freeze-dried frown may have belied her feelings. "I want to be out from this cloud. If Daddy thinks you are the one to do it, I wouldn't disapprove."

"Ah, very nice," I said, "but would *you* hire me,

if daddy left it up to you?"

"I don't know," she admitted. "I suppose I might want to check your references. I mean, you seem a nice enough sort of man...but this is beyond my expertise."

"Were you satisfied with the police?"

"No."

"And Detective Wessner?"

"Oh, no."

"What would have satisfied you?"

"If they found out who killed him," she said. "It wasn't me—not directly, not indirectly. If you can prove that, I will have a good life for what is left of it. If not, I will continue to be miserable as long as I live."

I said my goodbyes to the Kulps. The doctor told me to call him on the morrow before I got my flight out. I was wondering after that tête-à-tête with his family if one-hundred thousand dollars was enough. I was sure, unless I stumbled upon a miracle, I wouldn't please them.

I went out into the snowy night with my trusty overcoat.

Zimmy was waiting at the door for me.

I settled into the front seat next to Zimmy. The snow was falling heavily now. It *was* beautiful.

"This damn snow," Zimmy said. "I wish it would let up."

9

Settled in my hotel room I pondered: Did I really want this job? Ginger's sensitivity, still strong a year after the death of her husband, seemed to me an orange flag. Was she protesting too much? I didn't believe she threw him off the roof—not actually—but metaphorically? All that insistence that the marriage was idyllic, that her late, apparently lamented, husband was nigh perfect—had not an enemy in the world. Is truth all perception?

Well, perhaps I didn't have to worry—the doc was not going to step up to the saucer with a hundred grand, and I had to admit my intestinal feeling was I had made a lousy impression on the women-folk. Almost as though I had been willing failure.

I went to sleep, reliving the dinner with the Kulps. I tried to analyze our tête-à-tête with an eye for mistakes I might avoid in future confrontations with someone whose work I might want. I was eager to get home to my palms and cycads.

I decided the case was intriguing, but in a way I didn't care to be intrigued.

The call I got the next morning was not the one

I expected. I answered it presumptuously, "Good morning, Dr. Kulp."

It was a woman's voice that said, "Mr. Yates," and the rest of it was so muffled I couldn't ascertain what was said.

"Excuse me?" I said, "I couldn't hear that."

"I need to talk to you," she said.

"About what?" I didn't want to hurt her feelings by asking who she was.

"Last night," she said, "Ginger."

That narrowed the field. But was this Ginger calling, or her mother Priscilla?

"May I come up to your room?"

"Up? Where are you?"

"I'm outside the hotel on my cell phone."

"Oh, well, I'll meet you in the lobby."

"No," she said, quickly. "I don't want to be seen. I'll explain—"

"I could meet you on the street."

"I said I didn't want to attract attention."

Reluctantly I gave her my room number.

While she was coming up to my room I had jittery visions of her making a play for me, and whether accepted or rebuffed, her husband (or father?), the good surgeon opting to do heart surgery on me—surgery that unluckily failed—just one of those things—condolences to the loved ones.

There was a gentle, almost hesitant knock on my door.

I opened it on a mirage of a woman paying homage to the burka, her dark glasses peeking out between her scarf and ski hat. Her formless dress touched the floor.

"Oh, thank goodness," she said, rather breathlessly, "I thought for a minute you wouldn't see me."

I thought the same thing but didn't communicate it.

She tore off the scarf and hat and let me know with that single gesture I was facing the mother, not the daughter. I suppose I was relieved with that option.

Hosting a woman in a hotel room where the dominant piece of furniture was a bed was daunting.

"Will you sit down?" I asked, gesturing to the one stuffed chair in the room—away from the bed, which she seemed to be eyeing. She took off her coat and deposited it on the bed, revealed a high fashion item on her svelte body—a look that might be more at home at a high priced charity event.

"I have to apologize," I said, "for answering the phone presumptuously. I thought it was your husband. I suppose he may call while you are here?" That last was a quasi-question. Perhaps with a thought to keep her in her chair. (You flatter yourself, Gil Yates.)

"He won't be calling," she said, with a grim smile.

"Oh, he said he would."

"Yes, but he's changed his mind," she said. "That's why I'm here."

I raised an eyebrow, begging the question.

"He and Ginger decided you were not respectful enough of Ginger—maybe groveling would be more accurate. Like you didn't realize what a princess Ginger was."

"Why, exactly, is Ginger a princess?"

"Long story."

I nodded. I wasn't sure I was in the mood for a

long story, especially if I didn't get the joke. "So why are you here?" I asked. "There's no need to apologize."

"No, I'm here to tell you that you have to take the job."

"If it's not offered? Did I misunderstand you? I thought you said your husband wouldn't be calling me?"

"*I* want you to get to the bottom of this. It's driving us all crazy."

I raised an eyebrow without much effort. "Against your husband's…and your daughter's wishes?"

"I expect I can bring them around."

"And if you can't?"

"I'd still want to pursue it."

"By hiring me?"

She nodded with a resolution that could have launched a bunch of ships.

"Not to be indelicate, but did your husband share our tentative fee arrangements with you?"

"He doesn't share."

"Yes, well, we were talking some big numbers."

"He has big numbers," she said.

"Yes, but… do *you*?"

"How big would you say?"

"We discussed a hundred thousand dollars," I said.

I thought her eyes would leave her head.

"A… hundred…"

I nodded. "Ten days—then we could reassess."

"Isn't that an awful lot of money?"

"It is to me," I said. "Less so to him, I imagine. That's why I asked. Do you have a joint bank account?"

She shook her head. Further vocalizations

seemed doubtful.

"Well," she said, after we stared at each other for eternity—okay, I exaggerate—five years? "Could we make some compromise? Some *other* arrangement?"

"Your husband tried, believe me."

"I believe you."

"It is not a case that lends itself to my usual contingency arrangement."

"What would that be?"

"I only get paid if I solve the crime. In this case, I'm not sure there was a crime. If I gave it my all and concluded Ginger's husband did the suicide dance, I don't think I would find favor in the heart surgeon's heart of hearts—do you?"

"No, of course not."

"So I felt I would earn my fee if I could show *why* he jumped. If I stumble on some convincing murder scenario, I would, of course, share it."

"Yes, yes," she said, "I agree with you. None of us want to accept the suicide verdict. Not if it turns out to reflect on us. I'm just afraid I can't accept any other scenario."

"Why do you suppose your husband and daughter can't accept suicide?"

"Ginger thinks people will blame her—not being a good enough wife, or something."

"What do you think?"

"I think we are all responsible for our own actions. Suicide requires the deepest depression. You can blame others, but you have to have it in you." She seemed lost in thought. When she regained her footing, she said, "Look here, it's an intriguing case. Why not give it a try. I'll see your expenses are taken care of. If you solve the thing to the doctor's satisfaction I'll get him to pay you."

I smiled. She must have grossly overrated my desire to have the job.

"I just had an epiphany," I said.

"Oh? What?"

"Your husband sent you on this errand to get me to reduce my fee."

"No," she said. "No, no, he would be most unhappy if he knew I was here. In this part of the country, in the doctor's tribe, women are to be seen and not heard."

"Was Ginger any good at that?"

"Well, each generation loosens up a bit."

"And time heals all lacerations," I said. "I expect Ginger should be about getting over this soon."

She shook her head. "You don't know Ginger."

"Do you think she has something to hide?"

"I'm afraid I do," she said, twisting her lips. "I'm not proud of it."

"You don't think she pushed him, do you?"

"Oh, not—not physically."

"Psychologically?"

"Maybe."

"Okay, how would you propose to—I don't want to be too mercenary, but how would you... pay me?"

She gave me enough pause to tell me she hadn't thought that through. "Well, my husband is a very rich man. If I asked him, he couldn't deny me. We have been married thirty-nine years."

"But don't you think if he wanted me working on the case, he would have hired me himself?"

"Not necessarily," she said. "There's the dynamic with Ginger—if she got bad vibes he might back off—even if his preference was to pursue the incident to get it behind us once and for all."

"But this is a small town. Do you see any way I could work on this case without both of them knowing about it?"

"No, but once it is a *fait accompli* they will not only accept it, they'll be happy about it."

"*Happy?*"

"Yes," she didn't seem at all conflicted in her quest.

"Okay," I said, drawing it out to convey my skepticism, "your husband has my fee schedule. Get him to sign his approval of it, and I will give your proposition serious consideration."

"In writing?" She seemed to think that was an outrageous request.

"In writing," I repeated. "*And* put the money in an escrow account controlled by you."

Five hours later I was on the plane to Los Angeles, in the first stage of withdrawal from what seemed to me a hopeless situation.

10

I survived another plane ride. Two actually—for the life of me, I can't imagine how. I understand some of the mysteries of life, but flight of enormous mega-tonnage steel airplanes, is not one of them.

Anyone who can add and subtract can surely see the airline industry is putting one over on us. Say a plane has a hundred passengers with an average weight of one-hundred and fifty pounds—that's fifteen-thousand pounds. Add one hundred pieces of luggage, and the same number of carry-on baggage at an average of fifty pounds each—another five-thousand pounds. There's *ten tons* already without the weight of that hulking steel leviathan, its crew and accoutrements.

So, okay, add that all up if you can, and tell me how that gigantic hunk of metal can float serenely through the sky without dropping like a stone, sending the whole kit and caboodle of ignorant sheep to their well-deserved oblivion.

My father-in-law, that world-class windbag Elbert Wemple, sole proprietor of Elbert Wemple Associate Realtors, with his Neanderthal pay package, keeps me treading water in the poverty pond.

Since I backed into this detective game (cf. *The Missing Link*), I have acquired a taste for filthy lucre, and as I achieved some success in amassing said lucre, its filthy nature receded in my consciousness. In partial honesty, I developed a taste for—to be perfectly crass about it—money. But, since this lucrative sideline was a secret from Tyranny Rex and her Daddybucks, I was forever tiptoeing on the tightrope.

In the fullness of time I have come to realize I may have over estimated Tyranny's interest in my affairs. To wit: I left her a note in a sealed envelope advising her of my trip to Pennsylvania. On my return the envelope reposed where I left it on the kitchen table. Unopened.

If she missed me at all, she showed an uncommon flair for repressing it.

Since I was home, I couldn't figure out a way to avoid that bag of gas, my pompous father-in-law, and coincidentally, employer.

I pulled into the parking lot of the low rent Quonset hut office building with the new outsized sign that proclaimed this the home—or final resting place—of Elbert Wemple, Associates in garish tasteless type that could have been seen ten miles away. The rest in seeing eye dog letters—garish red on a bright yellow background.

Daddybucks had told me he was getting a new sign for the outfit—something befitting his stature, he said.

They don't make signs that small, I said. Okay, I may not have actually *said* it, but I absolutely thought it.

I have found Daddybuck's pronouncements to be eminently forgettable, so I forgot it.

Until I pulled into my parking space, as far from the door as possible in our parking lot, befitting *my* stature in the eyes of Elbert A. Wemple, Associates, Realtors. My memory was jogged, or rather jolted, by the sign Daddybucks considered befitting of his stature. It was the size of a freeway billboard with said circus colors:

ELBERT WEMPLE, ASS. REALTORS
BROKERAGE & PROPERTY MANAGEMENT
ELBERT A. WEMPLE, PRINCIPAL

Not mentioned was the fact that this principal was hardly a man of principle.

I imagine the sign was visible from the freeway, some blocks away, and if tilted heavenward, it could be seen from the moon.

Taste was not his long suit. Now that I think of it, he didn't have *any* long suits.

Though my parking space was as far from the principal as possible, my desk was the closest to his throne, elevated so he could keep his eye on the troops—principally on me.

As soon as he saw me approach my desk, Daddybucks made his patented come-hither motion—a remarkable combination of a shoulder jolt and a full-fingered swirl. I complied—my shoes made of concrete—but I bypassed the exclusive chilled water in a sudden burst of desire to get it over with.

There was the man himself, sitting on his throne in all his resplendent glory—king of all he surveyed (a room the size of an airplane hanger and more sales-people than there was any sense counting). Dapper Dan was in his signature chocolate brown dandruff-flecked suit, presiding over his nickel-pinching factory.

"Where the Sam Hill you been, boy? I been looking all over for you."

"I've been to London to visit the queen," I said. I'd gotten dangerously flip since I started earning big bucks at the investigation game. No matter, it went in one ear and out the other. He wasn't a guy who troubled himself to listen to what anyone else was saying.

"I don't know how the queen is going to help you with the ball of snakes we got down in Cypress."

And I'm a snake charmer, I almost said. "You never know," I said, instead.

It was the usual "ball of snakes" talk.

I always experience severe ennui when Gasbag goes on one of his rants. A few key words and you have it. You can safely snooze through the rest.

"You seem to be taking an awful lot of time off lately."

"Thank you," I said.

"For what?"

"For noticing."

"Yeah, well don't let that little head of yours swell up," he said. "The secretary could do your job on her lunch break."

Ah, I thought, but could she take your constant belittling?

"Let her," I said with the supreme confidence that went with my private investigation sideline where I was sometimes averaging more in year than in my career with Daddybucks. That may contain a touch of hyperbole, but just a touch. But thoughts of quitting this rabbit race were never far from my mind.

"Why do you take so much time off?" he needled. I sensed he was befuddled by my bravado. "You have a girlfriend?" he asked.

"Dozens," I said.

"Very funny. But seriously, why so much vacation?"

"Keeps it fresh," I said "sharpens the secretary's skills."

"Fresh?" he asked. "Who's fresher, you or a rotten banana?"

That one went over my hairline, but I didn't pursue it.

I thought about the chances of landing the job in Pennsylvania from the Kulp clan: skinny to zip. I was about convinced it was not my cup of java, but after five minutes with Daddybucks I ached for a return to Dr. Barracuda Kulp, who compared to the resident gasbag was Albert Schweitzer.

"I'll get right on it," I said, when it appeared Daddybucks had run out of steam. I was grateful for the escape.

On my way off his megalomaniacal platform, I helped myself to his chilled water—the only cooler in the place—room temperature water in the service of the peons saved him a few dollars a year.

The ball of snakes, it turned out was in "Cypress" which we called "Cypress" in tribute to our proprietor's pretension. To wit, the apartment complex straddled three cities: Lakewood fifty-five percent, Hawaiian Gardens forty percent, and Cypress five percent—a corner of the parking area. But the cachet was with Cypress, a touch more upscale, so Cypress it was.

It was one of our challenging properties due to

the unhappy fact that Gasbag insisted on installing his cleaning woman in the manager's position. Though I prefer a manager of a hundred and twenty-unit apartment to have had some experience, I am but a poor, powerless underling, who is left to cope with the challenges of inept inexperience.

The ball of snakes was, however, something less than the calamity it was portrayed by Señor Wemple, the dandruff king of Torrance, California.

Felicia Morales, the manager/cleaning woman in question was comfortably in her forties—and had just married a fellow who painted for us. He was comfortably into his twenties—Juan Gonzales was his name, and Juan had taken a shine to a young cutie closer to his age who fortuitously resided in the self-same property. Delilah Ramirez by name who was almost a high school graduate, who favored short skirts and skin-tight blouses. Juan was convinced Delilah had sent him strong signals of interest fostered by the patron saint of Eros. To that end he blew six hours of his painting income on a dozen American Beauty roses, which he deposited on her doorstep with a note declaring his love. He was, it must be acknowledged, no Robert Browning or Bill Shakespeare, but his recitations of Delilah's endearing attributes was from his heart.

For some reason Delilah was shocked by his sentiments—*shocked!* But she liked the floral tribute.

Enter the snake charmer, and his heart-to-heart chat with Romeo.

Juan was suitably chagrined, if not terribly contrite. The chick had led him on, he was sure of that. Sure, he was married, even if it were an arrangement of convenience. And just as assuredly I recognized the times were one of ultimate personal freedoms. I countered with the advantages of the appearance of old-fashioned propriety. And furthermore, I was bound to convey from Herr Wemple himself, his desire that the offending Juan cease and desist from working for his company. I neglected to add the gasbag's proffered advice that Felicia divorce him like a hot potato. I thought that was going a little far. Robbing Lothario of his livelihood seemed sufficient retribution.

Someone said men and women were not compatible, and I was having a hard time arguing with that. The machinations of the sexes, the deep recesses of the mysteries therein are as old as mankind. Every day we can be alarmed by the peccadilloes of some celebrity or other, as though their dalliances were endlessly shocking and unusual.

As that old slaveholder said, all men are created equal and have certain inalienable rights to life, liberty and the *pursuit of happiness*, which he himself pursued with his fourteen-year-old slave—she bearing him a passel of kiddies. Sex goes way back, but we have an undiminished capacity to be astonished by it.

C'est la vie.

Why that put me in mind of Ginger Kulp and her late husband, I'm not sure. Perhaps I had developed a notion that his demise was sexually related—girlfriend troubles—or maybe even Ginger had her extra-curricular romps.

But, by now I had written them off. I wasn't put off by Priscilla Kulp's last minute foray before I left Pennsylvania. She was not the custodian of the bucks, and without the buck, I had no truck.

So, imagine my surprise when I got home and

found a message on my machinery devoted to just such nonsense.

"Hi, Gil, it's Priscilla. Give me a call. I have good news!"

$10,000*

Good news is a matter of perspective. Good news to Priscilla Kulp was meeting my requirements—some might say "demands," but that is so pushy.

Bad news: I was back on an airplane. It should get easier each time, but it doesn't. I just can't conquer the math to see what keeps that monster up there.

Good news was my commitment for ten days for one-hundred thousand dollars—which without using any tricky formulas—worked out to ten-thousand dollars a day.

I'd arranged in advance to have a copy of the predecessor's investigation report at the hotel.

When I landed in Muhlenheim, miraculously without falling out of the sky, I picked up my rental car and the suitcase I had to pay an extra twenty-five dollars for. But that's not all. I had to pay for a lunch on the plane from Los Angeles to Chicago. The airlines have a

---

* I am quantifying these daily remunerative amounts—which could easily and fairly be considered in poor taste—somewhat self-consciously. They appear on the day they are earned and are listed cumulatively for the profound salubrious effect they have on my self-esteem.

lot of nerve trying to make a profit at their passengers' expense.

When I checked in, I asked for the package that was to be dropped off for me. There was none. Not a good sign. I decided to wait until the morrow to inquire of the good doctor about why this promise had gone unfulfilled.

I had settled into the stuffed chair in the room, and was reading a good book by David Champion called *Bomber Bombs*, when the phone rang.

"Hello?"

"Mr. Yates?"

"Yes."

"This is Zimmy. I'm in the lobby with a special delivery for you."

"The detective's report?"

"I don't know what it is. I'm just the messenger."

I went down. Zimmy and I greeted each other as though long lost companions, alumni of a shipwreck, or similar calamity.

I hied it up to my room, tore open the envelope and began to read.

If you've ever read a police report you know they are snoozers. CYB—cover your backbone or something. This was not much more exciting.

It was bound in one of those clear plastic binders readily available at stationery stores the world over. The title, visible through the plastic:

PRIVATE INVESTIGATION INTO THE CASE
OF THE DEATH OF (EDWARD) SANDY STRAUS

There was a date and a signature at the bottom of the page under:

Respectfully submitted

I liked that touch.

The next page was a Table of Contents, not unlike a Ph.D. thesis, viz. titles sounding more profound than the subjects were liable to be.

Cutting through the self-serving palaver in search of some rational theories, preferably illuminated with facts, I came up pretty parched.

The only ideas presented to counter the suicide verdict of the police were under the heading of

THEORIES UNABLE TO SUBSTANTIATE

1. The victim, finding it stuffy or claustrophobic in his office, went outdoors in the most expedient manner—the bridge leading to the scene of the accident—perhaps to simply get some fresh air. He sat for a moment on the ledge and somehow lost his balance and fell to his death. He may have leaned over to see something on the ground, real or imagined.

Alternatively, he could have been sitting there for some time, perhaps deep in thought, lost his balance, perhaps suffered a brief but fatal bout of vertigo, and fell as above.

2. Victim was surprised by intruders in the store after closing. In fear and desperation he sought the most convenient exit to escape their threat. He climbed the wall for an easy jump, but in his excitement fell on his head.

3. He surprised intruders in the store who led him at gunpoint to the roof and proceeded to push him over the parapet.

There was no mention of evidence of a physical struggle in the coroner's report (attached). There were no signs of struggle or physical exertion of any kind. There was no evidence found in this investigation that would indicate anyone wanted to kill Sandy Straus. By all accounts of everyone questioned by this investigator, he was a widely well-liked gentleman. No one could remember ever hearing him arguing or raising his voice with anyone.

Private Investigator Wessner took care to praise the police work in the case, with an eye, no doubt, to getting referrals from them in the future. I don't expect he was insensitive to the fact that his client, the good Dr. Kulp, would not be pleased by that, but Wessner must have weighed the relative likelihood of getting further work from Dr. Kulp—a one-case client—or the police with their many cases and contacts, and landed on the side of the latter.

Wessner's report didn't give me a lot to go on. I wonder if I had seen it before I signed on for the case, would I be here now? But ten-thousand dollars a day is ten-thousand dollars a day, and it adds up in ten days.

First thing in the morning I had an appointment with Priscilla Kulp at her house—after the doctor left for work. I wondered if she'd read the report. It wouldn't surprise me if the good doctor had kept it from her. Either way, I was curious to hear what her theories were.

After Priscilla, I was to see Ginger Straus. I imagined Dr. Kulp was not too happy about that, but with his wife Priscilla in charge of the case, the tobogganing should be smoother. I initially laid down the private audience with Ginger as a minimal requirement for taking the case and Priscilla readily agreed, whereas her husband had balked at the suggestion, expecting, I suppose, that I could conjure evidence to please him from the thin atmosphere. But he finally agreed to put the money in an escrow under his wife's control.

Sleep always came to me reluctantly after a west to east trip. This time I had plenty to mull over in the meantime.

$20,000

The streets were shiny, glassy slick at this hour of the morning, but somehow I managed—mostly by driving annoyingly slowly.

I pulled in front of the address given in a neighborhood of wide lots and generous setbacks, and houses that might be commodious for a few extra families.

There was a Cadillac parked out front. The house was an amalgam of beige stone and red brick, as though they had run out of one or the other, or perhaps a statement that the residents could afford both. It was two stories, probably a nod to the efficacy of heating such a mansion—heating the lower floor would rise to the second. It seemed a trifle ostentatious to me, but then I realized how modest it was vis-à-vis the doctor's income.

Priscilla opened the door, dressed to kill in some cashmere apricot getup, and hurtled out of the house as though there was something therein she preferred I didn't see.

"I want to show you something," she said and led me to *her* Cadillac parked in the street in front of the house, as though poised there for a quick getaway.

When we climbed in, she behind the wheel, I said, "You don't waste any time."

"At ten thousand dollars a day we don't have that luxury."

Obviously I was going to like Priscilla.

We left the posh area of her home, out onto a busy thoroughfare and into the lungs of the city. It was an eastern town in the aftermath of the industrial boom—and bust. Nothing much seemed to be going on—a couple of young'uns with aspirations to gang notoriety lurking around street corners, their visages a combination of latent menace and juvenile boredom.

The streets weren't busy. There was nowhere to go.

Priscilla was a bit of a talker and she rattled on with her life history, as though that would clear her of some suspicions I didn't have. When she got to the part about her early pre-Ginger work experience I asked, "How did you decide to become a nurse?"

"I wanted to be a doctor, but the money just wasn't there, so I opted for the next best thing. And it was a good thing too."

"Why?"

"I'd have never landed the doctor, if I was a doctor too."

"How do you know?"

"He's a landsman—Pennsylvania Dutch. Women here are still subservient for the most part—especially his generation."

"Was Ginger subservient?"

"That's a younger generation. Women's stock continues to rise the world over. Some places at a faster pace."

"So is that a no?" I asked.

"Ginger, subservient?" she frowned as though she were considering the question. For the first time, perhaps she was. "No... I don't think so. But Sandy had such a beautiful temperament. I don't think you'll find anyone to say anything bad about Sandy."

"And Ginger?" I asked. "Will I get any negatives?"

She paused too long. "Ginger...? Well, I don't know. I'm perhaps the wrong one to ask. I'm her mother."

"So, as far as you're concerned, Ginger is perfect?"

"Well, how many of us are perfect?"

"Not many," I agreed. "Was Ginger?"

"Oh, she may have had some shortcomings."

"Like what?"

"Oh, I can't be specific. She was an only child, you know."

"Yes—" I thought I nuanced that "yes" in a fashion that would encourage Priscilla to continue. She didn't. It was too early in the investigation to press her. I didn't want to turn her off.

"Did you and the doctor have a good relationship?"

"Oh—oh, my, yes. I would have to say yes. He certainly was a good provider."

"And you and Ginger? One happy family?"

"Yes," she said, but a little more emphasis would have sold me more. "The doctor doted on Ginger."

"Too much?"

"Too much?" She seemed confused. "Can you love someone too much?"

"I could imagine you could."

"No. No, love is what it's all about."

It was such a nice sentiment; I let it drop for now.

Priscilla turned her Cadillac off the main street into a narrow alley. It was wide enough for one car going one way. No room to park. It ran between two larger streets and that was it. I wondered what miasma of city planning blessed Muhlenheim with this geography—a blip on the city grid.

A blip, apparently, that produced the august Dr. Chester Kulp.

Both sides of the street had row houses, cheek-by-jowl, street-to-street; they crowded the alley like two small mouths, facing each other, both full of buckteeth.

Priscilla pulled in front of a tooth, brick-faced, in roughly the center of the block.

She checked the rear-view mirror. "If someone comes, we'll have to move," she said. "Well, this is it."

"It?"

"The doctor's *geburtshaus.*"

"Excuse me?"

"The house of his birth. His parents were the first generation in his German family who spoke English."

"Have you been inside?"

"Well, the doctor is strong on appearances. He'd rather not have people know he grew up in an alley."

"Is that possible in this smallish town?"

"Well," she said, her mind drifting, "*he* thinks so—and when the doctor speaks, we listen—we don't contradict."

She sighed. "These houses are all the same; living room, dining and kitchen, first floor; bedrooms and bath, the floors above. Each bedroom had two beds, two slept in each. The latest born shared the bedroom with Ma & Pa, the next youngest slept in the living room. Somehow they shoehorned the lot of them in there. I don't suppose it hurt that two of them died."

"Why?"

"Why what?"

"Why are you showing me this?"

"I want you to understand."

"Understand what?"

"My husband."

"Your husband?"

"Where he came from. What his roots are. Why he is so driven—so successful."

"Well, I imagine a lot of boys came off this alley who were less driven, less successful."

"That's true," she conceded. "His brother Fabian, for example. But whatever you find out in your investigation, remember the alley."

I nodded as though giving a solemn oath. "But why?" I asked.

"Things happened here," she said, under a shroud of mystery.

"What things?"

"Oh…I'm afraid you must ask my husband. I would not feel it was my place to disclose…"

"Will he tell me what it is you are referring to?"

The morning was replete with dramatic pauses. Here was another. "I don't know," she said finally, "perhaps not. It is not something he talks about. Anyway, I doubt it has any bearing on your investigation."

"Oh, but every morsel of knowledge interlocks like a jigsaw puzzle. You can't complete the puzzle without all the pieces."

She smiled. Was it amusement, derision, or complicity? "Perhaps so," she said, "but it is a piece you must get from him."

I realized I didn't have a lot of hope he would enlighten me. That was when I thought of my airplane seatmate, Jessamyn who worked for the local newspaper.

I made a mental note to call her when I had obtained a morsel of privacy.

13

"And what about you?" I asked Priscilla.

"Me? What about me?"

"Where did you come from?"

"Oh, just over there," she said, nodding in an eastern direction.

"Is it far from here?"

"Nothing is far from here."

"Can you show me the house you grew up in?"

"Why on earth...?"

"Well, you showed me your husband's. Give me a larger picture."

"But he's an important man. I'm just a little housewife. You aren't liable to find anything helpful in my past."

"Will it take more than fifteen minutes?"

"Nooo... probably not."

"You could give me the address and I could go without you, if you prefer?"

She didn't move the car.

"Why aren't we going?" I asked.

"Because I'm not important in this scheme. I had a much easier life than the doctor. Ordinary, really. I'm not interested in casting my shadow over him. Not in any circumstance."

"Very noble," I said, "but let's go anyway. Humor me."

With another gaze into my eyes, she slid the car into a forward gear.

It was perhaps fifteen or twenty blocks, and as we drove the neighborhoods got progressively more affluent. Was it there I developed my theory that affluence could be gauged in this neck of the forest by the distance the front door of the house was from the street? In the doctor's home neighborhood, the front door was *on* the street. The Doctor Kulp manse was set back far enough for another house to be built in the front yard, and still have a front yard of it's own.

The ancestral home of Priscilla Kulp was one car length back from the street—so a car could be parked in the driveway between the house and the street.

"There it is," she said.

It was a two-story red brick box, very much like its neighbors. A decided cut above the doctor's alley, yet still a far piece from the house and neighborhood they lived in now.

"How long did you live here?"

"From birth until I married the doctor."

"While you were going to nursing school?"

"Yes."

"Like it?"

"The house or nursing school?"

"Both."

"Yes, to both."

"Any lawyers in your family?"

"No, why?"

"I don't know, just seemed you made that a little more complex than it had to be. You could have said 'both' right away."

"I didn't think of it."

"Fair enough," I said, but I thought she seemed to want to be extra careful with her answers, as though she were in court.

"Your family still live here?"

She shook her head. "Dad died last year. Mom's in a home."

"In reasonable shape?"

"Reasonable. Still gets around with a walker. Mind's good."

"Have a good family life, did you?"

"I'd say so."

"Siblings?"

"A sister—younger. Married, two kids, lives upstate."

"Husband works?"

She nodded, but didn't specify.

"Doing what, may I ask?"

"I don't see how any of this matters," she said, a trifle testily.

"Yes, well, if you prefer, I can ask someone else."

"He's a truck driver."

"Is that something to be ashamed of?"

"No, certainly not. No, no...no. It's honest work."

"Is it the cause of any sensitivity among you? Your husband is the pre-eminent heart surgeon in the valley—her's is..."

"A truck driver, yes," she said, then added hastily, "They have a wonderful family life. They're very happy."

"And those are the important things."

"Yes."

"May I ask a delicate question?"

"Do you ask any other kind?"

"Touché," I had to like her, even though she seemed a touch more prickly than I thought warranted. "You have a sister."

"Yes."

"Your sister has two children."

"Yes, so what?"

"You had only one."

"So what again?"

"Well, that I guess is my question. Why?"

"Because that's all we had. Some people have zero children. We're one up on them."

I didn't really know what testy was until I absorbed that response. I thought of more questions in that line, but decided I'd gotten enough of an answer and I thought it best to keep her on my side.

So I stayed silent on substance on the drive back to her home in the ritzy section. I didn't have to guess that her sister and family did not achieve this standard of living—unless perhaps the man of the house was driving trucks for drug lords.

Priscilla more than made up for my reticence with a constant stream of inconsequential chatter, as though she were trying to tell me to keep digging because there were clues there that I had to ferret out myself.

Why was she so protective, and who was she trying to protect? Or the larger question was why was she so intent on me crossing the country to investigate this stale case if she didn't want to reveal anything that might help solve it? Could she have been culpable in some way?

When we pulled into her airport length driveway, she invited me inside. I didn't think she would.

I followed her up an upper-crust length stone walkway to the imposing over-sized front door in a rich burgundy hue.

Priscilla extracted a key from her purse and, with some notable embarrassment, turned it in the lock and opened the door. By way of explanation, she said, "The doctor insists I lock the doors. I'd rather a thief came in the door than break a window to get in. When I was growing up, we never locked our doors."

I followed her into an entry hall that no swell would have to be ashamed of.

It hit me like a ton of stone as I rounded the corner into the living room: over the mantel of an imposing stone fireplace reposed an even more imposing full-length portrait of the man of the house, resplendent in his white scrubs, standing with his right hand on the back of an empty chair. It was the most god-like portrait of a human being I'd ever seen. His facemask was settled around his neck, and if that was a smile on his cold lips it was at once grim and self-important.

"Wow!" I said.

"Yes," she said.

"Is the empty chair symbolic of something?"

"The chair is for scale. It is two-thirds regular size, so it makes the doctor look taller."

"Oh, my."

"Now that has to remain our secret. I would never say such a thing."

I nodded as somberly as I could, though I was

laughing on the inside. The size and scale to the large-enough room was laughable, but the larger question was why was she telling me?

She asked me to sit down and I had the immediate notion that I would defile this expensive-looking furniture.

The carpet was meringue deep beige. The expensive furniture credited to one of those dead French kings—an ecumenical move on the part of these trans-Pennsylvania Germans.

She offered me an assortment of libations and sweets, all of which I declined. I had an admittedly peculiar notion that if I took some refreshment from her I would be obligated to her slant on the story. The one-hundred thousand dollar fee didn't seem to enliven the same scruples.

Out of the blue, she asked, "Did anyone ever tell you, you have the most gorgeous blue eyes?"

That stunned me to silence. No one had, but I couldn't think it was a serious question. More bizarre, was that she was coming on to me like that. Did she really have something to hide and needed my help hiding it?

"You're the first," I said.

"I can't believe that," she said, still in her vamp character.

I hastily asked for directions to her daughter Ginger's house and bid starry-eyed Priscilla farewell—for now.

14

Ginger's house was less than a mile from the doctor and Priscilla's. It was suitably less ostentatious, but not by much. The driveway was one car length shorter, the façade was all brick, but the differences ended there.

I parked behind a Cadillac in front of the manse. This family seemed to be supporting the Cadillac dealer single-handedly.

The hike to the front door was less taxing than at Ginger's parents' home. The front door a modest size and color (white). My gentle knock was answered by the lady of the house, resplendent in a lime merino wool dress that neither hid nor underplayed any of her considerable physical charms. Everything was perfectly sized and right where it should be.

"Mr. Yates," she said with a conservative smile. "Nice to see you again. Please come in."

I followed her and the moment I was able to take my eyes off her I searched the walls for a full-length portrait of Dr. Kulp. I didn't find it—but I wasn't disappointed for there was a somewhat more modest oil of the good doctor—Daddy, in this case—over the fire-place. He was wearing a nice somber suit and tie and vest, and I could swear, sitting in the same two-thirds scale chair that he stood behind in the portrait in his own home.

Ginger noticed me looking at the portrait. "Do you like it?" she asked. "It's not as large as Mummy's but Daddy gave it to us as a housewarming gift. I was going to say wedding gift, but I guess the house was that."

"Nice gift," I said.

"Daddy is very generous with me."

Was it my imagination or was she projecting her voice over the imaginary footlights? "Here," she said, "let me take your coat."

As though on cue from the wings Dr. Kulp made his proprietary entrance—the house was, I assume, largely his.

"Hello Yates," the august doctor said, with what I took for a smile of derision. It does me no credit to confess that something inside of me snapped and I responded without thinking.

"Hello Kulp. Fancy seeing you here."

I could forever mark that as the nadir of our rela-tionship such as it was. But it achieved one thing, that derisive smile instantly faded to contempt.

He took a seat in the center of the long couch and splayed his arms out from his body in a territorial gesture, as though this were his house and I was the Fuller Brush man, an unwelcome intruder. "Kulp, indeed."

"I'm sorry," I said. "I had an appointment to see Ginger." I nodded in her direction.

"Yes," he said, the supercilious smile returning. "I won't interrupt. Just consider me an innocent bystander."

I shook my head with an impolitic hint of amusement. "My interviews are one-on-one. No bystanders, innocent or not."

Kulp showed no inclination to movement so I bowed to the ever-radiant Ginger and said, "I'll be leaving you now. No sense wasting the time of three people. I can attempt some further investigation without you—I wouldn't guarantee any useful result, or I can curtail it now with a plane ride home. You will only be out thirty-thousand dollars. Your choice." I directed a sappy smile at Kulp, "Consider it a heart operation gone badly," I said.

Eyes aslant, head cocked back, Kulp was giving me the third degree silent treatment. "Wait a minute, Yates," he said rising from his turf. He cocked his head in Ginger's direction and beckoned her to follow him through the dining room to the kitchen, a closed door.

I was too amused to leave, although I considered it. I had time to chastise myself for not connecting the Cadillac in front of her house with the good doctor.

There was a commotion in the kitchen that the closed door didn't silence—voices were raised, an argument was in progress.

While I was speculating on what the reaction would be if I slipped out, the warring factions returned to the living room; Ginger, red-faced again; Dr. Kulp, it could fairly be said, looked disgruntled. Ginger went to the hall closet and retrieved a hat and overcoat, not mine.

"All right, Yates," he said, "you won this round.

I'm warning you, you haven't seen the last of me."

"Okay…Kulp."

He got a look of all consuming hatred in his eyes. "And I'll thank you to show me proper respect. My title is *Doctor* Kulp. I'm a medical doctor. The effort required to attain this status is worthy of the respect of persons far more worthy than you. Good day."

And with that lecture on status he took the coat and hat from his daughter and was out the door.

I looked at Ginger. She seemed embarrassed, but didn't say anything.

So I did. "I must say I never had clients who seemed so intent on making it difficult for me to do my job."

She pondered the thought. "Daddy must be under a lot of stress," she said. "I mean, being a heart surgeon can't be that easy."

"Hmm, perhaps not. Others seem to cope with it. What's eating him?"

"Why do you ask?"

"Well, you're an adult, yet he is intent on running interference for you. I thought it was his idea to investigate this case again. Was it not?"

"He is doing it for me. He wants me to be as happy as I was before my Sandy was…taken from me."

"Are you dating?"

She got a stricken look. "Oh lord, no."

"Why not?"

"It would be blasphemy."

"Why?"

"It just would," she said cutting off further discussion.

"The more you can help me, the better chance I

have of solving this. Are you *willing* to help?"

"Certainly."

"You know, I have the strangest feeling that you all don't want me to succeed. As though you might fear what I find. That goes for the three of you—father, mother, and you. Is there any possibility…"

"Why, that's just silly. Why would we agree to pay your outrageous fee if we didn't want a resolution?"

"Ah, resolution perhaps, without a solution?"

"No."

"Or only a solution you preordain? Will you be able to accept a resolution that supports suicide?"

"He didn't commit suicide!"

"So then, I take it the answer is no?"

"I won't accept something I know not to be true."

"No matter what the supporting contradictory facts show?"

She shook her head. We sat in silence.

"I have a suggestion," I said at length.

"What?"

"If your mind is closed then you don't want it opened. I venture for half of my fee you could get someone to write the report you want. Or he might even sign a report that you write."

"You insult me, Mr. Yates."

"It's your daddy who wants the title. I'm just plain Gil." I said. "So I'm third in your investigation pantheon. The police and detective what's-his-name failed to please you. What makes you think—hope—I will be any different?"

"I have faith in you," she said. Then she added with a connection I couldn't fathom, "Gil, did anyone ever tell you you had the prettiest blue eyes...?"

Wow! I almost said, your mother did just today. Instead I smiled the smile of gratitude. "You just did," I said.

To keep the record straight, I must disclose I am not immune to this kind of base flattery. You might say I was painfully susceptible. A pushover. What I didn't understand was why I had been a recipient of it. Why did Priscilla and Ginger need my goodwill? Could they be involved in a cover-up? But why would Priscilla have gone to the end of the branch to get me on the case? Could it be my unthreatening demeanor?

"This is a nice house you have here," I said, changing an uncomfortable subject.

"Oh, thank you. The furniture's mostly from the store."

I nodded. "Many people as young as you in this neighborhood?"

"Daddy helped us buy the house."

"Helped you how?"

"Money. We couldn't afford this neighborhood on Sandy's salary. Daddy made it possible."

"Was Sandy okay with that?"

Another cloud shrouded her pretty face. "Well, we did it. Sandy might have rather been...oh, further from the folks."

"A smothering presence, were they?"

"Oh...no, I don't think so."

"Did Sandy think so?"

"You misunderstand Sandy. He was so easy to get along with. Nothing bothered him."

"Did your father's abundant attention come closer than anything else?"

She blushed. "I wouldn't say that," she said.

You just did, I thought.

"Daddy's been so supportive during this...upset. He may not always be the easiest person to get along with, but he means well."

"I'm sure," I said, not so sure. "How did you get along with your husband?"

"Famously. We *loved* each other."

"Any disagreements?"

Pause. "Well, nothing of any consequence. The usual marital squabbles, I guess."

"Such as?"

"Oh, I can't even think of anything now. All my memories are positive."

"Was he moody?"

"Oh, isn't everyone?"

"Were you?"

"Well, see above. But very seldom," she said. "You know, I don't want to be the focus of your suspect list."

"But you aren't. What makes you think you would be?"

"All these...questions. This...probing."

"That's what I do. I probe...everybody. It's a puzzle. I need all of the pieces to solve it."

"I didn't kill him."

"I expect, Mrs. Straus, that would be fairly obvious. You weren't on the roof to push him. And though you might think someone else pushed him, apparently the prior investigators didn't yield a suspect. Can you give me some names of people you think might have killed him, and why they would want to?"

"I don't know who killed him. I only know two

things: it wasn't me, and he didn't jump. "

"Why are you so sure he didn't jump?"

"Because he was a happy man. Contented—a wonderful husband."

"Did you have children?" I knew they didn't. I was looking for her reaction.

"No, we weren't blessed. But he would have been a wonderful father too."

15

My iphone was out of my pocket before I got into my car. The Cadillac was gone, which relieved me.

The iphone was a mind-bending invention especially to one (me) who had not come up through the ranks with more rudimentary models. It was all part of the thousand years of progress in a hundred—or even ten years—depending on your viewpoint.

The nifty phones were assembled in China by fellows before they leapt to glory from tall buildings from the stress of their eleven hour per day weeks in service of the aforementioned world progress.

I punched up Jessamyn's number.

"Oh, hi there," she answered on the third ring.

"Do you have a minute?"

"I just got into class. Can I call you when I get out?"

"Sure thing," I said.

I drove back to my hotel, parked the car in their lot and made my way across the main street of Muhlenheim to the nearest department store. I wanted to make an appointment to talk to Manny Ness, if he would deign to see me.

The sun had done its bit on the snow and only patches remained. The street reverted to shiny black, coated with melted snow like some ice skating rink retiring for summer.

I pushed through the revolving door and was hit by the warmth of Ness's heating system—some Eastern boiler contraption, no doubt. I passed the perfume counter with a young pretty woman offering free samples (I declined, I hope politely).

Gentle messages wafted from speakers: what to find where, incredible bargains to drag you through the store past other counters that may tug your impulse purchase strings.

I stopped at the jewelry counter to inquire of another attractive young woman the whereabouts of Manny Ness.

I noticed their clerks were fairly uniformly young and dressed in severe black dresses terminating at mid calf. Fashion would fluctuate these lengths from ankle to thigh but I suspected there was a Ness immunity to these impulsive elevation changes. Over the left breast of the young women clerks were jeweled brooches with their names engraved in gold (leaf, I would hope). This smiling face was signed Debbie. Behind her and elevated was a diamond display. It seemed rather garish to me but I'm not a connoisseur of expensive trinkets.

To be sociable, I asked, "How much is that pile of gems behind you?"

"The blank diamond?" she said. There was a name in the blank space but I don't remember what it was. Doubtless it would have meant something to diamond sophisticates. She looked at it longingly.

"That's only four-hundred and seventy-five thousand."

"That's all?" I said with a sappy smile. "Sell any?"

She matched my smile. "You'll be the first," she said.

"Well," I said, "will you let me think about it?"

She allowed as how that would be fine. I wondered with Muhlenheim prices if I'd charged the Kulps too little.

"Where might I find Manny Ness?" I asked her.

"His office is on the third floor behind the furniture department."

I took the escalator to the third floor taking in the appealing displays of merchandise en route: menswear, candy, cheese, toys, children's clothes, athletic equipment. On three there was a lot of furniture, which looked high end, but from the prices displayed, apparently it wasn't.

The door to the executive offices was modestly placed around a corner and discreetly signed—small delicate letters:

Executive Offices

There was nothing especially welcoming about the décor, but nothing foreboding either, so I went in.

Inside there were other offices with secretaries out front—two or three cubicles to a secretary. On a hunch, I went to the end where I found a woman sitting guard at a lone office. She was somewhat longer in the tooth than some of the females on the sales floor but perhaps more pleasant on the surface than her longevity would warrant.

"Yes sir?" she said, with a welcoming tone. I

could imagine the tone more challenging in a larger city. "How may I help you?"

"I wondered how I could get an appointment to see Mr. Ness?"

"When did you want to see him?"

"At his convenience."

"Well, let me ask him," she said. "Your name?"

"Gil Yates."

She picked up her phone, pushed a button and said, "There is a Mr. Yates here asking for an appointment to see you." She smiled listening to his response. She replaced the phone in its cradle and said, "Go right in."

At first I thought I misunderstood. No executive wait? No, "I'm too busy—call next week…" No, "What does he want" even—just go right in.

So I did.

It was quite an office—art and artifacts all over the place. Mussolini would not have balked at the size. I approached his desk, the bulk of which would have also put a smile on the face of any Italian. The guy behind the desk rose, met me half way to my destination, put out his hand and said, "I'm Manny Ness. Welcome to my modest digs."

Manny had a craggy face that wouldn't have been out of place on a lumberjack. Weathered and leathered with the lines turning up instead of down. He wore a tailored blue suit, white shirt and burgundy tie. Anything more daring might have rocked the senses of the conservative fold in this valley.

He motioned for me to take the seat across the desk from where he now parked himself.

"So, Mr. Yates," he said, looking through me.

"May I call you Gil?"

"Of course."

"I'm Manny," he said. "To what do I owe this honor?"

On my tongue was 'What makes you think it's an honor?' but I held it there.

"Informal," I said, to put him at ease, though this did not by his demeanor seem necessary, "not to put the touch on you."

He smiled.

"Though, I was—am—pleasantly surprised at how easy it was to get to see you."

He waved the proverbial hand of dismissal. "We're a community store. We don't high-hat members of the community."

"I'm from California."

He shrugged. "So you take a chance. What can I do for you, California?"

"I'm working on the Sandy Straus case."

He sank back in his chair, as though winded. "They're still at it?" he said. "Can't let go?"

"Apparently not. But I'm just a hired hand."

He nodded.

"Any theories on Straus's death?"

"Theories? I suppose everyone in town has developed some scenario. Myself, I think he jumped."

"Why did he?"

"The only guy who knows the answer to that isn't here to answer it."

"How was their business?"

"How much time do you have?"

"Lots," I said.

16

"Times are changing," Manny Ness began. "Times are always changing. The old country store to the department store to the mall to the internet. It's all happening right here to us. Adapt or die. We adapted. Straus slid along on tradition. We signed up for the mall—some spell that M-A-U-L," he said, smiling that smile of rueful acceptance of fate. "Straus held back on the mall. They did just fine with the store as it was. The Princeton boys were not a forward-looking bunch. Hidebound in their tradition, went to all the football games with their blankets and beer kegs. Active in the community, belonged to big clubs—I always wondered who was watching the store.

"By the time they came around to accepting the future in the mall, the best space was gone. So they are waiting and waiting for the next mall, and before that's finished everybody will be buying from the internet. You press a button and—click," his fingers mimicked the gesture, "—that pretty spring frock is on its way to your door."

"Can you survive where you are?"

"Survive? If by survive you mean make a profit, I don't think so. Straus always did less than we did—now we're off and the gap is widening. Downtown Muhlenheim ain't what it used to be. What downtown is? Neighborhoods change. They are closer to the rabble than we are, but it's going to hit us all. The mall is in a cornfield. But just when you get comfy with that isolation this techno wizardry known as the internet," he made a sour face, "comes along offering even *more* isolation from the riffraff."

"So," I interjected, "do you think all of this might have pushed Sandy Straus off the ledge?"

"Might have helped," he said, looking out his window on the streets of row houses. "Sandy was the sensitive one, I recall. You know that wife of his was a startling beauty. She had it all—looks and incredible wealth. There wasn't a red-blooded guy for miles around that didn't envy his catch."

"Why did *he* get her?"

He laughed. "Why indeed? Who was she going to pick—a gas station attendant? When she could have a Straus? Country-club inbreeding. How much reason has the heart? Proximity and timing play a big part in those things, but I don't pretend to have that answer, and the thing that snows me is, why do the Kulps keep at this thing? 'Let sleeping dogs lie' they say, for good reason." He looked up at me. "So tell me why are you still at it?"

"I could ask you the same," I said. "You know them better than I."

He shook his head once. "Can't figure it out. The girl is distraught, we're told. Okay, sure, it's got to be a blow to have your husband jump off his store roof, but that's got to be more within him than anyone else."

"Logic," I said, "doesn't always rule the minute."

He looked surprised. "Doesn't that go 'rules the day'?"

"Oh, maybe. Does the length of time involved make a difference?"

"I suppose not. Though if you're going to use a cliché you want to be accurate, don't you? I mean, isn't that why it's a cliché?"

"I'll have to take your word for that. Clichés aren't my fortissimo."

He had a good laugh at that.

"So, why do you think you are the more successful store?"

"Why? That should be a hard question, but it isn't. It's our relative approaches to retailing. I believe in drama, gimmicks, the loss leader, daily fascination, excitement—I'll take you through the store, if you want. The Straus boys are plodders. If it was good enough for granddaddy, it's good enough for them. If you don't sweat the program you have more time for golf."

"But all the more reason for Sandy to be a happy well-adjusted guy."

Manny shrugged. "Maybe that bombshell was too much for him."

"Ginger Kulp?"

"The same. The greatest catch in the valley and he gets her. Soft-spoken Sandy. Who'd have thought?"

"He have any competition?"

"I'll say!"

"Before or after marriage?"

"Well, whoa Nellie. I don't deal in gossip. Not that I have any to give you. But it's safe to say before he had to stand in line."

"Why'd he do it?"

"Dance off the roof, you mean?"

"Exactly."

"Must have been unhappy, wouldn't you say?"

"I'd say. But why?"

"Maybe the business was in the toilet? Times change. Saw the handwriting and rolled over. I don't know. Only Sandy knew and he can't tell us."

"Decent people, were they?"

"Oh yes—salt of the earth—with a detour to Princeton."

"Scholars?"

"I daresay good enough—you may consider and weigh anyway you want to: Granddaddy's copious contributions to the cause, only bested by Daddy's. So I don't imagine the admissions process was too taxing. They all went to jew-free private schools while they were at it."

"Really?"

"That's hard to believe nowadays. Today they'll even take a Jew or two into the country club."

"Now's your chance."

"Now that I might get in, I no longer want to. We only want what we can't have and no one wants to be looked at sideways the way they look at different people. I mean, Jesus, it isn't as though I were a religious fanatic or anything."

He looked at me curiously. "I'm not giving you much help, am I? It's only because I don't have it to give.

"Something always held those Princeton boys back—a peculiar kind of reticence for the merchandise game. It was almost as though selling was beneath them. They would offer the merchandise to the customer as a WASPy service, but they certainly wouldn't tempt or push. Look at our newspaper ads, look at our displays, our personnel. Theirs is rock-ribbed Pennsylvania Dutch elite. You can read between the lines. These guys were to the manor born. Me? I was the son of a rag peddler—my Pa thought that college was for sissies—for guys who couldn't make it on their own. Like the Strauses."

"Do you think they are sissies because they went to college?"

"Nah, wimps would be more accurate. Merchandising wimps—afraid to take chances. How would it look at the country club—a club that wouldn't take me, by the way, because of my religion.

"Did you resent it?"

"Damn right I resented it. Wouldn't you?"

"I don't know. Intellectually, I feel like Groucho Marx. I wouldn't want to join *any* club that would have me as a member."

He smiled. No belly laugh, but a smile.

"Spoken as one who has never been discriminated against for some accident of birth.

"You know what my Pa told me when the subject of college came up? 'Beethoven,' he said, 'stopped going to school at age ten. Didn't hurt him.'

"So I came to work in the store and Pa died not long after, and I found myself in charge. Come on," he said, rising from his chair, "let me show you the store."

"Oh, well, I don't want to bother you."

"No bother," he said. "It's good for the troops to see me on the battlefield."

"Boosts morale, does it?" I asked.

He smiled ruefully, "Perhaps—or you could say it lets them know I'm watching."

Later I wondered if he didn't pass the word that I was an investigator on the Straus case, the competitor's suicide—may he rest in peace.

17

Wherever we went, Manny Ness greeted his employees heartily by name. He was proud of his people, and proud of his merchandise, regaling me with stories of their histories.

"Hi Solly—how's it going?"

"Just fine, Mr. Ness."

"How's that beautiful granddaughter coming along?"

"Just fine. Started first grade and already she's reading to me."

"Wonderful, Solly, wonderful. Give her my love."

"Will do, Mr. Ness. Thank you."

And on we went throughout the store.

"What will I see at the Straus's store?"

"It's a nice store. Not exciting, but nice. With them, it's a business. With me...I get pleasure from the excitement. Every day is a merchandising challenge. It pumps up the customer. Well, see for yourself—measure everything—the size of the crowd, the excitement on their faces, the anticipation when they come in the door. Do they browse—take in aspects of the store apart from what they came in for?"

"Do the Strauses make money?"

He shrugged. "Ask them," he said. "They'd be in a better position to know."

"Yes, but do you ever speculate?"

"All the time. It's my business to get the largest share of the customers' money."

"So in your speculations, do you ever see them lose money?"

"All the time."

"Where would they get the money to keep the store propped up?"

"Well, I assume from the savings from past profits."

"How long can that hold out?"

He shook his head. "Not indefinitely," he said.

"The next obvious question is how any of this might have helped Sandy Straus off his store's roof?"

He nodded. "That's a legitimate question."

"Any answers?"

"Me? Not me. I'm a shopkeeper, not a shrink. There were three brothers minding the store. The other two are still earthbound. Maybe they can help you."

"You think they can?"

"I don't know. My sense of it is one of them might. The other, between us, is a bit of a jerk."

"Which is which?"

He held out a hand. "Oh, no, that's something you have to judge for yourself."

We were in the fur coat department. There was a striking full-length, silver fur coat on a mannequin in the center of the floor. Manny stepped in front of it.

"Like it?" he asked.

"Like it? Well, I don't know anything about fur coats. It's an anomaly where I come from."

"Ah, yes. The land of eternal sunshine," he said. "We get a little break from that lucky old sun in these parts. A nice fur coat comes in handy to keep out the cold and boost your status," he chuckled. "Truth be known, there isn't a lot of opportunity to wear them here either. Mostly walking to and from the car when it's really cold. Well, take a look at the price of this puppy." He indicated the price tag with his hand.

I checked the price on the tag. The numbers were bold, I suppose so no one would mistake it for an off-the-rack economy item.

$575,000.00

"Wow," I said. "Have you sold any?"

"No," he said.

"Will someone buy it?"

"No. But they come in here and see it, and the coats we have starting at ninety-nine dollars look a lot better. We sell a lot of them."

"Yeah, but what do you have to pay for a $575,000 coat?"

"We rent it."

"Rent?"

"Yeah. What do we want with a fur coat in summer time? And we aren't putting this on the ten dollar bargain table—so we rent it. I don't know what we pay, ten thousand to twenty thousand dollars a month."

"It's worth it?"

"Or we wouldn't do it," he smiled. "Hungry?" he asked.

"A little."

"Come on, let me take you to lunch."

We descended another escalator to the basement where the store's Terrace restaurant was located. "We were the first ones in town to have escalators," he said. "People would come to the store just to ride them."

It was after two in the afternoon and the line of people looked a block long. My first thought was if I had to wait in that line I'd pass out before I got any food.

Silly, he *owned* the store. He didn't wait in line, but breezed through the front chain where an accommodating woman with a bosom full of menus the size of billboards unhooked the chain and said, "Good afternoon, Mr. Ness."

"Hi Molly," he said. "Husband doing better?"

"Yes, thank you, we brought him home from the hospital yesterday. He's so happy to be home."

"I'm sure," he said. "Give him my best, will you?"

The corner table was kept open for him and we were ushered to it. We sat down. He pulled his iphone from his inside breast pocket and pushed some buttons.

"Lizzie, Molly's husband just returned from the hospital. Send him a nice fruit basket, will you?" He clicked off the phone. I was perusing the billboard menu. There were children at the next table and the waitress in a white dress with multi-colored Ness's printed all over it was serving one of the kids with something in a toy refrigerator that opened. Her mother was having a strawberry pie that was so large and tall I couldn't grasp the engineering that kept it upright.

"You *are* quite a showman," I said to him. He smiled. He was pleased I had noticed.

"The crab cocktail is delicious," he said. "Maryland blue crab —fresh. What do you like? I like seafood. The broiled assortment is great, so is the cold plate. It's all good—a very nice steak."

"Geez," I said. "I never saw a place this busy."

"Big portions, a terrific chef, and bargain prices."

"How do you do it?"

"Well, we take the profit out of the prices. Not many people run restaurants at under cost. Not for long, anyway."

"You do?"

He nodded.

"Why?"

"Brings people into the store. You don't sell anything if you don't get people into the store. They spend a lot of time in line, but they're standing in the sportswear department, and while they're here they might as well pick up that sports shirt and a pair of shorts. They see it as an efficient use of their time and we reward them with a super meal at less than it costs us."

Then a thin woman came parading by the table where she stopped and twirled, showing us all sides of the dress, while she intoned in suitable blasé monotone the designer's name, and where it could be had, and for how much: "Fashion Center, fourth floor, eight hundred dollars."

"Sell any of those?" I asked. It was a nice enough frock, but it seemed on the expensive side. I saw too many women hereabouts who could not squeeze into the thing without popping a few seams.

"Occasionally," he said. "There was a line in a play called *The Child Buyer*—saw it years ago, never forgot it. They were buying children in the ghetto for their brains and offering the parents gifts like a matched set of designer luggage, china, sterling silver place settings, and what have you. When the buyer was finished cataloguing the gifts to his associate he said, 'The more inappropriate the gift, the more flattering the offer.' I never forgot it."

"Hmmm, say, how about this theory on Straus's jump: An altruistic act to reduce the store's responsibility by thirty-three and a third percent?"

"Nice. As things get tougher, another one jumps? But who gets to be the last man standing?"

Two more clotheshorses came by, with their pitches for the fashion center. I had my broiled fish menagerie, and he insisted I try the strawberry pie.

"Where do you get strawberries this time of year?"

"Chile. Fly them up fresh."

"No wonder this loses money."

He nodded with good humor. "It's our signature dessert. The customers expect it, and if you want to do this business right, you don't disappoint the customers."

I nodded my admiration.

"If I had to, I'd send Brobst, the restaurant manager, to Chile on a bicycle to get them."

I laughed. "They might not be so fresh by the time he got back."

"But he'd be well-fed."

The pie came. It was incredible—tasted as good as it looked—not an easy feat in the food business.

He waved away my offer to pay for the meal and walked me to the front revolving doors. We shook hands. He said, "A pleasure to meet you. If you want anything else, you know where to find me."

18

I was on the main street of Muhlenheim on my way
from Ness's to Straus's when my phone rang.

"Hello?"

"Hi there, it's Jessamyn."

I stopped in my tracks and moved toward the
building. Multi-tasking was beyond my expertise. In a
way, I admire those mortals who can drive a car while
chatting on the cell phone. Myself, I would have a fatal
accident. I wouldn't even dare it while I was walking. Of
course my admiration decreases when I hear that one of
those multi-taskers has killed someone with their car,
driving while on the phone.

"Are you ready to go to work?" I asked.

"Sure am," she said.

We made a date. I was going to pick her up for
dinner.

I continued on my way to Straus's department
store.

Adjacent to Ness's there were boutique shops
that seemed to draw their survival from the big department store—almost like a mall—outdoors on the main

street. But the closer I got to Straus & Sons I noticed a thinning of these shops. The transition area held thrift stores, second-hand clothes, a derelict auto parts store, and more empty shops. No customers were seen. Were these still-open shops paying their rent, or were the landlords being indulgent, waiting for a miracle turn-around when their tenants would magically be replaced by paying customers? One looked like its inventory had been obtained under cover of darkness.

A block before Straus & Sons was a tall thin monument to the gallant soldiers and sailors from the area who gave their lives that this town would endure. Heroic poses at the foot of, what looked like, a tall thin cannon barrel pointing to the sky—straight up.

I wondered how many opportunities there were in battle to strike that heroic pose. I decided none. But the poses of enlightened courage and heroism made for better statues.

Do monuments like these make war attractive? What would happen if all commemorative war monuments showed battle as it was? Instead of the combatants in heroic far-seeing poses, in immaculate dress uniforms, it showed a bunch of grunts on their bellies in fox holes, their bleary-eyed faces splattered with mud, wounds leaking blood, the gruesome impact of a mortar shell tearing into virgin flesh, ending the hopes and dreams of a young person before he had the time to act on them.

But what town would sponsor such a monument? The heirs of the victims much prefer glory to reality. Wouldn't you?

At the end of the block I came to Straus & Sons, a building not different from the others around it, which I might characterize as downtown pedestrian brick.

Across the street stood a vacant department store. Its windows made opaque with whitewash, its name still curving over the front door—a ghostly reminder of more auspicious times. There were still two department stores standing in town, but it wouldn't be long before there was one, then none. The big boys from Philly had already moved into the mall on the outskirts of town and the Big Apple stores were signing leases.

Revolving doors were a curiosity for those of us who hailed from warm climates. They let the customers inside without heat loss.

Lipstick and perfume counters greeted me on my entrance, but there were no young women in the aisles pushing samples. I inquired of a grandmotherly clerk who, in my humble opinion, had overdone the perfume makeover, where the executive offices were.

"Third floor," she said, without cracking a smile, possibly to keep from mussing her lipstick.

The physical surroundings put me in mind of a Sears store managed by someone who cared, but was not long on flair. Perhaps it was my imagination, but the merchandise compared to Ness's looked like they were leading up to a closing sale (everything must go).

I didn't see any escalators so I took the stairs. Elevators are for wimps, and you didn't see any merchandise while cooped up in a moving box.

On the third floor another hefty clerk beyond her childbearing years directed me to the store personnel and executive offices tucked away in the back corner.

Windows were superfluous on merchandise floors—nothing should compete with the goods—but here, in the prime movers' office space, were windows that eerily looked out on the walkway on which Sandy had made his final trek.

I was in an open waiting room, not unlike the doctor's office, but larger. At the end was a reception desk—the desk jockey was on the phone. On two of the walls were doors to other offices. On the wall adjacent to the receptionist were five life-sized photographs in three rows. On top was the founder, with a metal sign below the frame that identified him as Samuel Straus, The Founder. He was a starched-looking fellow who probably did not suffer fools, period. Beneath him, his son, John Amos Straus—a jovial smile lit up his face with no attempt to camouflage the bald spot.

Beneath him, the third generation, who had apparently forestalled the adage, shirtsleeves to shirt-sleeves in three generations, for here they all were in their blue blazers and regimental striped ties on their button-down oxford cloth shirts. They were handsome boys; there was no gainsaying that. Should they be suddenly called back to Princeton, they would not have had to change clothes.

Odds and experience would lend one to believe there would be at least one renegade in the apple barrel, but, apparently, there was not—at least until the middle boy went over the wall. That would be the picture marked Edward R. (Sandy) Straus. He was the only one with a nickname.

On his left, I assumed, his older brother, with a dead serious set to his eyes and mouth—his face a little fleshier than his brothers. On Sandy's right was the youngest and the only one with a full-teeth displaying smile. The teeth were perfect without hint of orthodontics. He seemed the most serene of the bunch. I thought I had the best chance of insight from him.

But the biggest surprise was Sandy in the middle. His face was pleasant, if bemused, but there was something about the placement of his eyes, the extension of his jaw, the large and angular nose that made him, at first glance, the least attractive of the three. And yet he landed the beauty, Ginger Kulp. I was amid changing my assessment of his expression from bemused to bewildered when it hit me. This was the first photo I'd seen of Sandy Straus. There were none in his home. Not that I'd seen. I suppose there could have been one in the bedroom—that thought piqued my interest in getting into Ginger's bedroom, though I had no notion of how I could bring that off. There was, of course, the grand portrait of Pater Kulp, M.D. in Ginger's living room.

So deep was my reverie, I was startled to hear the voice of a woman over my shoulder. "Like our rogue's gallery?"

"What?" I said, turning to see the receptionist in a beige skirt and white blouse, buttoned at the neck. "Oh, yes, though I wouldn't presume to call them rogues."

"That's all right. They refer to it themselves that way."

"Oh," I said, "but how did you sneak up on me like that?"

"You were so absorbed," she said. "May I help you with something?"

"Yes. What kind of bribe would you take to get me in to see one of these guys?"

"Oh, it wouldn't take a bribe," she smiled a smile that could stand as an aspiration for all receptionists. Then, as though she realized she was spouting a cliché, she said, "and what is the nature of your visit, Mister...?"

"Yates," I said. "Gil Yates."

She waited for the other part. I decided to let her wait.

She broke the silence. "Is it a line of pots and pans you are flogging, Mr. Yates? Or something...more intimate?"

"Why don't I just tell the fellas?"

She smiled a killer smile. "Because long experience has told me you wouldn't get over the threshold with that game."

"Oh," I said, trying to sound surprised. "I just came from Manny Ness, who I got to see without a question."

"Oh, Manny Ness—he *is* a breed of his own," she said, without disrespect.

"Say," I said, "I didn't get your name."

"You didn't ask," she said, teasingly, the eyes and mouth working in harmonious concert.

"My mistake—my apologies."

"It's Alice," she said, as though proffering me a gift.

"Alice Straus?" I asked.

She laughed. "That would be something," she said, "but no, I am just a hired hand."

Alice was what I came to think of as a Pennsylvania Dutch beauty—pleasant of face, ample of body. For verily in that paradise of ice and snow and humidity the opportunity for exercise was severly curtailed. In the winter God knew you had to heat the body with ample calories (*calorie*: a unit of heat...) or cool it in the summer with sugary drinks—or ice tea which nefariously stimulates the appetite.

"Well, it was nice meeting you, Mr. Yates," she

said, turning toward her desk, unmistakably dismissing me.

"Hey," I said. "What about seeing your bosses?"

"Without telling them why?" she shook her head. "I value my job here. Not that I don't value our acquaintance, however brief, but I do hope you'll forgive me if I put the pressure of the former slightly ahead of the pleasure of the latter."

"Okay," I said. "Touché. What would you say if I said I was writing a book about department stores and their future?"

"What would I say? I'd probably say I didn't believe you."

"Oh? Why not?"

She wrinkled her nose. "Maybe you don't look the writer type."

Further sparring seemed pointless. "Okay. I'm investigating the death of Sandy Straus." I nodded toward his photograph on the wall under his father and between his brothers.

She seemed to deflate before my eyes. "I've just been depleted of my optimism," she said.

"Oh, why?"

"I can tell you, Josh will not see you. He's had it up to here with the investigations. First the police, then that private investigator." She shook her head. "Another isn't going to fly with him. Hank may see you. He's a pleaser, but I wouldn't look for miracles from him either."

"Fair enough. Thanks for your honesty," I said. "Will you give it a go?"

She sighed and returned to her desk where she punched a short number.

I heard his gruff voice on the other side of a door perpendicular to Alice's desk.

"There's a Mr. Gil Yates here to see you. He'd like to talk to you about Sandy's..." She couldn't finish—there was a crescendo rumbling from behind the door. Alice listened with forbearance, nodded and said, "Yes, sir. I'll tell him."

She looked up at me with a grin that was actually more like a grimace. "The short answer is no—not in a million years. The longer is, 'Will we have to rehash this for the rest of our lives? All we have to say has been said ad nauseam. I can't waste any more time on the Kulps' ego.'" She looked at me with a sympathetic twinkle in her eye. "You want me to ask Hank?"

"Please."

She repeated the routine and I heard no shouting or grumbling. She looked up at me. "He says he can see you tomorrow. What time is good for you?"

"First thing—early as he can."

We settled on nine a.m.

19

I picked Jessamyn up at her college—a rambling campus of red brick buildings, rolling grass, and well-seasoned trees.

I told her I wanted to take her to her favorite place. It turned out to be one of those semi-lit places with red and white-checkered tablecloths. I expect those are so ubiquitous in Italian restaurants because they camouflage the tomato sauce stains.

She had dressed the part in an outfit picked up at the Goodwill thrift shop. She prided herself that nothing in her wardrobe cost her more than twenty-five dollars. There was a name for the look, though I was embarrassed to ask her what it was. Distressed, poor boy, retro-depression, thrift chic—something.

Our waitress was Pennsylvania Dutch masquerading as an Italian.

I was pleased to see ravioli on the menu; it is so labor intensive I was persuaded to have it. Besides, the likelihood of Tyranny Rex ever making it was a lot slimmer than she was.

Jessamyn ordered the veal marsala.

She looked good to me—a warm healthy glow. It had to be acknowledged, she was not a knockout. With age, I notice my cuteness quotient in the appraisal of young girls has slipped precipitously. The more out of reach the girls become, the less fussy I am.

I thought Jessamyn was cute. I expect had I been her contemporary I would have found her solid, but uninspiring. If I wanted to be brutally objective, Jessamyn was petite and well shaped with an overbite and a touch too much nose, mousey hair pulled back in a bun; but she had a personal perky flair which overrode all else.

After the waitress retrieved the menus Jessamyn fanned her hands beside her on the banquette. We did small talk: "How's school?" "Fine. I can't wait till I'm out."

Then we segued into the business at hand.

"My dad said you can call him anytime. He doesn't know what help he can be, but he'll tell you what he can." She reached into her pocket and produced a slip of paper where she had written his name and phone number. She didn't carry a purse; too feminine perhaps. I was impressed she anticipated my interest in speaking to her father.

"Let's cut to the chaser," I said, and she laughed.

"Did I say something funny?"

"A chaser is something you wash down booze with. 'Cut to the chase' comes from the movies—means okay cut to the car chase—the action of the piece."

"That's good to know," I said, but I wasn't sure it was. "Your remunerative pay. It's negotiable. I suggest fifty dollars an hour."

"Fifty!" she said startled. "That's five times the best job I can get at school. I work at the paper for nothing."

"If it's too much we can shave it a little. Shall we say forty-nine?"

"No, no, fifty is fine. What do you want me to do?"

She was so eager I had to laugh. "Well, whatever you do will have to be in the next seven days or so. I have a ten-day maximum contract that is already at the end of the second day, and I have a day to travel back. I don't want you to skip your classes or anything."

"Are you kidding? For fifty an hour I'd quit school."

"No, no—not necessary. One thing I'd like for you to do is take advantage of your newspaper's archives. There was an incident in Dr. Kulp's past. What can you find out about it?"

"Okay."

"I'd like to see all the paper coverage of the Straus boy's jump—any other references you can think of."

She nodded.

"Anything on the Straus family or store personnel. Oh, by the way, do you know any computer hackers?"

She laughed. "A tougher question would be, do I know any guys who aren't computer hackers?"

"Good. Anyone we could hire and count on for discretion?

"Also, use your contacts at the paper—the old-timers who might remember the Kulps from years ago—any dirt. The big question is, why is this so important to the man—to bring me across the country, at embarrassingly large expense, to dredge up this case again? I'm interested in any gossip you can find, any rumor, no matter how unfounded. Sometimes you find a germ of truth in unsubstantiated gossip or rumor."

Jessamyn looked at me with a deep inquisition in her eyes. It unsettled me.

"So far I have found nothing to substantiate the murder scenario."

"What if you don't?" she asked.

"I have a ten-day window. If, after five days, I am convinced it was suicide, I'll give them the option of ending it, or spend the next five days developing a theory on why."

"Will they go for it?"

"I doubt it. The why will most likely point to one or more of the family, and I would be surprised if the prospect appealed to any of them—with the possible exception of Mrs. Kulp."

Jessamyn was raring to go when we ended the meal on some fat-laden dessert with chocolate mousse, caramel, pecans (ninety-five percent fat), and crème fraîche.

I drove her back to school and asked her to call me at the end of each day—or more often, if the spirit moved her.

She said she would.

So I called it a day—another day, another ten-thousand dollars. It was fun to make it, but my goal was to earn it.

20

$30,000

First thing the next morning, after I got out of the bed, I called Jessamyn's father in Arizona. When I got Axel Nolan on the phone I told him how impressed I was with his daughter. "I've hired her for some legwork."

"She told me. A nice thing to do."

"No—I expect I'll get my money's worth." I said. "So, can you tell me about your sojourn with the Straus's?"

"Basically they are decent people. The father was a brick—I was crazy about working for him—but everything ends. And he did. The kids are doing their best in a difficult environment. Department stores, like so much else, are falling victim to internet technology—and of course, death of the inner city. Plus the Straus's had the misfortune to work in a town dominated by Manny Ness. Nobody could take him on and survive. Not in these times."

"And they aren't surviving?" I asked.

"No," he said. "That's why I left."

"Voluntarily?"

"Well, in a way. I left because I saw the writing

on the wall. They were paying me out of savings. Everything is paid out of savings from better times."

"So Sandy took over?"

"Yes, I stayed to teach him."

"What had he been doing?"

"He was a buyer. But they were buying a lot less, so he had the time."

"How was he?"

"A fast learner—and a peach of a kid—well, not that young. He seemed like a kid to me. All relative I guess. He only had five or so years on my oldest," he said.

"Jessamyn?"

"No, she's the youngest. We got along well," he said.

"Was there anything in the books that might have nudged him off the roof?"

"No," he said. "Not that I can see. He didn't have time for it to have gotten much worse—at any rate it was hardly *his* fault. It wasn't anybody's fault—just the times."

"Could he have been depressed at the prospects for the store supporting three families?"

"He could have, I suppose," he said. "I never got that impression, but it's certainly possible."

"That would turn the spotlight off the Kulps. They should like that."

He didn't respond to that. It piqued my curiosity. "Did you know the Kulps?"

"Not really. I'd met Sandy's wife."

"And?"

"Seemed a polite sort—certainly good looking."

"They get along, did they?"

A pause. "As far as I know."

"Did you see any indication that things weren't perfect between them?"

"You know any perfect married couples?"

I got a chuckle out of that. Naturally I thought first of Tyranny Rex and yours truly. "Could she have had a boyfriend?"

"I saw no evidence of it if she did."

"He—a girlfriend?"

"Ditto. Since I was in the office with him all day that would have been more difficult to bring off."

"While you were there."

"Yes."

"How long before he...jumped...did you leave the store?"

"Oh, six months or so."

"And nothing untoward struck you about either Sandy or Ginger?"

"Extracurricular hanky-panky? No, I..." He seemed to be considering something.

"Yes?"

"Oh, nothing," he said. "All I can say is that half the guys in the Valley would have given anything—eye teeth, wife, kids—for a woman that good looking. Maybe I'm wrong."

"How so?"

"Not half, three-quarters." he said.

"And Sandy?" I asked.

"He was devoted. Muhlenheim is a small enough town and any affairs are usually widely known the next day."

"And you never saw any indication?"

"None!" he said.

"But you weren't around Ginger much, were you?"

"Hardly at all."

"Well, thanks for indulging me. If you think of anything—no matter how unimportant it seems to you—would you be good enough to call me?"

"Sure," he said uncertainly. "Come to think of it, I did get some vibes the last time I saw Sandy and Ginger together."

"What kind of vibes?"

"Not such good ones," he said. "Like it maybe wasn't all sweetness and light between them."

"Did you ask about your suspicions?"

"God no. Wasn't my place. I was just a numbers cruncher. Probably just my imagination anyway."

"Hmmm," I said. "Oh, by the way, did Sandy have a computer?"

"Everyone has a computer now."

"Know what happened to it?"

"No, he kept it in the store—somewhere…in his office. After he…died…I don't know."

"Who there could I ask—discreetly of course—someone who wouldn't blow the trombones to the family?"

He chuckled. "The whistle," he said softly.

"What's that?"

"The expression is 'blow the whistle,' call in the whistleblowers, those who snitch—I get the picture—someone who could tell you where Sandy's computer was, on the off chance no one else got to it."

"Exactly."

"I'd have to think about that," he said. "That secretary,—what's her name?"

"Alice?"

"That's the one. She liked Sandy. He was less bossy than his brothers—more down to earth."

I cringed at the description. He indeed ended 'down to earth.'

"She might help—I can't think of anyone else who might fill the bill."

I thanked him. 'Fill the bill?' What I could do with that! 'Pad the check,' 'stuff the accounting,'—the options were almost endless. How about 'fill 'er up, Bill?'

I thanked him again for his help and hung up the phone like we did in the old days.

I went down to the dining room for my hotel breakfast. You'd think it would be difficult to hurt eggs, but they tried their best.

I planned to be at Straus Department Store when it opened. Three targets—the two surviving brothers, and the secretary.

21

On to Straus and Sons down the main street from my hotel. Down was toward the river. You didn't see the river unless you were down upon it—hidden in the bowels of the city as it was. But, when you thought about it, every locale had a river somewhere. All that water demanded the attention of an outlet. Even in my Southern California shoulder of the woods we had rivers that were largely concrete channels—dry most of the time—but in the rainy season they carried the rain water from the Los Angeles basin to the ocean as fast as they could, as though we didn't want to acknowledge rain in sunny Southern California.

It was only a slight elevation decrease between the hotel and the Straus store. Shortly thereafter the terrain plunged to accommodate the river which must have had a name—though I never found out what it was.

The hotel I just left in Muhlenheim was peculiarly already seeming like home.

On my way I mused that home was many different things to many different people. Home is where the stomach is or for some it was a place to get away from—out of the house because of the cry of the discontented, and I was out...

Entering Straus and Sons you can't escape the feeling of a neat, clean, well-lighted, uninspiring place. All the showmanship was uptown with Manny Ness.

Upstairs in what passed for the executive suite, I exchanged pleasantries with the secretary/receptionist, Alice Bluegown. Well, that wasn't her last name, but she sure was dressed in blue. And maybe it wasn't a gown exactly, but some full fitting dress.

I gravitated to her desk. "Good morning, gorgeous," I said. You seldom get a sincere argument from flattery. She beamed as people are wont to do when you say something nice to them.

"I had an appointment with the young gentleman this morning—informal to be sure..." I said.

"Yes, he's expecting you. He'll be out in a minute."

The older, less friendly Straus came in the door. He carried a leather briefcase as though he were some mid-level striver in an auto plant—trying to impress someone (who, was not clear) that he had burned some midnight gasoline, when, of course, he had spent his evening vis à vis a glowing television set. He had broad shoulders, an enviable chest, he looked like he had lettered in some he-man sport at Princeton.

He saw me at Alice's desk and she introduced us.

"Oh, Gates." He was at no pains to underplay his superior stature.

"Yates," I muttered in humble cake not to correct him—oh no—just to set the record straight.

"I think it would be best for all concerned if you

turned off the snoop and turned tail and headed back to your intellectual wasteland of sunshine and sand and left us all alone," he said.

I nodded my understanding, not an agreement. "Just," I said modestly, "doing my job—honest living and all that."

He frowned.

"This wasn't a pleasant thing for our family, so here are these people prolonging the agony with one snoop after another looking for some kind of miracle or something. Why? The cops, the other detective, now you. You got any idea why?"

"I guess it was as hard for his wife to take as it was for you," I said.

"Yes—sure—but doesn't she want to get over it?" He asked.

"Maybe she can't."

"I mean, get a life. Believe me, we've been all over it—again and again—we have nothing to tell you. Zero, nada, zilch. Sandy was a great guy. Apparently he wasn't happy and his wife is afraid someone will blame it on her. Well, so what? C'est la vie—but to fish around for some mysterious killer is just preposterous. There ain't such a creature anywhere."

"What do you think pushed him over the wall?" I asked.

"Depression," he said. "Happens all the time. It's a chemical thing."

"Is it triggered?" I queried.

"I don't know. I'm not a psychiatrist."

"I mean everyone who is depressed doesn't go jumping off roofs."

"I'll take your word for it," he said, itching to get away from me.

"How's the store doing?" I asked.

"Doing? Times are not what they used to be. All you have to do is look outside."

"Did it worry Sandy any?"

"Well, he'd have been an odd man out if it didn't," he said. "But you'll notice the rest of us aren't jumping."

"He ever confided his personal life to you?"

"Sandy was a very private man. He never complained about anything."

"Not his wife?"

He seemed startled at the suggestion. Either because it was so prescient, or such a surprise consideration.

"Look, I've got a store to run. I could sit here and jaw with you all day, but I'm not gonna. See you," he said turning away lugging his manly briefcase, laden, doubtless, with important documents.

What was the saying about getting turnips from a stone or something? I gave it up.

When the big guy disappeared I reset my attention to Alice at the reception desk.

"Would you be offended if I told you that you look especially radiant today?"

"Oh no," she said. "I wouldn't be offended—of course not—but no I'm not especially radiant today."

I smiled. "Don't argue with me," which I said in mock seriousness. "Why would you turn your back on a compliment?"

"Oh, I know I'm heavy and I should do something about it, but I've come to terms with it. That's just me. Metabolism or something. Besides, I like to eat. It's the most pleasure I get in life. And exercise leaves me cold—in the winter it's too cold to be exerting outdoors—in the summer it's too hot and humid. I mean it's *unpleasant.* So when you have a choice between pleasure and pain—I mean, it's a no-brainer."

"Well, good for you," I said. "I like a person who knows what they like and goes after it."

She blushed, but she was smiling. A compliment doesn't have to have a lot of weight to it.

"So along that line, could I entice you to let me take you to lunch today?"

She looked up at me with glittering eyes, "Today?" She asked with no attempt to veil her excitement so much so I feared I had inadvertently built her expectations beyond mine.

"Let me check my calendar," she said and extracted a paperback sized calendar from her purse. She kept it close to her chest and peered at it as though she were myopic. I didn't see the writing but I was fairly sure she was staring at blank pages.

"Looks like I might be able to squeeze you in today."

"Oh, good!" I said, delighted. "What time do they unlock your cage?"

She chuckled. We were batting it off.

"Oh, they're very flexible here. Almost any time will do."

"Where shall we go?"

"Where?"

"Your favorite place."

"My...well...can you keep a secret?"

"No one better."

"Have you ever been to Manny Ness's Terrace?"

"In fact, I have. Great place. Let's go there."

"Let's," she said. There was no hiding her excitement. "But we'll have to get there early otherwise it's hours before you can sit down."

"Great!" I said. "Shall we leave around eleven o'clock?"

"That would be peachy," she said.

Young Hank Straus appeared at his door with a smile more generous than he could possibly feel.

"Mr. Yates—come on in."

I followed him into a room that could have been the den of a dean of admissions at Princeton—rah rah regalia everywhere—some loving cups and plaques from rowing triumphs, barrel chairs with a coat of arms carved in the semi-circular back—one of which he waved me into while he sat on the stuffed swivel chair behind his imposing desk.

"It's good of you to see me," I said staring at the Princeton banner behind his desk. It was the size of Daddy Bucks Wemple Enterprise's billboard in Torrance, California—well, okay not quite, but that's what came to mind. And at the moment the contrast in intellectual achievement level did not occur to me.

"I expect you are as tired of these inquisitions as your brother."

He waved a hand. "I understand Dr. Kulp's feelings. It was a mild sensation around here for a while. Not necessarily the suicide itself, but the apparent fact that a young man in the prime of life with a staggeringly beautiful wife and no worries about where the next meal was coming from wanted to close the store and go."

"Is that what motivates the Kulp family not to accept the suicide verdict?"

"I don't know what motivates them. Guilt is a big motivator."

"Guilt about what?" I asked.

He shrugged his shoulders. "Who knows? But in this life there is no shortage of opportunity for guilt. Granted, a lot of it is imagined."

"Any chance someone could have pushed him—or surprised or scared him into falling?"

"Anything is possible they say—but I don't see any evidence. I guess that's why they hired you across the country to find some."

"Any idea where I should look?"

He shook his head. "No ideas. The ground has been covered and covered again. Maybe they are just keeping demons at bay putting on these investigation shows. Look, as long as they can pay someone to go through the motions the evil spirits will not get a foothold."

"You think that could be a conscious motive?"

"Who knows," he said. "You know the Winchester mansion out in your bailiwick?"

"The rifle folk?"

"Yes—a widow kept adding rooms and stairways to the mansion. I was out there a while back and I tell you it's a kick in the pants. Stairways leading nowhere. Doors that don't open or lead anywhere. She was convinced as long as she kept building the evil spirits couldn't take a foothold."

"So the Kulps are paying me a queen's ransom to

keep the evil spirits from taking hold?"

He threw up his hands, "You have a better explanation?"

I had to admit, I didn't.

"Would you say your brother was a happy man?"

He looked askance at me. "Happy? Relative to what? You? Me? I guess really happy guys don't go off the roof."

"I guess not." I agreed. "How was his marriage?"

"As I said," he said. "How is anyone's? I once read marriage was like a dull meal with the dessert first."

I couldn't disagree from my experience—except that my dessert was very low calorie. "So," I said, "you noticed nothing out of the ordinary in Sandy's relationship with his wife Ginger?"

"Not really," he said. "Well, he did convert to Catholicism. We thought that was a bit extreme. Many I suppose think nothing of it. But how deep is our understanding of people we don't live with?" He chuckled, "Even those we do live with."

Amen brother, I thought. "And his father-in-law?"

"A tougher customer in my view."

"Any...altercations?"

"Wouldn't surprise me," he said, "though I have no evidence."

"Can you think of any enemies Sandy had?"

"None!" he answered too quickly. "Not Sandy—universally loved."

"So you don't think anyone helped him off the roof?"

"Of course not. Sandy was fit. He could have jumped with his eyes closed and come up without a scratch...he went head first."

"No one could have drugged him and thrown him over the parapet?"

"Did an autopsy. Zero drugs in his system."

I nodded. It made sense. So why was I still dubious? I hope it wasn't to run up my bill. How many people could turn their backs on ten-thousand dollars a day? And if there were such animals, was I one of them?

22

Eleven a.m. was early for me to have an appetite for lunch. But Alice was eager and I wanted information.

We waited only five minutes in line at eleven o'clock—at the Ness Terrace restaurant. Coupled with the ten-minute walk from Straus and Sons I got the lowdown on Alice's vicissitudes—and they were considerable.

When I am trying to ingratiate myself, I listen more intently.

The waitress who could have been a nurse in the Boer War handed us the billboard-sized menus sans flourish or smile—and this was the *beginning* of her shift. Rumor had it that the only people who made money in this restaurant were the salaried help and the waitresses. When I surveyed the current crop of the wait staff the word that came to mind was 'droll'.

The upside was Alice could feel slim in this company.

"You come here often?" I asked Alice.

She looked at me sheepishly, "Once in a while," she said.

"But the Strauses don't know it?"

"Oh, I exaggerate there—but I don't go out of my way to tell them. Sandy brought me here for my birthday last year...before he..." She teared up and didn't finish the thought. She didn't have to.

"What kind of guy was Sandy?"

"Oh, the best," she said abandoning the old emotion, lighting up with a ton of wattage. "I adored Sandy."

"Took a personal interest in him, did you?" I thought I had phrased that cleverly.

"Oh, I had a crush on Sandy all right. I mean, I couldn't hold a candle to Ginger lookswise..."

"Why would you want to hold a candle to anyone?" I asked.

She looked perplexed until she realized I didn't know what she was talking about. "Oh, it's just an expression," she said.

"Has nothing to do with igniting them...with a candle?"

"Oh no," she laughed—the engaging throaty laugh of the weight challenged. "She's just so...beautiful. I could never hope to compete..."

"Did you want to?" I said, "Compete with Ginger?"

"Oh, well, no—she was married to Sandy after all. There wasn't any thought of competition."

Of course, I could see in her moist eyes that there was.

"Well, you know what they say," I said in consolation, "pretty is as pretty does."

"Yes—you can say that," she said, "if you are pretty. If you're not, it sounds like sour grapes."

The food came. She looked at it and giggled.

"What's funny?" I asked her.

"Oh, nothing," she said. "I was thinking I'm looking at the enemy."

"Enemy?"

"At my age, food is the enemy."

"Enemy?"

She got one of those pensive, far away looks in her eyes.

"A nickel for your thoughts?"

She came back to earth. "Inflation?" She asked rhetorically. "I was just thinking."

"About what?"

"Sandy brought me here to celebrate my fortieth—if you can call it a celebration. It was the last time I was here." She looked through me and to the growing line of hopeful diners.

Why was she telling me this again? Was there going to be a payoff if I played my checkers right?

Her gaze drifted in and out. "Well," I said, "it's a celebration. Round numbers have a certain appeal."

"Oh, it's just another dreaded milestone of the spinster. First thirty—when you officially become a spinster, then ten years later when you are confirmed in the dastardly condition."

"Oh, I don't know about that. Half the people are not married these days. Maybe it's not such a stigma after all."

"Yeah—unless you're one of them."

"Did Sandy's brothers do anything for your birthday?"

"They signed the card."

"No check?"

"Oh, no. They're into saving money these days. But Sandy, he wasn't like the others. He was a real gentleman."

"So you mean, there was—nothing—no hanky panky in your relationship?"

"Oh, goodness no."

"Would you have objected to any advances?"

"Oh, Mr. Yates—you can't ask about that unless you're a single woman."

"Fair enough."

"Oh, but I'll admit I fantasized," she said, her eyes afar. "What girl wouldn't?"

"So why did he do it?"

"What?"

"Jump…"

"Oh, no one knows."

"Knows? But surely everyone speculates. What's your guess?" I asked.

"I don't know—everyone said he was so happy," she said. "Maybe he wasn't."

"Yes—happy guys don't go off the roof."

"Exactly."

"But the thing is—*why* do they say he was happy? It's like protesting too much…if he was unhappy someone might have to take the blame…" I said.

"Yes—who and why?"

"Well, it's the Kulps who are protesting, so I don't think we have to look far afield," I said. "And that's where you come in."

"Oh?"

I nodded. Was I trying to impress her with my erudition? My gravitas? I hope not, but the evidence was not validating me.

"Did you ever meet Ginger Kulp Straus?" I asked.

"No, I never did," she said, then thought better of it. "Oh, at the wedding, but that was only for a second."

"Would you like to?"

"Well...I don't know. Sure—I don't know—would I?"

"Get your woman's intuition take on her?"

"Okay. How do I do it?"

"Hm," I said and said it again. "That's the tub."

"Tub?" she giggled. "You mean rub, don't you?"

"If you say so." I said. "I guess it wouldn't work sending you to the door selling Girl Scout cookies?"

"Guess not—I'm a little old for the Girl Scouts."

"Maybe you could find some excuse to call her up, invite her to lunch."

"Oh, she'd never do it."

"How do you know? Her social calendar couldn't be too jammed these days. She's playing the bereaved widow. And you do have her late husband in common."

She shuddered at the thought.

"Nah," she said. "I couldn't do it."

"Think about it. It could help us get to the bottom of this—why are you smiling?"

"I was just thinking you got a cliché right."

"I did?"

"'Get to the bottom of this.' You could have said cellar or basement or...butt."

Alice did justice to clam chowder and the mountainous crab cocktail before tackling the porter house steak, medium rare.

At some point, mid-steak, she turned the spotlight on me.

"My, it must be exciting doing detective work."

"I guess there's some excitement buried in there somewhere—mostly it's drudge work. How about you? Any excitement in your work?"

She frowned, then pursed her lips.

"Excitement? Nooooo—intrigue—perhaps."

"How so?"

"Well Mr. Yates, you are at the center of it."

"Me?"

She nodded. "Nobody is comfy under…" she searched for the word, "…scrutiny."

"Hmmm," I pondered. "Even the innocent?"

"Is there such a thing?"

"Innocence? Well, certainly—to age three anyway."

The slender models had begun their parade among the tables, deadpanning their monotone recitals of the floor, availability, and price.

Why did models always seem to take everything so seriously?

Sometime after the skyscraper of a strawberry pie appeared on our table (one for each) I sashayed into the question which had loomed so large in my imagination. I was almost afraid to ask it—fearing a response from which there was no salvation.

"Alice," I said with a fork full of strawberry pie piled high with whipped cream stop-framed between plate and mouth—as though I was suddenly seized with an afterthought—"did Sandy use a computer?"

"Well, sure," she said. "We all use them."

"Do you know what happened to it?"

"Happened?" She looked puzzled. "Well I don't suppose *anything* happened to it."

"Is it still in the office?"

"Well, I don't know. If someone took it out, I don't know who or where they would take it."

"Ginger?"

"His wife? Why?"

"It just seems the Kulps' would leave no stone unturned in their quest to disprove the suicide. Wouldn't a computer be a good starting point?"

"But why?" she asked. "He only used it for business."

"How do you know?"

"Well," she chewed another forkful of strawberry paradise, "you don't know Sandy—didn't. He was all business in the office."

"Did the police look for it?"

"I don't know. It wasn't at his desk."

"Or the other detective?"

"Not that I know of."

"Who would they have asked?"

"Well, me, I suppose." Her brow was creasing in thought. "But if Sandy *had* anything incriminating on his computer wouldn't he have erased it before he...jumped?"

"Ah—maybe. But only maybe," I said. "Having never seriously contemplated suicide, I can't be sure—but it would seem to me that if your mind was set on self-destruction those peripheral considerations might fall by the sideway."

She got a glimmer in her eyes and a smile on her lips.

"What?" I asked for clarification of this barely

veiled merriment.

"Way*side*," she said.

"Fair enough," I rejoined. "You get what I mean?"

"I get it," she said. "And you could be right—but you could also be wrong. If something he had on his computer would have caused, encouraged or explained his suicide...he might have..."

"Destroyed it? Yes," I said, "but he could also have *wanted* it read—like a suicide note explaining..."

"Hmm."

"In which case it could be our duty to find it," I said.

"And out him."

"Out him? Does that mean you think he might have been a homosexual?"

"No," she said. "I mean it in the sense of getting whatever secrets he might have had—out—in public view."

"Maybe that's what he wanted."

"Maybe," she said. "Okay—I'll look for it."

When the check came I paid it. It wouldn't put a dent in my ten-thousand dollars for the day.

On our way back to Straus and Sons I asked Alice, "What would it take to make the call to Ginger?"

"Take? Oh, you've done enough with this lunch. I really enjoyed it. You know, I don't get out much—usually it's just me and the cat."

"Well, I'm glad."

"You know," she said with a sparkle in her eyes, "I think I will. I'll call her."

"Good for you," I said. "Will you look for Sandy's computer?"

She frowned. "What will we do if I find it? I mean, I don't know his password or anything."

"I'm lining up one of those nerd experts. He'll know what to do. When may I call to see if you found it—and if you do, how we might get it out of the place?"

"Give me the afternoon—I can't be too obvious about it. Maybe the boys will be at lunch when we get back."

"That would be great," I said. "Do you know what time the night watchman comes on?"

"Eight I think."

"How can I talk to him?"

"Come by—we're open until nine tonight."

"Do *you* work that late?"

"No," she said. "But I'll call you when I know something."

23

I gave it an hour before I called Alice to see if she had found the computer.

Her cheerful, upbeat answering of the phone was followed by hushed tones of mystery.

"The item in question has been located," she said—and the subdued tone of her voice kept me from whooping my pleasure.

We made arrangements to meet after I spoke to the night watchman. He came on duty an hour before the store closed, put in his eight hours, then turned the care of the store over to the janitorial crew who worked until opening.

I don't want to call George, the night watchman's, lair a hellhole, but nothing else comes to mind. It was set apart from the boiler room by a partition, but only a blind man could have been fooled.

He had a metal desk that I expect was acquired at some World War II clearance sale at a price that would make a pauper smile.

George himself might have been on the shelf at the same clearance sale. Rumpled he was. Not his clothes, but George himself. His attire was fastidious enough, but inside the clean but worn suit of serious black cloth which would not have been out of place at the bargain funeral parlor, George was simply rumpled.

George stood to greet me. Blessedly there was a chair for me to sit on. We shook hands, he said, "Have a seat," followed by minimal pleasantries and some phrase or other of mine then set him off like a wind up toy.

"I remember him coming in that night. It wasn't unusual for him to work late, but it was unusual for him to come in that late."

"Did he see you?"

"Oh yes, I said 'Good evening, Mr. Straus.'"

"What did he say?"

"He seemed distracted. If he said anything I didn't hear it. It was like I wasn't there."

"That was different than the usual greeting?"

"Yes. Usually I'd say good evening Mr. Straus and he'd say, 'Oh George, call me Sandy,' but I never did."

"Why not?"

"It didn't seem properly respectful to me. I mean, they *owned* the store, I was only a night watchman. A guy who did the dirty work."

"That was modest of you," I said.

He waved that off with a fluttering hand.

"Do you remember anything else about that night?"

"The night he jumped?"

I nodded.

"Enough to know the theory that some people—who shall be nameless—have that someone hid in the store and pushed him is hogwash."

"Couldn't have happened?"

"No possible way."

"Okay," I said. "Can we go back and reconstruct the evening to see if there is any possible scenario that could bolster Kulp's case?"

George's eyes narrowed—was he signaling that he thought I was being contrary—stupidly contradicting him, or was it rather a "show me" stance? I cleared my throat as though that would give us a fresh start.

"Okay—about what time did you see him come back in the store?"

"Ten-ten."

I lifted an eyebrow at his precision. "You can be that precise?"

He tightened his lips and graced me with a curt nod.

I was flustered. I didn't believe him. "But...but...how?"

"I keep a log," he said. "Part of my job. I logged him in at ten-ten."

My demeanor turned to admiration. "Good for you," I said.

He accepted the compliment with a modest shrug.

"What time did the store close that night?"

"Six."

"How does it close?"

"I close it."

"How?"

"Announcements are made on the sound system that the store will be closing in fifteen minutes, then ten and then five, and people are supposed to head for the exits."

"Do they?"

"Most. Every once in a while I have to encourage someone to get a move on."

"That night?" I said. "Do you remember any unusual resistance to leaving the store?"

"No," he shook his head. "Not a bit."

He seemed almost absurdly certain—as though he might be bolstering a predisposition to his vigilance.

"Okay," I said, "if someone wanted to hide in the store, could it be done?"

"Highly unlikely."

"Well, but, there are certainly places where someone with a mind to do it could duck into and not be noticed."

"Oh, but it's so far fetched—someone is going to hide somewhere, then pop out to get into the locked executive offices, pick Mr. S up like a sack of flour, go out on the walkway and toss him over the parapet without a struggle? Remember, it was only two floors and almost anyone who wanted to survive falling that distance could do so."

"Sandy was in good shape?"

"Excellent. Not an ounce of fat on him."

"Could he have been knocked unconscious, then been taken out and thrown over the parapet?"

"Outrageous," he said.

"But—anything is possible—wouldn't you agree?"

"Well, somethings are more possible than others. That idea is at the bottom of the list."

"Okay," I said. "What are the places a person could hide inside the store to bring this off?"

"I suppose anywhere—bathrooms, dressing

rooms, under a counter. Except we check all these places at closing."

"How?" I asked. "How do you check?"

"Someone goes into each bathroom opens the stall doors. The clothing clerks check the dressing rooms."

"Because you think someone might—what? Take some merchandise out?"

"Possible, but not easy. All doors are locked so someone would have to steal something small— jewelry?—while I was not looking."

"Possible?"

"That part is, but the jewelry is locked in a safe overnight. It's hard to think of anything else small enough to hide on a person of sufficient value to make the whole thing worthwhile. I mean, no one is going out of here with a refrigerator."

"But if someone wanted to murder someone?"

"They'd have to know the victim was going to come back in the store at night—very unusual."

What he said made perfect sense. "Could Sandy have had an appointment to meet someone?"

"At ten at night? Why?"

"I don't know—speculate. A gambling debt? Assignation?"

"So a woman threw him off the roof?"

"Could have been a man."

"Oh, no—not Sandy. No," he said. "But with all that you're forgetting one thing?"

"What's that?"

"All the store doors are locked from the inside. How would he get out?"

"Spend the night, then mingle with the morning

crowd and go out after the store opens."

He shook his head. He wasn't buying it.

"Do you make rounds all night long?"

He nodded. I wasn't sold. "Being alone in an empty store without any sound intruding on the silence—the necessity for constant vigilance might be compromised. We all gravitate to ease."

"Perhaps—but I take my job very seriously. I don't gravitate to ease."

"Of course," he had to say that. What was he going to say? 'Yeah, I fell asleep—anything could have happened,' even if it were true.

"You know what bothers me?"

"What?" he said.

"If it *was* a suicide and it was successful, he meant to do it—yet a two story jump is hardly a guarantee of success. Why didn't he jump from the Ninth Street bridge, or the hotel roof, something offering a higher chance of success?"

"I don't know. You'd have to ask him and that won't be possible."

"Touché," I granted him that. "Okay, did you hear anything? The door to the walkway opening? A thumping sound of a body hitting pavement?"

The lips pursed again and he shook his head.

"What time was the body discovered?"

"In the morning—someone coming to work."

"Did you think it peculiar?"

"Why?"

"You didn't see him leave the store did you?"

"No."

"Didn't make you suspicious?"

"Of what?"

"Where he was? Was he still in the store, should you maybe check on him to see he was all right?"

"Why wouldn't he be all right?" he asked. "*Nobody* suspected suicide."

"Or murder."

"Right. And he could easily leave the store without my knowing it. I could have been on another floor—another part of the store. He had a key. No," he said shaking his head sadly, "I never gave it a thought. It isn't my place to intrude on the executive suite. I'm a night watchman, remember. Just the watchman."

I remembered.

I thanked him and went to keep my appointment with Alice and the "item" she had located.

24

I was sold on the watchman's theory. The larger question was, could I sell my client? Did I have a convincing rationale for continuing to take his or her money?

Would it strengthen the case for suicide if I provided a motive for the act? Did the Kulps care—or would they be devastated by my report, or refuse to believe it?

I decided my immediate priority was to get Sandy's computer in the hope that the local nerd could solve its secrets.

I stepped outside to use my cell phone. I got Jessamyn's voicemail. "Hi, leave a message." I left a succinct message that I had a gift I would like to deliver to her friend at his earliest convenience.

With time to kill (Question: should you kill time before it kills you?) I walked the store searching for opportunities for a mystery man (or woman?) to stow away after the store closed. Bathrooms (basement and third floor) and dressing rooms (first and second floors) were the obvious targets. I started in the basement. A hodgepodge of bargain items, lawn mowers, snow blowers and other mechanized wonders to ease the burdens of these sojourners in this corner of the frozen northland.

The bathroom was nothing special with nowhere to hide—unless you let your imagination run wild and allow for someone to stand on a toilet in a locked stall when the nightly inspection took place with an inspector who didn't have the gumption to attempt to open the door. There was also a locked closet I assume held supplies.

I didn't go into the women's room for obvious reasons. I didn't think this speculative caper conducive to the participation of a member of the fairer gender.

The dressing rooms in the clothing departments were accessed through a door. There were a series of curtained rooms which were closed when occupied and drawn open when unoccupied. These partitioned spaces were closely watched because of their potential to house folks with larceny in their hearts. All were checked at the end of the day.

In sum: I was unable to find a rationale for this purported heinous act that differed from the police report. The Kulps had to be reaching for their speculative scenario. But *why*?

Some things may defy logic, but I didn't see anything here. Then I did some shopping. I bought two shirts I didn't need—for the bag—large enough to slip a laptop computer into.

I made my way to the executive suite to Alice and my hoped for prize. I realized even if it were in fact Sandy's computer, there might be nothing of value on it. I would be pleased to say I had many other avenues up my sleeve if the computer didn't dish out, but that would be a merciless stretch.

Alice lit up like a Hanukkah tree as soon as she saw me—and I had an uncomfy foreboding she was setting her eye teeth for me.

"Oh Gil," she said when I was within eyeshot of her desk, "it's so good to see you."

"Well, yes," I said. My eyeballs darting all over the room. I was already on edge for my mission being discovered.

Alice leaned over and whispered, "I so enjoyed our lunch." I hunched my shoulders, scrunched my eyebrows in reaction. Was she really flirting? How could I cope? She was the key to the case; I couldn't afford to cross her and yet—how far would I go?

"Do you have it?" I whispered.

She cocked an eyebrow—"I hope so," she said, then smiled. Was it lascivious?

I looked around the room at the closed doors. "Anybody here?" I asked, still *sotto voce*.

She smiled. She stood at her desk and with a cocked index finger said, "Follow me."

She led me to a door across the room. When she opened it, my first thought was she had made a mistake. She switched on the light revealing a room perhaps fifteen feet in length, ten feet in width with shelves all around laden with office supplies, paper, toner for the fax machine and printer which stood in the corner.

I immediately tried to spot the computer but could not. Alice closed the door and unless I am sorely mistaken, she locked it.

I tossed her an inquisitive glance.

"Sensitive business," she answered my unspoken question.

"Is the computer here?" I asked, then immediately wondered if this were a trap and being recorded.

Her grinning response was simply lascivious; I swear it was. "You aren't afraid, are you?" she asked with that particular cocking of head and eyebrow.

"Maybe," I said.

She laughed.

"The...computer?" I sputtered. "Is it in here somewhere?"

"You're here," she said. "I'm here. Does anything else matter?"

"Well..." I said... "Yes. The computer—Sandy's computer. Do you have it?"

"What do you think?" She winked and started toward me.

Suddenly she lunged at me and threw her arms around my body. My first irrational thought was, is this quid pro quo—affection for computer? Could she?

But there she was—my passport to a computer that could solve my case, crushing me in a bear hug—making eyes at me like she was one of those praying mantises who bit off the head of her lover after amorous consummation.

It was at that thought, that I said to myself, "*It's not worth it.*"

"This feels nice, doesn't it?" she said—more of a statement than a question.

"If you will forgive me," I said, "it would feel nice to see the computer. Do you have it?"

Suddenly my cell phone chirped in my pocket. Alice twitched in shock. I reached for the phone having my usual trouble extricating from my pocket. Achieving success with the phone I said, "Hello." It was Jessamyn announcing her readiness.

"Oh, sweetheart," I enthused as though speaking to my lover, "what good news. I'll be there in a few minutes."

Alice was watching me like a distraught hawk. "And just what was that all about?" she demanded as though she and I were in a committed relationship.

"Oh, nothing," I said. "Do you have the computer?"

She paused for a time—a lot shorter than I feared.

When she sighed, her whole body seemed to collapse as though it sprung a pin-hole leak that grew with every breath.

"Oh," she said. "I thought...it could have been...soooo...nice."

"Perhaps under different circumstances or another time..."

"No," she said, tearing up. "I know better now."

Believe it or not, that scared me. Perhaps her offer did not come free of strings, and I'd never see the computer.

"It's all right," she said, patting my upper arm. "I understand." She took a step back. "I left it right where I found it. I thought it might help you to see where he put it."

She took my hand and led me to the corner of the room away from the machinery. There were stacks of paper reams and rows of beige metal filing cabinets—the kind with pull-out drawers. I didn't notice them when I came in. Now they loomed as agents of promise.

"There?" I asked her.

"There," she said.

"That's a hiding place? In drawers that are pulled

out every day?"

She shook her head.

"I mean, wouldn't someone be curious what a computer was doing stashed in a file drawer?"

"Sure," she said, nodding. "That's why he put it behind the cabinets."

I followed her gaze to the back of a cabinet, then stepped aside so I could see behind it.

There it was, in plain but obstructed view. Someone put it there, most likely as an attempt at concealment—which was short of annihilation. Was the idea to stoke the fires of conspiracy? Or was it simply inconvenient for a janitor to get it out of the way? Only a gander at the contents could tell the tale.

I retrieved it from its lair to reveal a silver cased contraption. I opened it up and attempted to turn it on.

Dead.

25

As soon as I cleared the store with the computer, allegedly Sandy's, in my store bag, I called Jessamyn on my cell phone.

"Got it," I said when she answered. "Is Mr. Nerd standing by?"

"He's close—I alerted him," she said. "Do you want us to come to your hotel?"

"No, I'll come there." Further from the store, I thought which perhaps did not exhibit top of the drawer logic. "Oh," I added, "tell him the thing is dead and I didn't find a cord with it. Ask him to bring a cord."

"What kind of computer is it?"

"How should I know?"

"Well, you could look at it for starters," she said with a thinly veiled assessment of the level of my intelligence.

I had the Straus Brothers shopping bag in my arms, like a beloved baby.

I looked in the bag being careful no one saw my prize. I didn't want to lose it so soon after the acquisition—not before I found out if there was anything of value to me in those mysterious, elusive innards.

"There's an apple with a bite taken out of it."

"Can you find the model number?"

"Where?"

"On the side or underneath."

"I'll call you back," I said, still paranoid about the possibility of detection. I made my way back to my hotel parking garage, got into my car and locked the doors. I surreptitiously removed the computer from the bag and found the model info which I conveyed to Jessamyn on my cell phone.

I started the car, checking all directions for an undefined enemy. After all, if the computer was still in the closet, no one could be too interested in it.

The distance to the college and Jessamyn's room was covered without incident.

I parked outside her place and in my excitement exited the car with the Straus bag—shirts and all.

Jessamyn met me at the door. Lurking behind her in the living room was an apparition with a shaved head and an over-full beard which he ceaselessly stroked with a mechanical hand.

"Hi there," she said standing back giving me a full view of baldy. "Com'on in. This is Elwin," with her arms signalling him, then the arm swooping over to me.

I admit to being startled by Elwin's appearance. He looked more like one of those food gurus whose main message was "death to sugar" than he looked like a nerd. The right hand, free of stroking his beard dangled an electric cord, sure, I expected, to fit the Straus computer. You could tell he was, bitwise, chomping to put the experiment in motion.

I handed over the computer sans bag and shirts. He found an electrical outlet behind a couch that had paid its dues in the service of giving rest and succor to the student population historically, hysterically and histrionically.

He plugged it in, sat on the tired couch with the computer perched on his lap. He opened the lid, performed some mumbo jumbo and said, "Know the password or user name?"

No one answered—no one knew.

"Didn't think so," he said. "What was his name?"

"Edward Straus," I said. "Nickname Sandy."

Elwin typed at lightening speed.

"Hmm..." he hummed. "Got it. Password," he said, not as a question and resumed typing.

"What are you doing?" I asked him.

"Putting in the most used passwords. See if anything clicks."

"You have them memorized?" I asked, prepared to be impressed.

"They're pretty simple—1-2-3, A-B-C, 1-2-3-4-5, A-B-C-D-E-F-G. Nothing too taxing. The vast majority of the populace are lunkheads exhibiting sub-zero mental ability. If none of this works, we move on to birth date, phone number, address, social security. We'll get it." He spoke as one who knew what he was about and didn't gladly suffer those who didn't.

"Sorry, I don't know any of that—but I know someone who does."

"Call him," Elwin demanded. He never looked up from his screen.

"Her," I corrected him. "And I don't know how to reach her before the store opens tomorrow."

I only wished I had gotten Alice's phone number—but on reflection I realized the signal of my personal interest could likely have caused her to think more wrong thoughts.

Perhaps my best ploy was to pay another visit to Priscilla Kulp. She seemed the most rational of the Kulps. Tomorrow after the Doctor went to work in the morning. I was still nagged by the feeling she could be my best source of information and contacts with people who could furnish the same.

Jessamyn sat on the couch beside Elwin, looking over his shoulder at the screen that was showing basic black.

Jessamyn turned to me, standing helplessly before the couch. "What do you hope to find with this thing?"

"Clues," I said.

"What kind?" she asked.

I shrugged. "Lots of questions."

"Like?"

"Like why was it where it was in the store room? Did he want it found? Not want it found but too distracted to purge it of its information? Or did he not even think about whether or not he had anything to hide?"

"So what do you think?"

I nodded to Elwin and the computer on his lap. "That's my hope—he'll be able to find something that will tell us something," I said. "You having any luck at the paper?"

"Nothing new yet. I'm getting there."

"When will you have something?"

"*If* I get something," she said. "Tomorrow or

164

the next day."

"Good."

Then I got Elwin's cell number and gave him mine. I declared it a day and returned to my hotel to ring down the shades on another ten grand.

$40,000

It is often said that one does not succeed by focusing on money. I had two friends who claimed in their early twenties that they would be millionaires by the time they reached thirty-five years. One settled on teaching school ("I'm going to make my million a nickel at a time," he said with a half smile). The other was driving a cab and still hopeful. Today he is unemployed (driving a cab being such a drag and all).

But to think in four days I had racked up forty grandolas tickled my sacroiliac. Though after you get over the thrill of anticipating the big bucks, orientation turns to results. Other than landing the still impotent computer, I couldn't point to any result I found significant. The client wanted me to prove the victim did not commit suicide, and I was convinced he did—albeit on evidence the client would never accept.

Ergo I was obliged to offer stronger proof in the form of a rationale for the act.

Proof that was so far eluding me.

I surmised the weak link in the Kulps' united

front was Priscilla. She offered the most fertile dirt for progress in my humble opinion, which was becoming more humble by the $10,000 day. I would seek another audience with the mater familias.

But first, Alice. Alice in Wonderland, you might say, though I wouldn't. I called the store before it opened and left a message for Alice to call me. Would she? Was she angry in re: my non-cooperation, or would she think I'd had second thoughts so possibilities still abounded? I hoped the latter but feared the former.

My cell phone was on my person for my perfunctory breakfast in the hotel dining room, which bespoke cleanliness and a certain sterility of décor. The fare featured ersatz orange juice, the sugar squeezed into plastic while squeezing out the nutrients. Plus one of those cardboard cereals salvaged by the sugar that coated it.

Breakfast over, there was no message from Alice. I called the store. The clever computer system directed the call to Alice's mechanism.

Alice answered herself, "Executive Suite, Alice speaking."

"Hi Alice," I said smothering her in good cheer. "It's Gil."

Frosty the snowman.

"Alice?"

"…Y….e….s….s."

"Are you all right?"

"All right? Well…I cried all night—so if that's all right, I'm all right."

"Oh, Alice, I'm so sor…ry. Is it my fault?"

"Well…" she said, "I bet you're calling because you want something."

"Ah...maybe a little info," I said, then hastily added, "You'd like to solve this case wouldn't you?"

"Yes...and no..." she said. "I have mixed feelings."

"We're trying to guess Sandy's password. The resident nerd has asked for his birthday, address and social security number."

There was a silence.

"Alice?"

"What's it worth to you?"

"What do you want?"

"Ooo—I don't know," she cooed, "make an offer."

"Dinner?"

"Dinner?" she asked, her interest piqued. "Tonight?"

"I was...hoping to make it after I solved the case—we if you give me the info and it works, you pick the place."

"Well..."

"Hey it's nothing that would put you out. I'll bet you have it all in your head already."

"Well...maybe."

"Like when he was born?"

The silence that followed was finally broken when she said, "October 30, 1970."

"10-30-70. Thanks.

"Know his social security?"

"174-29-2930."

"You are a gem," I said.

"Yeah," she wasn't convinced.

"You gonna have a chance to take Ginger out to lunch?"

"I'm thinking about it."

"Tell you what…"

"What?"

"You get her out, I'll take you to dinner that night plus my last night."

"Really? I'll call her today."

"Thanks a lot, Alice. I really appreciate it."

I called Elwin with the info. He said he'd call me if anything worked.

It was time to call Priscilla Kulp. She would see me in the time it took me to drive over to her house.

When I pulled the car to the front of the house I was relieved to see two things. The doctor's caddy was not out front, and Priscilla herself came out in the cold to greet me.

I hugged her. She hugged back. "It's good to see you, Gil," she said, leading me into her living room.

We sat side by side on the couch.

"I appreciate you seeing me," I said.

"It's the least I can do," she said. "I'd really like to get this horror behind us."

"I understand. That's why I'm here," I said. "For some strange reason I think there may be strings, strands, loose parts—however the saying goes."

"Oh, Gil," she laughed. "Loose ends."

"Good enough." I often wondered if my inadvertent malapropisms didn't, however slightly, endear me to my contacts. It seemed to be working with Priscilla. People have compassion for misfits.

"Ginger," I began, then letting it hang there like a blimp leaking gas, "Ginger," I repeated. "Why do I think she may hold the key to this thing?"

"Ginger? Well, no—I mean…I couldn't imagine…"

I held my gaze steady on her eyes. "Y..e..ss you could," I said slowly, "you do."

"I do?" She sounded perplexed but she was faking it.

I nodded slowly still. "What's the *real* story?"

"Why Mr. Yates, what do you mean?"

"I mean Sandy did the suicide thing. Nobody pushed him—it's not only remote in conception and execution, it's virtually impossible."

"But Mr. Yates, that's why we hired you. To sort it out."

"Perhaps if you called me Gil—like you did before—just perhaps, understand, you might let your guard down. So tell me about Ginger—Ginger's community."

"Tell you? Tell you what?"

"Ginger's extraordinarily beautiful," I said. "That's indisputable."

"She *is* attractive."

"I'll chalk your understatement up to modesty. After all, you are her mother and you're no slouch in the looks department."

"How sweet of you…Gil. But my day has passed…I know that."

"Ginger, how did she do in school?"

"Fine."

"Where did she go to grade school?"

"In town."

"Junior high—same."

"High school?"

"We sent her to…religious school."

170

"Why?"

"Well...we thought she might be...safer."

"Safer?"

"Yes, in a religious...all girl environment."

"And was she?"

"Oh...yes."

"Did she have any boyfriends—other than Sandy?"

"Well, she could have had dozens."

"I'm sure," I said. "Did she?"

Her brow scrunched. "She was very fussy."

"Four to five fussy, or zero?"

"A lot of fellows were interested," she said. "I know that."

"Yes? Did she bring any fellows home?"

"Home?"

"Yes, home—here," I said spreading my arms wide in her living room.

The brows squeezed again, "I'm trying to remember."

"Um hmm. How about college? Any boyfriends?"

"I'm sure she could have had all she wanted."

"I'm sure too," I agreed. "Did she want any?"

"Ginger was fussy, you know."

"Yes, you said—you might say Ginger was...standoffish, wary of men perhaps?"

"Oh, I don't know."

"Close to her father, was she?"

"Of course," she said with a firm cast to her jaw and cheeks. "She was his only daughter."

"Yours too."

"Oh, but that's different."

"Yes," I said. "I've heard mothers and daughters have issues."

"Issues?"

"Things they disagree about," I said. "Did you and Ginger disagree about anything?"

"Well, I suppose we did," she said. "It's normal, you know."

"So she was a normal girl?"

"Well, yes. I think so."

"Knowing the facts, would others think she was normal?"

"Well, I don't know about others. I suppose they would."

"Um hmm," I nodded. "Priscilla, if you want me to get to the basement of this, you've got to do better. What was unusual in Ginger's childhood?"

Priscilla was silent. Was she thinking or searching for a way to evade my questions?

"She's my daughter," she said, "my only child. You aren't going to get me to say anything bad about her."

"No."

She was silent a minute, then stood. "Follow me," she said.

She led me down the corridor to a bedroom, then without a word she opened the door and stood back, beckoning me with her head to enter.

I entered the room and was immediately shocked to the quick. It seemed every conceivable space was covered with bride and groom dolls paired on shelves, bed tables, dresser as well as on the bed itself.

On the dresser, the focal point of the collection featured a groom that looked an awful lot like Jesus.

"Jesus?" I said, barely skirting profanity.

"Jesus," she said in confirmation.

"Aren't nuns considered brides of Jesus?"

"I believe so."

"Was she a nun?"

"Noooo," she said. "At some time or other—a girl's dream—sort of a child's fantasy.

"But she didn't?"

"No."

"How close did she come?"

"I think it remained just that—a fantasy."

"When did she get over it? Or did she?"

"When she met Sandy and realized she was in love with him and wanted to marry him." Her eyes drifted to Jesus and his bride, who looked not unlike Ginger. "He was such a gem. No woman could have done better."

Better? I thought. Perhaps someone less perfect would still be alive.

Casting my eyes over the nuptial menagerie gave me more questions than answers.

"Does her father know about this?" I asked waving my hand over the overstuffed room.

"Of course."

"What does he think?"

"We've never discussed it," she said knocking me off track. How could she not? I mean, I am a big fan of denial, but this was over the upside.

"Did he with Ginger?"

"Oh—well—he—I guess. But I don't know what was said."

"Did you notice any change after he talked to her about it?"

"No."

"When was that?"

"Before she went to college."

"Did she want to take the dolls with her?"

"I don't know."

"Did she take them to her marriage abode?"

"No. They stayed home."

"Any new dolls since she went to college?"

"I...don't...think so."

"Any deletions—any change since the marriage?"

"Not that I'm aware of," she said, "but I don't intrude here. This is her room. I respect that."

"What do you make of it—this collection?" I waved around the room again.

"Make of it?"

"Think it a little odd? All these depictions of weddings."

"Noooo."

"Know anyone else who ever had a collection like this?"

"I'm sure there must be others...lots of them," she said with a hopeful tone.

"Hmm. I don't know," I said. "What does it mean to you?"

"Oh, nothing special. Little girls fixate on things. Ginger's was apparently weddings."

"Apparently."

27

The wedding menagerie put me off my sustenance. Was it only a childhood fixation? But there it was enshrined in her childhood bedroom for some decades—even many years after she'd had a wedding of her own. Okay, I thought, but you will notice the wedding collection did not travel with Ginger to the nuptial palace. Why not? They had empty bedrooms. Did the late groom even know about all these ghoulish dolls?

It gave me something to ponder as I called Elwin. He took his time answering.

"Yeah," he said. It wasn't exactly a challenge, but I wouldn't mistake the greeting for friendly.

"Anything clicking?" I asked.

"Yeah, I just got a password—a clever combo of his birthday and social security number. Now the fun begins."

"How much fun do you figure? In hours?"

He laughed. "Days would be more like it."

"Days?"

"I don't know. I might get lucky," he said. "You'll be the first to know."

Did he hang up on me? Or should I have realized the conversation was completed?

I hoped for better telephone luck when I called Sandy's mother.

She answered cheerfully on an early ring and told me—rather upbeat for the circumstances—she would be delighted to see me.

Hazel lived on a farm on the outskirts of Muhlenheim in one of those towns whose pronunciation by the locals I could not reconcile with its spelling.

It was a big spread with a couple horses corralled behind a fence. Their interest in me was short lived. Not the sort of animals that lived vicariously.

No sooner had I reached the door than it opened on a petite woman shrunken by age. Chipper, upbeat she put out her hand for a shake as though she were one of the boys which she very nearly was.

Hazel Klepinger Straus was a wisp of a woman—an anachronism in this Pennsylvania Dutch mecca of fried potatoes, butter and sugar drinks. Wiry, you'd say.

"Nice to see you Mr. Yates," she said with a smile that socked you right to her bosom.

"My close friends call me Gil," I said realizing how silly that sounded. I didn't have any close friends and if I did they would be using my real name, Malvin Stark. Mal at best.

She led me into the living room—spacious, old school furnishing and horsy. She turned to me, "May I get you something to drink?"

"Oh, no thanks," I said. "Thank you very much."

She chuckled, "Well your gratitude seems out of proportion to the offer."

Suddenly I was drawn to the mantle of the huge fireplace. The fire box could have housed a jeep—a small jeep, okay? A tad exaggerated, but I'm trying to say BIG.

But the mantle—it was loaded with trophies—an *ideal* ice breaker—though there wasn't any ice within sneezing distance of Hazel Klepinger Straus—warm as they come.

"Are these yours?" I asked trotting out my best awe.

"Oh, I'm afraid so," she said. "The trophies used to be in the barn where they belong, but my horse didn't like them."

"He told you?"

"We communicate."

"In English?"

"Of course not," she said as though considering the proposition for the first time. "Perhaps had the prizes been for horsemanship...but we understand each other," this followed by a crinkling of her nose.

I was going to like her—in one of those make believe mysteries she would emerge as a suspect—perhaps incest or something for a motive. She was so likeable it was difficult to believe it was mother issues that propelled her middle son off the department store roof—and dad was long gone at the time.

"What are they for?" I asked moving closer to inspect them.

"Flying," she said. "It's nothing really. If you land safely at one of those meets they give you a trophy. I put them up so I can pooh pooh them so everyone says how modest I am."

"Well, you are."

She laughed. "My mother would say I had a great deal to be modest about."

"But I mean flying? Are you an airline pilot or something?"

"Oh no—nothing so grand. I just fly for fun."

"*Fun?* You get *fun* out of flying?"

"Oh, yes. Small planes, propellers, just like the olden days—I push back the canopy and I revel in tasting the clouds."

"Clouds? You fly in the clouds?"

"Well, sure—I don't fly around them…"

"But, but you can't see."

"Well, yes, that depends on if the visibility is, well, clouded," she clapped her hands once at her funny.

"Is it…safe?"

"Well," she said with a broad show of teeth, "I'm still here."

I was getting queasy feelings as far down as you can go and it was rising fast. I feared I would soil her carpet from one end or the other—perhaps both.

"Oh, enough about me," she said leading me to the couch. "Come. Let's sit," and we did.

"It's very good of you to see me," I said.

"Oh, pshaw," she said. "Not at all. I love to have company. My dear Ollie passed away going on three years now. We had fifty-six glorious years."

"Really," I said, "is that possible?"

"Fifty-six??"

"No—glorious years of marriage."

"Well, it was for me," she said. "I can't speak for anyone else."

"May I offer my condolences," I said. "I never met your son, Sandy, but from what I hear, he was widely loved."

"Thank you," she murmured.

"Did he have a happy marriage, would you say?"

Her face appeared to have absorbed all the clouds in the sky.

"I don't know, I'm not a meddler."

"But—but you're his mother, you could hardly help having some ideas."

"Ideas…" she said, trailing off.

"Yes," I said, encouraging.

"Everyone has ideas," she said. "What they might be worth is another matter."

"Try me," I said. I sensed she wanted to talk, get it off her lungs, and only lacked for the slightest encouragement—which I had just given her.

"What, specifically, would you like to ask?"

"Your thoughts on the whole thing—relationship, marriage—anything that might have bothered him enough to…end it."

"Yes, everybody asks those questions," she said. "Sometimes there are answers, sometimes not."

"In Sandy's case?" I prodded gently after that seemed called for.

"Well, the Kulps don't seem satisfied," she said. "I suppose that's what you're here for."

"Can we satisfy them?"

The nose crinkled again. "I fear if they require motives and proofs for someone to have pushed him off the roof, we cannot."

"So what is the plausible counter to that proposition?"

"Perhaps chemistry."

"Chemistry."

"One school of thought has it he was seriously depressed."

"Did you see signs of that?"

A deep breath shook her. "I don't know. I never saw signs before he married... Ginger." She paused just enough to give the name a certain spin.

"And how *was* their marriage?"

"Fine," she answered quickly, then added in softer tones, "I suppose."

"He ever talk to you about it? About Ginger?"

"Not directly."

"Indirectly?"

"He said some things that made me wonder."

"What kinds of things?"

"Oh, just for instance her father called her every night at dinnertime."

"And she talked to him?"

Hazel nodded, as though a verbal response might be painful.

"So you mean instead of having dinner with her husband, she had it with her father?" I asked, trying to picture it.

She nodded. "I didn't see him that much after they married."

"Why? Because he was too depressed to visit?"

"Oh, I don't think so. Though depression can set in at any age."

"Any of his ancestors...?"

"Depressives? None we can think of."

"Well, I suppose people who are happy don't jump off roofs."

"No." There was a catch in her voice.

"So we might conclude he could have been happier."

"Yes."

"Why? How?"

She shrugged her shoulders, but I knew she had theories.

"Was he happy on his wedding day?"

"Oh, I'd say so," she said. "Very happy. But you realize I was a peripheral figure at the wedding."

"And after?"

"They just seemed to settle in like a seasoned married couple," she said, "but as I say, I didn't see all that much of him afterwards."

"Was he a happy child?"

"Oh yes," she said, smiling at the memory. "I *was* there for that."

"No signs of depression?"

"Oh, no. None. Maybe the opposite…"

"Manic?"

"Well, *happy*."

"Not bogged down being the middle child?"

"No, no," she said. "He could keep up with the best of them."

"So you were just a big happy family?"

"Not that big."

"Happy as oysters?"

She looked perplexed. "Isn't it clams that are happy?"

"I'll be darned. Lots of happy fish in the sea, I suppose."

She laughed—she had a good laugh—contagious.

"Did you know the Kulps before Sandy married Ginger?"

"I knew of them. We weren't friends."

"What did you know?"

"He is a prominent heart surgeon. Part of the country club crowd."

"Did you belong to the club?"

"Oh, yes. But my interests were elsewhere— flying, horses. We went for dinner occasionally and the kids went swimming. Then as they got older, golf."

"Did Sandy meet Ginger at the club?"

"I think it was a party. Perhaps at the club, perhaps not."

"Love at first sight?"

"Oh, my, he was gaga—absolutely beside himself. He took a terrible ribbing from his brothers."

"Jealous?"

"It wouldn't surprise me. Ginger was *the* catch in these parts."

"How so?" I asked.

"Well, you've seen her I take it?"

"Yes."

"She's incredibly gorgeous, wouldn't you say?" she asked.

"On a purely physical plane, I guess I would say she was nice looking," I said, "but she seemed sort of morose—and if you subscribe to the theory that pretty is as pretty does, I'd say she'd have to lift herself out of the doldrums before I could agree that she was gorgeous— incredibly or not."

"Fair enough. I haven't seen her since the funeral where she was swathed head to foot in mourning clothes."

"And—in addition—what were her assets?"

"She is well educated, private schools virtually from the beginning, she is well read, well spoken and can be charming."

"Can be? You mean by that she isn't always?"

Hazel shrugged. "Is anybody *always* charming?"

"I don't know. Some more than others I suppose," I said. "I imagine *you* are *always* charming."

She laughed a, yes, charming laugh.

"Oh, dear boy," she said, "If you only knew."

Well, I guessed I didn't really want to know. I liked her just the way she was in the original. I told her so.

"Why Mr. Yates, I do declare you are making me blush. No easy task at my age."

"Perhaps if that is so, you blush too easily."

"Perhaps—and of course," she continued as though no break had occurred in her train of thought, "she came from a good family."

"Good? Does that mean rich?"

"Oh, you wouldn't rule it out, but I mean good as in good values, upstanding citizens, contributing members of the community, all those good things."

"Yes," I said, "you are talking about the man who called his daughter every night at dinner time."

Another slow nod from the lady of the house.

"Tell me, what did Ginger do about her dinner?"

"Do?"

"Did she eat while she was talking to her daddy? Did she wait until he hung up? And how long did they talk?"

"Until Sandy had finished his dinner."

"Really?"

"More or less."

"What did they talk about?"

She smiled. "Did you forget I wasn't there?"

"Sandy never told you?"

"Not much more than that. And now he can't—but Ginger still can. You could ask her."

"I will," I said. "How about breakfast? Did he call then?"

"Sandy made his own. Ginger liked to sleep late and Sandy had to go to the store."

"A weekend lunch? Did they ever have a meal alone together?"

"I suppose they did. Sometime why don't you ask her that too?"

"Okay. Would you like me to tell you what she says?"

"Oh, I don't know. I'm afraid it wouldn't bring him back."

"I don't suppose you'd object to my finding she might have deserved some of the blame."

"Oh, and I don't know about that either. You know," she said, "mothers and daughters have issues some—okay most—say. But they pale compared to mothers and their daughters-in-law. Try as we might, differences surface. A competition for our man—the wife displaces the mother and that doesn't always go down so easily."

"I suppose not." Our son wasn't oriented toward taking a female to wife, but if he did I imagine my dear Tyranny would eat her alive.

"I remember," Hazel said, "my mother-in-law criticizing the way I cut vegetables. A perfectly nice woman you understand, but there was the irresistible competition."

"I suppose going to the level of cutting vegetables bespoke your perfection in all other important areas," I said.

"May I thank you for that without acquiescing to the sentiment?"

"Sure," I said, "but then why thank me? By the way, how did your husband like Ginger?"

"Oh, he thought she was the cat's pajamas."

"The cat's what?"

"Pajamas."

"I suppose that means something good, but I never knew cats wore pajamas. How do they get them on?"

She laughed. "Just a figure of speech. Ollie, my *late* husband, loved Ginger. She knew how to turn the eye of the male of the species."

"How did she do it?"

"Oh, big toothy smiles, playing on the vanity of the macho, but let's face it, *weaker* sex. We didn't see Ginger that often as I said, but when we did Ollie lit up like a Christmas tree. Ginger knew how to attract men. I told you Sandy's brothers could barely hide their envy."

"Could there have been anything, extracurricular going on?"

"With Sandy's brothers? Oh, no. That would have been impossible to hide."

"With someone else? Could she have had another extra-marital relationship?"

"Of course, I don't know. But somehow I don't think so."

"Can you give me the names and whereabouts of any friends Sandy might have had—people he might have confided his thoughts to?"

"Oh, Sandy didn't seem to have a lot of close friends. You might say he was something of a loner."

"Girlfriends?"

"Occasional. Again, not close or lasting. Ginger was his first real love."

"Anyone he might have confided in, some buddy in college, at home?"

"I'm perhaps not the best person to ask. Sandy was a private person. Perhaps he might still be alive if he'd sent warning signals to anyone." She sighed at the hopelessness of it all. "Tell you what. I'll put my thinking cap on, talk to the boys. See what we can come up with."

"Great," I said. "Appreciate it."

I considered it a fruity afternoon, something to do with fruit anyway. Full of fruit perhaps. Calling your married daughter every night at dinnertime seemed weird at best, perverse at the other end. Annoying as it must have been, it probably would not have pushed a stable guy off the roof. It had to be symptomatic of something deeper.

I left there with a warm feeling for Hazel Klepinger Straus.

She was a woman liberated before women's liberation—before all that flag waving hoopla and she didn't fuss about it when she climbed into her airplane for a spin around the countryside. She was a man's woman or a woman's man, depending on your gender disposition.

But dinnertime phone calls. Did that mean there was a father/son-in-law competition for the good opinion of the daughter/wife, similar to the mother/daughter-in-law issues? Not as common, perhaps, but not impossible either.

I could always hope Elwin could crack Sandy's computer and provide some sense to all this information.

I thanked Hazel for her time and cooperation and we parted after a warm hug.

28

"Elwin!" I shouted into my cell phone in my car outside from Straus's digs. He must have taken ten rings to pick up. "Gil Yates," I said. "How's it going?"

"I'll call you when I have something," he virtually snarled into the phone.

"But…"

"Buzz off," he said and buzzed off.

Patience would be the mood of the moment.

Meeting Hazel Klepinger Straus was a boon to my thinking. She gave me another boulevard for investigation. The wedding dolls and daddy calling at dinnertime were leading me in a new direction—a shifting. I decided some insight into Ginger Kulp might not be amiss.

I waited for the mother superior at the catholic girls' school in Muhlenheim in a Spartan waiting room. I could imagine legions of girls cooling their heels in terror in the same position.

I knew one mother superior joke which I turned over in my mind. I would tell her or not depending on my assessment of her sense of humor:

A young catholic girl joined a convent where she could speak only two words every ten years. After her first ten years the mother superior summoned her to her office.

"Sister, you have put in ten faithful years, and now we express our appreciation to you by allowing you your two words.

Without thinking as though she had pointed her whole last ten years to this moment, she blurted, "Bad food!"

"Oh," said the mother superior, "thank you for sharing that thought. I will certainly see what we can do to improve the food."

Ten years later, the sister was again solicited for her two words.

"Hard bed!" she exclaimed.

The mother superior apologized and said she would look into getting her a softer mattress.

After ten more years had passed—on the sister's thirtieth anniversary, she was again given the opportunity to express her thoughts in two more words.

"I quit!" she said.

The mother superior studied her charge and nodded slowly. "Well, it's a good thing," she said. "Ever since you got here you've done nothing but bitch."

The longer I waited in the sterile holding tank, the more I felt the wait was unreasonable—perhaps even arrogant—an emotion I would prefer not to ascribe to the truly holy. And as time dragged on I increased in my doubt that my joke would fall on receptive ears.

I thought for a moment I should have called for an appointment, but I feared she would not see me at all, so I took my chances.

When I was finally ushered into her august presence I immediately sensed my joke would be out of the question.

I explained I had been hired to look into the cause of the death of Sandy Straus. "I understand his wife Ginger Kulp was a student of yours. I wondered if you might tell me something about her."

"What makes you think I'd want to divulge confidences?"

"I'm not asking for confessional confidences, merely about her school years, if there was anything untoward. I wouldn't expect you to breech confidences."

There was nothing untoward, she wanted me to know.

"I didn't think there would be," I assured her. "Was she a good student?"

"Exemplary."

"No problems."

"None."

"Got along with everyone?"

"Yes, she was very popular."

"With the boys?"

"Mr. Yates," she said sternly, "there were no boys. This is an all girls school."

"Oh, did you ever have mixers? With local boys' schools or anything?"

"The environment here you will find a serious one. There was no time wasted on frivolity of any kind.

"Men of maturity are necessary for the prolongation of the race. Boys of school age are generally unserious and—frivolous, yes."

"Is that a thought you taught?"

"It wasn't something I *had* to teach. It was obvious to the girls in this school."

"How obvious? If there were no boys here—to make it obvious." I don't know why I added that last bit.

She stiffened, "Well, here—school—is not the only place they came across boys."

"Where else?"

"Goodness," she said, "*everywhere* else."

"Why don't you teach boys here?"

"We have found it distracts the girls. They perform better without them. When boys are present the girls get silly trying to attract their attention—and being careful not to raise their ire by outperforming them."

"Have you taught boys in your time?"

"Yes, I have." I need not go further from the expression on her face to learn what she thought of that. I decided to ask her anyway.

"And..."

"And what?"

"How was it?"

She graced me with a sour prune face. "Boys that age..." she repeated the prune.

"Yes?"

"Well, you know what I mean..."

"No...I don't."

"Well," she harrumphed, "their minds are on one thing. If you get my drift."

"Oh," I said, getting her drift.

"But surely, in this environment, those …urges…can be kept under control."

"At what cost?" she asked shaking her head with her arms. "No, it just won't do."

"Well, isn't the vast majority of education in the country co-ed?"

She pursed her lips, "Doesn't mean it's good."

"Well, but surely you—the church—has a stake in reproduction of the species. Aren't you famous for encouraging large families?"

"Young man," she had me in her gun sights, "Church doctrine is none of your affair. Are you even a Catholic?"

"No…I…"

"I thought not," she said satisfied God was in His heavens and all was right with the world. And I had been put in my place.

A thought had occurred to me—I'm not sure from where. "I am persuaded it is in the church's interest to get boys and girls together, keep the congregations' vital and all that."

"Procreation is sacred—it's not a pastime."

Wow, I thought. She should be writing advertising slogans. "Is that something you teach?"

"Certainly," she said as though I was some sort of mental deficient not to realize without asking.

"Was Ginger Kulp a good student?" I asked as though shifting gears, but I wasn't.

"I told you she was an exemplary student."

"By the way, were you acquainted with her father, Dr. Kulp?"

She looked at me as though weighing how much info I could process.

"Yes," she said as though she weren't sure she should.

"Did they have a good relationship? Father and daughter?"

Her eyes narrowed. What was so difficult about that, I wondered. It required only a yes or no answer.

"Young man," she said rising to her full height which was considerable, "I will bid you goodbye."

"Why? Have I asked an embarrassing question?"

More imperial glare from the superior mother (sans children), "You do not have it in your power to embarrass me."

"No? So was their relationship…normal?"

"That is a personal question the insinuation of which is insulting to the principals. I have no special insight into the Kulps, but I can tell you they are loyal, upstanding members of the church, whom we are proud to have. So I've no idea what your motives are in this probing, but I can tell you I doubt if any answer I could give you would satisfy your morbid curiosity, so I will thank you to vacate our holy premises and take up your inquiries with the Kulps themselves."

I thanked her for her time, more or less graciously, and she responded in kind. It was a toss up about which of us was more inauthentic.

On my way out I took a different route—you learn nothing by treading the same ground. I went through the large church which was attached to the mother superior's digs. I paused in the vestibule to reattach my bearings. Mother superior had indeed been daunting—not even my years with Tyranny Rex had prepared me for it.

I can't say that life with Tyranny Rex didn't give

me an insight into the upside of chastity. It had become a foregone necessity, though Roman Catholics did seem to have a corner on the idea. The head female honcho they called mother superior, and that kind of mother doesn't engage in the practice that would legitimize the appellation. Or to put it another way, they can achieve the common but lofty title without the mess and bother heretofore attendant on it.

My eye was caught by one of those ubiquitous walls resplendent with a surfeit of names. I don't know why, but I looked at them (there were hundreds) and they seemed to be listed by categories of donations. Numerically by the amount contributed.

At their top of the list, in the five million dollar category were the names

Dr. & Mrs. Chester Kulp

That was fifty operations worth before taxes— but these operations would not be taxed.

29

Alice's selection for dinner after her lunch with Ginger Kulp was a romantic retreat on the outskirts frequented by the gents in the area when their wives were out of the area.

It did not escape my notice that Alice had aspirations.

My aspirations were for information. Making the most of mine and the least of hers was my challenge.

Fish was in the sack—crab cakes, clam chowder, steamed clams and Maine lobster were their specialties. I couldn't decide among them, so I had them all.

In fine fettle was our Alice. She thought my selection sounded good, so ordered the same. It would be enough food to keep us in the restaurant until we fell asleep. Perhaps at the table.

Without fanfare—after the orders were placed, Alice launched into her soliloquy.

"She sure is beautiful. I forgot how stunning she was. It's easy to see why Sandy went for her."

Implicit, but unspoken was the lament "and not for me."

"So what is your sense of their marriage?"

"Fuzzy," she said. "Ginger insisted they were happy as clams," Alice tittered, perhaps in reference to our dinner order. "But something didn't compute, I can't put my finger on it, like she was almost too eager to protest too much."

"Protest what?"

"How great their marriage was."

"Did she tell you her father called her every night at dinnertime?"

"No," she frowned. "I did get the impression she was crazy about her father."

"*Crazy?*"

"Well, okay, she liked him a lot."

"How was her childhood?"

"Idyllic."

"High school?"

"Same."

"College?"

"Everything was picture perfect."

"Also heavy on protestations?"

"Yes."

"Mention her doll collection?"

"No."

"What were your impressions of her?"

"She seemed happy to be out. Who knows, maybe she is perpetually happy, though I got the sense that mourning was a drag. She did seem out of sorts that no one seemed to believe Sandy didn't do himself in."

"But she still believes it?"

She nodded. "Why they have you. She is expecting a miracle from you."

"Yeah," I said, "but those gems are in short

supply. You think she really believes someone pushed him off the roof with murder in their hearts?"

"Oh, for sure."

"Give you any insight on what might have been the motive?"

"No, but she believes it in her heart."

"Her mother and father believe it, did she say?"

"Daddy believes what she wants him to believe. Mommy is another matter. I sense some issues there."

"Me too. I wish I could exploit them."

We had gotten through the clam chowder and the steamed clams and were awaiting the crab cakes.

"I said I bet she missed him. She said, 'Oh, terribly.' Then I went out on a limb and asked what she missed most."

"What did she say?"

"Oh, nothing startling. I wanted her to say she missed sex."

"But she didn't?"

"No."

"What's your feeling?"

"No feelings," she said.

"You mean Ginger has no feelings or you have no feelings about your lunch?"

"Perhaps both."

"How do you assess Ginger as a person?"

Alice wrinkled her brow to show me she was giving the questions serious thought.

"Like many if not most beautiful women, she has an air of entitlement. Self-absorbed would not be off the mark. I think Sandy spoiled her."

"And what did she do in return?"

"I don't have a sense of that."

"Did he ever talk about her in the office?"

"Seldom," she said. "Then only impersonally."

"Never complained about her?"

"Oh, never. Sandy was not a complainer."

"How were his spirits—before and after the marriage—and at the end—before he..." I didn't have to complete the thought.

"Sandy always made an effort to be upbeat in the office," she said. "Which of course was the only time I saw him."

I had a flash—was *she*, Alice, protesting too much? But I couldn't cast her as a villain, let alone a murderer.

The crab cakes came and in the process of devouring them my cell phone pounded out my ring tone, a little ditty from the hands of Beethoven calculated to wake up the bearer, and I fear, everyone in the restaurant.

My first hope was that it was Elwin with good news about the contents of Sandy's computer. The screen showed simply

Bozo Kulp

(I was getting good at programming the thing.) I quickly turned the racket off.

I could tell by Alice's expression that she was dying to know who called. I tried to convince myself it was a normal reaction and I should not resent her nosiness. I don't think I succeeded.

"Dr. Kulp," I supplied her curiosity.

"Goodness," she said. "What do you suppose he wants?"

"To keep me under his finger."

"Thumb."

"Of course," I conceded. "Technically that's a finger."

"I suppose," she said. "Do you want to call him back? You can leave me here. I'm not nosey."

"He can wait," I said, then added with a smile, "you're more important."

She liked that, I thought. I hope not too much.

We got the lobsters and wrapped up our 'date' dinner. She invited me to come to her place, I danced around it, trying to sound like nothing would give me more pleasure, but his master's voice had summoned me—and since he was paying me ten-thousand dollars a day, it would behoove me to swim through a few hoops that he could effortlessly, perpetually spin.

After we parted I speculated about what the doctor wanted and whether I should call him that night (forty thousand dollars) or wait until the morrow at fifty thousand dollars.

Finally on the hope that he had a hot tip for me, I called him.

I was back in my hotel room and I took my time in the hope it would be too late for him to answer.

No such luck. He grabbed it on the first ring with a fury that should have melted the airwaves.

"Doctor, this is Gil," I said in my humblest pose.

"Yates," he said. "You have some explaining to do."

"Oh?"

"And you know damn well what I'm talking about. Don't pretend you don't."

"I'm not pretending," I said in the humble I-must-be-an-idiot mode.

"You know why I hired you?" Before I could answer he added, "You don't seem to."

Well, it was really his wife who hired me— without any noticeable support from the sourpuss—but I let him ramble.

"Well, I'll tell you why I hired you: to find out who pushed my daughter's husband off the store roof. I did not hire you to go snooping to respectable people about *my daughter!* She is not on trial."

I didn't respond.

He said, "Are you there?"

"Yes," I said.

"Well?" he said. "What do you think you're doing?"

"My job," I said.

"And just what do you think your job *is?*"

"Investigating the death of Sandy Straus and the reasons for it."

"Reasons? We want to know who pushed him."

"And why?"

"Well...I suppose that would be helpful."

"And if we find he wasn't pushed by anyone other than himself don't you want to know why?"

"Young man, you are entirely too big for your britches. In spite of your ridiculous fee I can see you are seriously out of your depth in this case. I suggest you pack it in unless you can come up with the criminal who pushed poor Sandy."

"Is that the wish of your family?" I asked gently.

"That's my wish, damn it," he snapped. "Where do you think the money to pay your ridiculous fee is coming from?"

"No doubt from you—who earns ten times my 'ridiculous fee' each day."

"I'll thank you to keep your comments about my medical practice to yourself."

"All right."

There was a long silence.

"All right, Yates—you come to the house tomorrow morning at nine sharp. The three of us will sit down with you and give you an opportunity to tell us what you have discovered and what plans you have for further investigating this…tragic…accident."

I paused a moment, then said, "All right Kulp," and hung up before he could blow up.

30

$50,000

The snow dusted the ground but it had stopped falling.

The doctor's Cadillac was parked in front of his house. Irrationally I had hoped he had changed his mind about the confrontation, or had perhaps let it slip his mind—he being such a busy guy and all. It wasn't to be.

I opened my car door, but instead of moving toward the house I sat immobile and did a deep breathing trick I had learned from one of those good health gurus who sported a belly that swung like an eighth-month pregnancy. I drew in air for the count of five, held it for seven more counts and exhaled it noisily for eight more.

I did it to gain courage for our meeting. The indomitable Kulps against lil' ole me. Three to one if my math is correct.

After completing five sets of the breathing exercise, I said to myself, 'Okay Malvin, buck up. You gotta go in there like a ten-thousand-dollar-a-day man. Hold your own. Don't panic or give them cause to doubt your worth. Don't let them brow beat you. You are acting on an at will contract. If they want to end it, just say fine—you've already earned fifty grand by virtue of your attendance at this meeting on the fifth day. Keep your chin up and if they cut off your head, make sure your chin is still up.'

With that bit of jack foolery I planted my feet on the sidewalk, my body following directly and I made my way to the Kulps' front door.

Thank goodness Priscilla opened the door with a gracious smile. It was always preferable to ease into the ogre. There was a chill in the room though the heat seemed to be working. The doctor and Ginger were glum. Priscilla, the mom, was doing her best to keep a happy face.

The Kulp living room was arranged for a world-class inquisition. It was to be three against one, then, as we sat, there occurred a chink in the armor. Instead of me alone on the hot seat facing the three, Priscilla shifted gears and instead of joining the inquisitors, took a seat next to me so we seemed to square off two against two.

Had it only been that simple.

The doctor didn't waste time on small talk. He was a far more important man than that.

"Now Yates, Mother Superior said you were snooping about Ginger and you were rude to boot."

"Rude?"

"Yes, rude. Now see here, we hired you to investigate the accidental death of Ginger's husband. There was and is no call for you to snoop around about Ginger. Our focus is on the death of Sandy. Now what progress have you made on the murder thesis?"

I paused to go through the deep breathing drill one more time—without the noisy exhale.

"Today," I said, "I am half way into our contract. I can fairly say I have found not the slightest evidence—even suspicion—that Sandy's death was a murder or even an accident. I have five days left to pursue the matter without giving up on how he died, my focus is shifting to the *why*."

Dr. Kulp was rocking back and forth like a man who was listening without hearing. One whose mind was not to be cluttered with facts, and who was letting me prattle on at his magnanimous sufferance without the slightest danger of his being convinced.

The doctor spoke slowly, befitting his role in the center of the universe.

"You'll forgive me if I confess I am not a man who got where he is by failing or by acceptance of failure in others. We hired you for results—we didn't get them, so," pausing for emphasis, "thanks but goodbye."

"Dear," Priscilla said, "it's only been five days."

"Yes, and already he's given up."

"Oh, dear, I didn't hear him say he was giving up. He just hasn't fulfilled our preconceived notions on the matter. When you hire an expert, honest, conscientious detective you run that risk. Detectives who will tell you what you want to hear are, I imagine, plentiful and less expensive than Mr. Yates.

"Doctor, and Ginger, may we remember how we brought Mr. Yates here in the first place? The process fell on me. You were both against it, but I insisted, threatening divorce if necessary because I could no longer live under this sinister shadow. It's like not living at all. I don't understand it—it's a tragedy but lots of people live with tragedy. The sickness—I call it a *sickness* for that is surely what it is—has not cured itself in over a year. I want a *cure*, closure. *That's* why we brought Mr. Yates here. His findings for suicide I find persuasive. All that's left is the why. Do we fear that? Is that why there are two votes to send him home?"

"Priscilla, you are out-voted, two to one. Now just accept that and bid Gil goodbye. He tried to please us, but he failed. Prolonging the agony will serve no purpose."

"*Oh?* I beg to disagree. *My* purpose is to return our lives to us. I was given that responsibility. 'You handle it,' the doctor said. So I did. The money is in an account that I control. I for one, want to get to the bottom of this. Five more days will get us his opinion."

"And *only* that," the doctor cut in.

"It's not an eternity. I feel Mr. Yates has demonstrated his willingness to go on to the reasoning phase of this dilemma and recognizing my position as dictator in this regard, I say go on."

"No!" Dr. Kulp exploded.

"Ah," she said and paused. "And why not? Is there something you fear?"

"I fear a needless waste of money that in no way serves our purposes."

"Did you consider the favor Mr. Yates is offering you? He could as easily have put in five more days, told us the same thing and left with his one-hundred thousand dollars. I say he stays five more days and I thank him for giving us this opportunity to end the agony."

"Exactly!"

"But if only it would," Priscilla said. "The only thing that will end it is for us to *know* why Sandy jumped."

Ginger winced. The doctor said, "We don't believe that."

"Then don't fear the evidence."

"Just a minute, young lady," his master's voice was about to make a pronouncement. I could feel it in my bones—my bones that were becoming weary of this argument. "Do I need to remind you where the money for this folly is coming from?"

"No, indeed," she said. "It's coming from the same godlike source that all our sustenance has come from. And you know both Ginger and I are eternally grateful for your magnificent earning power. But vital as this is, there are other factors in a reasonable life. While I have no illusions that we could have gotten anywhere near here on my nurse's salary, I see my role as a provider of things money can't buy. Things like peace, serenity, well being, mutual love and understanding. Equanimity is another word. We've lost it in the last year. I want it back—at all costs—if Mr. Yates can help with that he will be worth many times the fee."

Dr. Kulp opened his mouth to speak, then closed it again along with his eyes.

Ginger was sobbing softly and I was on for another five days.

31

After my stressed out session with the Kulps I decided to go back to my hotel. I had designs on flopping on the bed and sleeping away my ten grand for the day. I'd earned it. If I had been offered another twenty-five thousand dollars to repeat the session, I wouldn't do it.

At any rate I realized sleeping all day would not be practical, but I fully intended to carve a little nap out of the ten grand.

But my mind was in the lickety-split mode and when I got to my room in the hotel my phone played Beethoven.

It was Jessamyn.

"Hi there," she sang.

"Hi, Jessamyn. You get something?"

"I got something." Silence.

"Well, are you going to share it with me?"

"Better not on the phone."

"Okay, I'll come over there."

"How about a nice lunch at the store across from you? I have a class I'd like to go to if it's okay."

"Well..." I said, "is what you have worth a lunch?"

"It's worth it."

"Okay, come to my room when your class is over. It's a little more private."

"Roger," she said as though we were in one of those airplane movies.

After she hung up the phone I was too plumbed to take my nap. Maybe later.

I called Hazel Straus. When she didn't answer on the first few rings, I pictured her doing barrel rolls in her vintage plane, her cockpit open to the sky. It made me queasy.

I didn't have to tell her why I was calling. She knew what I wanted. She had one of each gender.

"The girl was a pal through high school, some of us thought he might marry her—I guess the chemistry wasn't right. The guy he went all through school with, starting kindergarten, and Boy Scouts too. He's as close as I can come to a friend."

"College?"

"No, he didn't go to college. Worked at Sears. Some kind of clerk, but wound up in middle management, I believe. Rumor has it Sandy offered him a job at our store, but he didn't think it would be right so he didn't take it."

I took the contact info she had. "But I can't swear by it." I thanked her and hung up.

Wesley Iobst was the name of the fellow, Christina Wagner the female. Since I knew where he was and wasn't sure where she was, I called him first.

He answered the phone, "This is Wes," his voice tinged with the intonation of the local constabulary.

I made my pitch. He said he would be glad to see me anytime in the afternoon.

Finding Christina Wagner was no piece of fudge. Her phone had been disconnected.

I phoned Elwin for his internet expertise. He told me there were Christina Wagners here and there but none matched her stats. There was a knock on my door. I had lost track of the time and when I opened it Jessamyn came rushing in like pent up water through a broken dam. She headed for the small couch. I sat facing her on the chair at the small desk. I think she took a quick breath before she began jabbering, but I'm not sure.

"Okay, here's the deal. The great and good god Dr. Chester Kulp got an early start in his medical career." She fell silent, as though she wanted to be coaxed when more likely she was considering for the first time her presentation.

"So?" I prodded.

"Yes—so—he—the doctor—was about twelve at the time," she said. "His sister, Lucy, fourteen or so, found herself with child *without* benefit of clergy."

"Good God," I exclaimed, thinking the worst. "It wasn't his?"

"I don't think so," she said. "So far no evidence that it was."

"Can we ask her?"

"Don't think she'd be receptive."

"I know, but there are ways."

"Not this time."

I asked the question with my eyes. She answered it with hers.

"*What?*"

"Abortion," she said, "gone sour."

"Can we talk to the doctor?"

She shook her head once. "There was no doctor," she said.

"Then…"

"Back alley specialist."

"So what was Kulp's connection if he wasn't the father?"

"Well, not the biological father, but he was the oldest male child in the family. The real father worked two jobs and had he known about the abortion he'd have killed her—very strict Catholics, you see. Chester Kulp was the facilitator, the bag man."

"Where'd he get the money?"

"A mystery," she said. "Apparently he didn't have much, maybe not any, but the aborter wasn't very good at his trade. Could even have been his first customer. All very creepy," she shuddered.

"What a motive for a medical career."

"Yeah, at least it wasn't gynecology."

"Well, I suppose his career could have been a coincidence."

"Hardly. No one else in the family even went to college, let alone medical school."

Though I couldn't see it, my frown was world class.

"Where'd you get all this background?"

"Small article in the paper—obituaries—girl named Kulp, aged fourteen, died. That's all. No cause of death mentioned."

"So how did you connect all this?"

"My boss at the paper. He wasn't eager to talk about it. I had to squeeze it out of him."

"Well, that's good work. May I talk to him?"

"I asked him," she said. "He said sure.

Tomorrow morning would be best."

"Good, good work, Jessamyn. Much appreciated. Would you be able to smoke out the doc's siblings? Names, addresses, phone numbers, and lend a hand to locate one Christina Wagner?"

"Who's she?"

"One of Sandy's friends. One of two actually, but she seems to have disappeared. Lived in town, then, poof, vaporized."

"Any leads?"

"All I know is she left without a forwarding address. Her phone doesn't forward either."

"I'll get on it," she said.

"Good. Are you hungry?"

"*Starving.*"

"It's rush hour at Ness's. Want to brave the line, or should we go somewhere else?"

"It's worth the wait," she said, and I agreed.

When I saw the length of the line I wasn't sure. It snaked around tables of sports clothes and pajamas.

"Geez," I said to Jessamyn, "we may be here all day."

"How many do you think are in this line?"

"I don't know," I said. "I can't count that high."

We stood there only minutes when another twenty-five or so formed behind us.

There, amidst all this anonymous humanity, I spied Manny Ness making his way toward the restaurant. "Well," I said, "here comes the owner. It might be worth it to have the headaches of a store to get to the restaurant without having to stand in line."

She said, "Can you trip him? Maybe he'll get us in."

"A little drastic," I said, "don't you think?"

"I don't know. I must be hungrier than you are."

I won't say I didn't consider confronting him for special treatment, but I couldn't think of a rationale for him to do me any favors, so I laid low down. I always was underneath—as Malvin Stark, husband to Tyranny Rex, employee of Windbag Wemple, a milquetoast.

But somehow, Manny Ness spotted me and lit up as though he had seen the President of the United States in his store. "Gil!" he exclaimed so everyone turned to gape at me. Everyone knew who Manny Ness was, his picture was in the paper all the time. But they wanted to see who this Gil was.

Wouldn't it be funny, I thought, if someone who knew me in Southern California, three-thousand miles from here, recognized me as Malvin Stark and blew my cover? Apparently no one did. By the time I completed the thought Manny Ness was upon us shaking my hand like he couldn't imagine anyone he'd rather see.

"Come with me," he said.

He must have seen my startled reaction. "No, no," he said. "You're my guest and this beautiful young lady….What's your name, gorgeous?"

I introduced them and hoped there wasn't some government human relations type around who might have found the greeting inappropriate. Well, it was his store, and how many women would object to being called gorgeous by its owner?

Sheepishly we followed him. The woman in a Ness Brothers dress who was manning the velvet chain across the entrance (or womaning as the case may be) unhooked it with a flourish. "Good afternoon Mr. Ness," she said and the three of us passed through just as though it had been a birthright for Jessamyn and me.

He looked over at the large corner table, where nine men were already ensconced. He turned to the hostess, "Get them the next table for two, will you?"

"Yes, Mr. Ness."

The manager appeared from the kitchen to great the king.

"Ah, Larry," he said, "these people are my guests, give them the extra love and me their bill."

Instead of joining his staff in the corner, he waited with us until a table cleared. We made some small talk. He asked Jessamyn about herself, how she liked her school, how she met me. For myself, I was not that comfy being stared at by everyone who must have thought I was some kind of celebrity.

The turnover was brisk. I was sure Manny saw to that somehow. He went with us to the table to be sure it was to our liking.

We assured him it was.

32

Jessamyn and I had another wonderful lunch—no bill was presented and although I heard Manny Ness tell the hostess to put us on his tab, I asked for it. "Oh no," said the waitress, "Mr. Ness is paying for it."

I went over to his table. He looked up and smiled the old President of the United States smile. "How was everything?" he asked.

"Wonderful. You have a great place here," I said.

"Was it okay, Jessamyn?" he asked, looking her in the eye.

"Oh, yes. Thank you very much."

"My pleasure."

"Yes," I added, somewhat belatedly, "many thanks."

He waved a hand. "I hope you'll come back."

"Well," I said, "the price is right."

The table got a good laugh.

Jessamyn was fired up to block, or is it pass? something to do with football, her next chores.

We parted in the hotel parking lot. She in search of Dr. Kulp's siblings and Christina Wagner, I to Sears and friend Mr. Wesley Iobst.

It was a one-story, plain yellow brick building on the edge of central Muhlenheim. Sears there was noted for its low prices so it behooved them to keep the rent down. They were teetering on the brink, thanks to the competition from Manny Ness.

A nice young woman directed me to Wesley Iobst's cubicle. He stood to greet me. He was medium tall like me, fit like someone else, friendly, open and unthreatening, a man easing into his middle years. Perhaps a testament to the simple, steady mostly undramatic passing of time hereabouts.

"It's very good of you to see me."

"No problem."

I sat in the lone chair across from him at his desk.

"Did you know Christina Wagner?"

He wrinkled his nose. "She was Sandy's friend. I didn't know her. I knew who she was and I think I met her once, but I never really knew her."

"Know anybody who did, or might know where she's gone?"

He shook his head almost without thinking.

"Do you have any insight on their relationship?" I asked. "Was there…intimacy?"

"I don't know. Somehow I doubt it. At any rate he never spoke to me about anything involving her."

I had—I can't remember what triggered it—an epiphany. Perhaps sitting there asking Sandy's one male friend about his female friend.

Sex.

Could it have something to do with Sandy's suicide?

Could it *not?* There were few things worth hiding

from the eyes of our peers. Sex is one of them—and I can't think of another. Money perhaps. There is the lack of it, no need to hide great wealth, though some few do.

Money was not Sandy's problem. True the store was not doing well, on its last arms and legs no doubt, but you could count on the family to pull the plug before everything evaporated. Sandy's brothers were carrying on without self-immolation.

Here I was with Sandy's lifelong male friend. He didn't seem in the slightest homosexual. But, I suppose, you never knew. Perhaps I would garner the courage to ask him—but could a denial be believed? Who in this town wouldn't deny it? That kind of news would play havoc with your shelf life.

"Did the police question you after Sandy's...death?"

"No."

"Did you volunteer anything?"

He shrugged. "What could I have contributed?"

"Did you ever see signs of depression in Sandy?"

"Oh, I've thought about that. I can't say that I did. He always seemed happy to me. But I didn't see that much of him after he married."

"How much did you see him before the marriage?"

"Oh, a couple times a month maybe. We'd go to lunch."

"What did you talk about?"

He smiled. "I guess I did most of the talking. Sandy just seemed interested and I was lazy about questioning him. We talked sports, some—about my family, kids. What they were up to. Some politics. We didn't agree on that. I used to tease him about being a robber baron. He called me the proletariat."

"All in good fun?" I asked.

"Oh, yes."

"When were you closest to him?"

"Oh, I guess the Boy Scouts."

"What do you remember about that?"

He looked out his smallish window to search for his past. "A lot of years ago," he said. "I remember Sandy took to it like nobody's business. He got the handbook and practically memorized it before we were old enough to join up. Then he set his sights on moving through the ranks as fast as the organization would allow. Were you a Boy Scout?"

"No, I…"

"Well, you start as a tenderfoot and after you accomplish certain things you get promoted to first class—or is it second or third? I forget. Anyway, you get a new insignia to sew onto your uniform and he kept his mother busy sewing. You started earning merit badges for camping, carpentry, health, music, you name it there was an endless stream of them. They had certain badges you had to get and others were electives sort of. Then you got to be a Star Scout, then a Life, then the big prize, an Eagle. It was a load of work. Kids took their time, two to three years to get Eagle if they lasted that long. Sandy did it in record time, moving from rank to rank to rank in the minimum time allowed by the rules of scouting. I think it was a year and a half or something. Anyway, he did it. I mean, this was quite an achievement. No one in the local council had done it in that short a time. A triumph, really. Except this kid in another troop did the same thing at the same time which Sandy didn't know about.

"So there's this interview with these big shots in the scouting council. An older guy in the troop tells Sandy they are going to ask if he masturbates—to see if he's honest or if he lies about it. That struck terror in the thirteen year-old's heart. So he sweated through the interview with these old fogies and was so relieved when it was over that he hadn't been asked. An enormous tension was released. He was so glad he had gotten over the hurdle.

"Except he hadn't. He got the news that he was being held back for the next awards ceremony six months later. He took it as well as could be expected, but I knew he was devastated.

"The other Eagle kid from the poor ward was treated to a half page picture in the newspaper."

"A half page?" I said. "Surely that's a bit of hyperbole."

"Half page. Not a column inch less. It ladled on the flattery of this stellar, unprecedented accomplishment. Brian O'Brian was the kid's name. I remember liking the lilt of it. But amidst all the puffery about the uniqueness of this accomplishment, our Sandy was never mentioned."

"Anybody find out why he was passed over?"

"Sure, his father, the big department store owner and pillar of the community called the scout executive to ask. He hemmed and hawed but what it apparently came down to was the board felt Sandy had achieved this wonder for his own glory, rather than, I suppose, the glory of the Boy Scout movement. I always wondered if Brian O'Brian was swimming in altruism at thirteen or even if he had the foresight to convince them he was."

Wesley Iobst shook his head. "I think it was

rather the proletariat scoring one on the robber barons. The Straus's were Republicans as robber barons are wont to be. The kid's family were Democrats, as the unwashed tend to be. The scouting council, the heavies who made this decision were largely Democrats. And even if they weren't, this was a perfect example of the do-gooders giving the prize to a poor kid who had very little in his life, rather than to one of the richest kids in the valley. They weren't denying the award, just giving him six months to shore up his altruistic bona fides."

"That's quite a story," I said. "Who knows what kind of scar that could put on a kid that age."

"He took it okay, as I said. At any rate, I don't think that was factor in getting him off the roof."

"How would you describe Sandy as a person?"

"Well, speaking of the Boy Scouts, he was the epitome of the scout laws."

"What are they?"

"A scout is trustworthy, loyal, helpful, friendly, courteous, kind, obedient, cheerful, thrifty, brave, clean and reverent."

"He was all that?"

"Yes, he was."

"You know," I said, "I've yet to hear an unkind word about him. But surely he had some less than admirable qualities?"

"Perhaps he did," Wesley Iobst said. "But I don't know what they would be. He did his duty, was kind to his elders, friendly, the whole ball of wax. Poster boy for the scouting movement."

"Something wasn't as perfect as it seemed."

"I guess not."

"Was everybody a Boy Scout to him?"

"Hah! He expected it—others to do their duty, be friendly, courteous, kind—but it didn't happen that way. Your family owns the store, you get bullied. Physically and verbally, and maybe it was the words that hurt the most. He was the last kid picked for the recess teams, that kind of thing."

"How did he take it?"

"He never showed much emotion, but you knew it had to hurt."

"Yeah," I said, "I get it. Were you at his wedding?"

"Sure. I was in it. An usher."

"What was it like?"

"Spectacular. The bride's family pays, you know, and not only were they *beaucoup* rich, she was their only daughter. The wedding was at the Catholic church and it was packed to the rafters. The reception was at the country club. It was probably the wedding of the two richest families in the valley."

"Everything seem normal to you—the bride and the groom?"

"Normal? It was way beyond normal. It was over the top. I've never seen anything like it. I'd never seen Sandy happier."

"And the bride?"

"Oh, well, the bride. The wedding's a bride's show you know. She's so damn beautiful. I remember thinking how poised she was. A lot of brides are bubbling with excitement. I've even seen them cry through the whole ceremony."

"Not Ginger?"

"Not that I could tell. She could have married anyone, but I think she got the best."

"Did she agree?"

"Oh, I'm sure—it's just…" he stopped. I waited. He stayed stopped.

"What?"

"Hm?" His mind was adrift.

"You're sure it's just what?"

"Oh, I don't know. It's not a rational thought, I'm sure…not worth mentioning."

"I'd be grateful if you shared your thoughts. Then we can decide if they're worthy of anything."

He considered this. "Oh," he said, "it's just a feeling I remember having. No facts, no evidence. A feeling, and you know how unreliable feelings can be."

"What was your feeling?" I prodded.

"Oh, I don't know. I just remember feeling he seemed more excited than she did. But I haven't been up close in many weddings so I don't have much to compare it to."

"She does strike me as a reserved woman," I said.

"Maybe that's the last line of defense for a woman that gorgeous."

"Maybe," I said. "Any idea what the marriage was like?"

"I don't know, but I can't remember seeing Sandy that happy again."

33

Leaving Wesley Iobst I realized I had got my first slight insight into the nature of the Ginger Kulp, Sandy Straus wedding and subsequent marriage. Certainly it was based on feeling and suppositions—and those slight—as opposed to any hard evidence, but it gave me an opening for another avenue to investigate.

Christina Wagner might help, but she'd disappeared. I set out to find her at the address in the phone book.

I parked my car across the street from an apartment building we would call pedestrian in California. Here it seemed about average. You had to build for the weather in this frozen northland to keep the heating bills to a reasonable level. Of course in the summer the air conditioning had to be going full blast. I don't know how these folks made it before air conditioning.

There were a lot of bricks on the exterior, just not much design.

The manager's apartment was at the front of the building. I gave them points for that. I knocked on the door. It didn't open instantly or even soon. It was as though the manager didn't want to seem too eager lest he be taken advantage of. But he answered, opening the door part way as though to keep his defenses up. As though he had a sense of how long a prospect would stand there without walking away.

"Yes?" he said.

"I'm Gil Yates, a private investigator working on the Sandy Straus case."

"Sandy Straus? The department store guy?"

"Yes."

"Who jumped off the roof?"

"Yes, I believe so."

"That was a long time ago," he said.

"Yes, the wife's family wasn't satisfied with the police results."

"Huh! Anything new about it?"

"May I come in?"

He grudgingly opened the door. Seeing him in the light he looked like George Washington with a bargain facelift that did not seem to be holding. He wore a Philadelphia Eagles sweatshirt.

"Play some ball, did you?" I asked.

"Not lately."

This was news he did not need to impart.

There was a sign on his desk, of the finest plastic. It said

Harley Taggart
Manager

He hadn't asked me to sit down, so I did anyway.

Then he followed, though if his expression was any indication, not happily.

"One of your tenants was Christina Wagner?"

He nodded.

"Know what became of her?"

"Poof," he snapped his fingers. "Disappeared."

"What was the last time you saw her?"

"Can't remember. Expect it was going to work one day. but I didn't see everyone come and go. You can see the way the place is laid out. It's not a manager's dream from that standpoint."

"When was the first time you knew she was gone?"

"Didn't pay her rent. I went for it. She wasn't there. I put a notice on the door to see me. She didn't. In a few days I took my keys and opened the door. She was gone."

"Anything peculiar?"

"Well, she took some clothes it looked like. But left the furniture."

"When was this?"

"I don't remember exactly."

"Roughly?"

"Oh, a year or so."

"Could you find out exactly?"

"Exactly? What for?"

"Might help my investigation."

"Christina Wagner? How?"

"She was a friend of the deceased."

"Really? I never saw any evidence of that."

"Did you know what he looked like?"

"Not till I saw his picture in the paper. But he

didn't look familiar. If he came around here I never saw it. But as I say, way it's laid out I wouldn't see anything from here."

"You disappointed in the layout?"

"Nah, it's just that it's hard to keep an eye on things with me isolated like this."

"You're in the front. Isn't that good for renting?" I had the unstated advantage of being in the same line of work—across the country.

"I guess, but I don't know what goes on here unless I hear a complaint."

"How many units do you have here?"

"One hundred twenty."

"Hard to keep an eye on that many."

He nodded. "'Specially hidden away like I am."

"How long did she live here?"

"I don't know. Five to six years I expect."

"She get any mail after she left?"

"Not so's I know. She probably had it forwarded."

"Ever get packages you had to hold here while she lived here? You know, delivered while she was working."

"I wouldn't be surprised. Lot of packages come here. I hold 'em till they're picked up."

"Can you remember any?"

"Oh, I don't pay attention. None of my business."

That I didn't believe. A guy disappointed because he couldn't see everything was going to be uninterested in who sent packages? "You sure?" I asked gently. "It could help the investigation. Anything a little out of the ordinary?"

He pursed his lips and shook his head. "Long time ago," he said. "Must have had five-hundred people in here in that time."

"Any way you can look up her last day here? And maybe her first if you can?"

"Nope," he said. "All them records goes to the front office."

"Can I ask them?"

"I suppose you could."

"Could *you* ask them for me?"

"I could." From his expression, that was not a prospect that added any joy to his existence.

I took a fifty from my wallet, placed it on the desk. "For your trouble," I said.

He looked at it without a trace of disapproval. Then he opened his desk drawer, took out one of his cards, laid it before me. "Call me tomorrow afternoon."

"And anything else on her records? Anything."

"Like what?"

"Well, she had an application with her references and former addresses, didn't she?"

"It's customary."

"Another fifty dollars for a copy of it."

"Don't know if that's legal."

"Well, can you find out? If it isn't legal..." I said, "I'll raise it up to a hundred."

He looked at the fifty on the desk. "A hundred more than that," he said nodding at the bill.

"Yes," I said, and was on my way.

I was such a generous guy, I thought. One hundred and fifty dollars out of my ten-thousand dollars for the day. What a guy.

Back in my hotel room I set out to record what I had so far on a legal sized piece of paper–known to the trade as a spreadsheet. In the center I drew a facsimile picture of Sandy Straus. It wouldn't have garnered any blue ribbons in the third grade, but I knew what it was.

Behind Sandy I drew a representation of the wall he descended. I drew him in the swan dive position. If he had jumped feet first from that height, he most likely would have lived.

The next question was, was this a spur of the moment act—everybody said how happy he was—you'd think if he brooded about it at length someone would have noticed it. Yet most suicides are built up depression or perhaps anxiety.

But perhaps I am not getting the whole story. The Kulps have a vested interest in characterizing Sandy as happy as an oyster till the bitter end. They want me to determine he was so happy that suicide was out of the question.

Somewhere in this cast of characters there had to be a clue. I listed my contacts to date and future hopefuls on either side of the Sandy Straus figure. I drew a line to other persons who weighed in somehow. Next to Sandy I drew a female figure, but as you can imagine, in no way could I do her justice. But that was the limit of my drawing.

PRIOR INVESTIGATORS — THE POLICE
ELDON WEBSNER, P.I.

WESLEY DOBST
CHRISTINA WAGNER
ALICE — SANDY'S
SECRETARY

STRAUSES
SANDY
JOSH
HANK
HAZEL

KULPS
DR. CHESTER
PRISCILLA
GINGER
TABIAN
LUCY

HELPERS —
JESSAMYN
ELWIN, THE NERD

228

One or more of these may have been complicit in the death, but the other possibility was that Sandy was just depressed, a not uncommon condition that could not be blamed on anyone else. Psychiatrists, psychologists speak of triggers, and they must exist, at the same time we should acknowledge that triggers are often within, the causes sometimes (perhaps often?) imaginary.

I looked the list over. I'd met them all except for the doctor's brother, Fabian Kulp, and Christina Wagner. The latter presenting something of a challenge since she seems to have disappeared without a trace. Somewhere, somebody had the key. I had five more days to find it.

My phone sounded. It was Jessamyn. She gave me a phone number and address for Fabian Kulp. Christina Wagner was eluding her, but she hadn't given up. Elwin's progress was slow, but he didn't seem discouraged. He did want me to know that with this kind of technology hope often outpaced reality.

I thanked her, then called Fabian Kulp. He didn't answer and there was no opportunity to leave a message.

$60,000

First thing the next morning I called Fabian Kulp again. This time he answered. "Hey-loh," he said in authentic Pennsylvania Dutch inflection which his brother Chester had overcome.

He would be glad to see me, he said, but he had his lunch and pinochle game at the Owls' home at noon. He'd be back today around 5:00 p.m. My choice.

I thought I could get free of the paper editor in time to give me an hour and a half with Fabian. So we settled on 10:30 a.m. His place was just a short walk from the paper.

Charlie Urfer was my first appointment for the day. I walked to the *Muhlenheim Chronicle* a few blocks from my hotel. Charlie was a democratic leader. We sat at a desk in the middle of a vast room, surrounded by his staff. No corner office for the chief.

He was a lanky guy—time having likely shorn some inches from his height. Some talented writer might call his fading blond hair unruly. I just thought it was a mess.

"Thank you for seeing me," I said. "I appreciate it."

"This business depends on the public trust," he said. "I couldn't not see you."

"Dr. Chester Kulp," I said, "and his late sister. What can you tell me about her death? I'm told you were on the beat, so to speak."

He frowned, then pushed himself away from his desk and signaled with his head for me to follow him.

Here was the corner office he could have had—used only for special occasions when he felt the need for privacy.

It was another venue Good Housekeeping magazine would overlook. But there was a table and some chairs and we sat, he democratically *not* at the head of the table.

"So," I said, folding my hands on the table to lend me some gravitas, "Dr. Kulp and his young sister. Did you know what happened?"

"Of course we knew, but this is a small town. We don't go tabloid which is a great temptation for even the *New York Times* these days. And it's not as though Dr. Kulp is everybody's best friend…but he is good at his trade. A lot of people in these parts sing his praise. You want to disillusion them? I certainly don't. Besides, you never know when you'll need him. So you picture him standing over prone you with a knife in his hand and he says, 'Say, aren't you the fella that wrote that nasty piece about me in the paper? Well don't worry, I'm not going to murder you—though it'd be easy enough—it's just my nerves are not as steady as they once were.' Here he shows you his right hand the one with the knife, trembling to beat the band, just before the anesthesia kicks in.

"I don't know about you, but that's not a vision I relish, and that's why it didn't make the paper and why it won't."

"But wasn't he only twelve at the time?"

"At the time, yes. But why ruin a kid's future with some gratuitous guilt-by-association picture? An unknown poor kid from the ward. Not our style in Muhlenheim. And now that he's an adult, a pillar of the community, how would we justify making a show of him through a childhood indiscretion? We chose not to. I'm not sorry. You may tie it to his son-in-law's suicide fifty-some years later, but I don't see how. I mean, you will admit it's a remote connection."

"I admit it."

"And most likely worthless in the scheme of things." I said nothing. "You will admit that?"

"Perhaps I am not ready to write off any information just yet. I have found in my years in this racket that sometimes the most unlikely bit of information becomes part of the puzzle that leads to solving the case," I said. "Okay can you give me the blow by blow—what happened?"

"The story we pieced together the best we could, and, understand this is really only from a kid twelve years old at the time—now Dr. Kulp—and let me tell you he was hysterical in the telling. I remember having an awful time trying to understand him. The police were at their wits end. I expected any minute to have one of them punch out their frustration on the kid. I wanted them to get medical attention for the boy."

"What did they want from him?"

"The story—what happened."

"He wasn't forthcoming?"

"Oh, they got it out of him, piece by piece," he

said. "The girl got preggers—less than two years older than the kid. The usual way—never found the father. The kid claimed not to know. I always wondered that the cops flat out didn't believe him, but I suppose it could be true."

"And the facilitator?"

"Abortionist—call it what it is. Disappeared. Scared to death for good reason. He'd have been lynched."

"At what point did he scram?"

"Soon as he realized he'd botched it. These back alley operations are not foolproof, even if they think they are."

"Who made the contact?"

"Apparently the kid asked around some of the shadier sections of the ward. This guy came cheapest."

"Did Kulp remember his name?"

"Oh, it was a fake name. Cops ran a check, nobody came up."

"Any of those cops still around?"

"No, sorry. We're talking fifty years, remember? Lucky I'm still around."

"So what happened after the butcher left?"

"I don't know. Near as we can tell from the kid, he almost passed out from panic. The sister bled to death while he cradled her and cried his eyes out. I got this from the cops. By the time they called me, she was gone, the butcher was gone and the kid was borderline catatonic.

"Might she have lived if he'd gotten her to a hospital?"

"I wondered about that. Was he too panicked to think about it or did he fear having her condition and his complicity know? I don't know. The cops hauled him to the station after the undertaker came for the girl. Called his father. That was something to see."

"Why?"

"Can you picture this? A twelve-year old boy at the police station, an accomplice in the manslaughter of his sister whom he dearly loved. And this authoritarian German comes in and gets the news in the kid's presence. I was there. I thought he was going to kill him. He lunged at him but two cops were able to restrain him. I don't know how. He looked like he could tear a Mack truck in two."

"So what happened?"

"The cops, God bless 'em, saw the handwriting on the wall and told ole dad they'd have to keep the kid in jail until a judge set bail. It was a lot of melarky but the old man didn't know better. 'Good,' he said. 'I hope you rot in jail.' And looking at young Kulp at that moment he looked like nothing would please him more. Bottom line, he was terrified of going home—one on one mano a mano with his old dad."

"Well, Kulp is still alive. I guess it worked out."

"I guess," he said.

"How do you suppose?"

"The mother came in the next day. Another German, strong, but calm and collected. Women have more sympathy for unwed abortions. At least she did. She consoled him, told him she understood he was trying to help his sister and he shouldn't blame himself. She was some woman, that one. She had to be to be married to that tyrant. Those authoritarian, bully Germans are all over the map around here. But the right woman can turn them into pussy cats."

"How?"

"Sex."

Was Dr. Kulp now one of that breed? I wondered. And did Priscilla have that kind of hold on him? She did manage to keep me on the case when he wanted me off. Sex could have been as good a motive as any. But living with him with his history was no piece of pie. I was pretty sure of that.

"I followed his career," he said, "and you know, it gave me a lift to know I probably could have ruined him by running that story. Oh, it would have sold a few papers no doubt, but what is that next to a human life? And look at the life, a heart surgeon who has gone on to save hundreds of lives. It was some transformation, I'll tell you."

"Was he ever in the paper after that?"

"Well, sure. We did a piece on college grads every June. Then he had med school. There weren't that many in those days. When he set up practice, when he became chief of staff at the hospital. And his daughter's wedding, of course."

"Did you go to the wedding?"

"Oh, no. I wasn't invited," he said. "I didn't expect to be. In a way I'm glad I wasn't. He doesn't need a reminder of that experience."

I thanked Charlie Urfer for his time and wisdom and he assured me he was happy to help, if in fact he did. And further, if I needed anything else to please feel free to contact him again. He was definitely an old school gentleman. We shook hands and I left the paper with just enough time to get to Fabian Kulp and the view of the tragedy from in-house.

35

Fabian Kulp lived in a narrow brick row house with a concrete stoop in front. Four or five stairs to reach the first floor. If I read the mailboxes correctly, he lived on the second floor with another name on the first. There was no bell, so I trundled up the wooden stairs and knocked on the door.

It opened on a man—I think. You've heard of bears of men, I'd say Fabian was more a walrus. Incongruously he was clad in work pants and one of those sleeveless undershirts. He looked at me all bundled up against the mid-winter cold as though I were the one out of step.

"Fabian?" I said. He admitted it. I stuck out my paw and he met it with his fin. "Hey-loh," he said again, like it was his signature. "Came to schmooze about my famous brother. Well, come in, you can see I'm from the unfamous branch of the family."

"A lot of downsides to fame, I expect," I said.

He led me into a compact room, carelessly divided into living room and dining room. Following him I noticed he had a limp, which he compensated for by swaying from side to side like a jolly swashbuckler.

On top his head was domed with a few hold-out hairs which he could point to should anyone accuse him of being bald.

No effort to tidy up the place for a visitor had been expended. On the formica topped table there sat a half-empty coffee cup (half full for optimists), a cereal bowl, a box of cornflakes, the flaps up in open position. Utensils perhaps from more meals than this cluttered the table.

Fabian sat in a threadbare lounge chair that he had sat in all his adult life. He told me so without shame or artifice. He was nothing if not a straight shooter. I sat on a half couch—both seats faced a TV set in the corner which seemed to be perpetually on. Fabian made no move to silence it. So when he spoke it was at an oblique angle to the back of my ear.

Off to the side a door was ajar on an unmade bed, the covers rumpled in unstudied disarray.

"I hope you'll have time for your card game," I said. "I'll try to be to the point."

"I'm okay," he said. "You know, I live for my cards. Pop never let us play cards at home. Said it was the work of the devil. But I figure I'm going in that direction I better be able to hold my own at cards." He chuckled at his funny.

"Pop?" I said. "Being your father?"

He nodded. "That's right," he said. "But I expect you're here to talk about Stinky."

"Stinky?"

"That's what we called," he paused to draw himself up, "the doctor."

"Why?"

"I don't know. I guess he stank."

"Everybody called him that?"

"Far's I know," he said. "But the old man, we called him Pop, but don't let the familiarity fool you...he was a tyrant of the first order. Stinky was terrified he was going to kill him. But instead the terror rained on him more subtle-like—it was with a glance or glare, or words with pointed double meanings. You might have figured if Pop was going to kill Lucy for getting pregnant at fourteen, Stinky saved him the trouble. On the other hand you could say Stinky was an accomplice to murder. He got away with murder, didn't he?"

"Well, there was no premeditation. He wasn't thinking of murder."

"Pop would say he was—he wanted to kill the child but he got the mother with it."

"What do you think?"

"Me? I was what—eight years old at the time? I wasn't heavy into abortion debates. But I'll tell you this, Stinky became another person overnight. I should call him doctor, I know, but old habits die hard. Where he was happy-go-lucky, he straightened up and flew right. He had lousy grades, he became an A student. Overnight. I tell you—*overnight*. You could say the doctor owes his success to his sister's death. Not a very pleasant thought, but I think it's true. I mean, I saw it with my own eyes, the transformation."

"What kind of relationship do you have with the doctor now?"

"Oh, I'm not in that class—a doctor!? I'm a janitor. I couldn't pretend to be otherwise. I mean, I've been to his country club—makes me uncomfortable.

No, it's okay, he has his life, I have mine. They don't cross."

"And that's okay with you?"

"Sure, I'm happy playing pinochle at the Owls'. He can have his country club." He sat back and interlaced his fingers over his prodigious belly. "Hell, you know it takes me four years to make as much money as he makes in *one* operation. We had the same mother and father, lived in the same house—I shared a *room* with him for God's sake—and look at us now. Go figure."

"So do you *never* see him anymore?"

"Oh, we used to get together over Christmas. He made a big show of being just one of the family. But it didn't fool me for a minute. You can tell the minute he steps out of his brand new Cadillac this is not just one of the Kulp boys. Oh, no—this is Doctor Kulp and don't you forget it."

"You ever want to be a doctor?"

"Doctor? Me? Nah. In life we settle into who we are. He's the doctor, I'm a janitor. I didn't have the trauma of sis's death—my hand in it if you know what I mean—to spur me—kick start a career."

"You think he was responsible for her death?"

"That's obvious. Don't you?"

"I don't know. You said he wasn't the father."

"Far's I know—I was just a kid. Mom lost two between sis and me, so I was eight years old. You think I had any notion what made a baby?" He paused to take in the ceiling of his living space.

"Pfuh," he expelled some spittle. "Nah, I never even *thought* about being a doctor, but then I didn't kill our sister."

I let that rumble around the room. I was frankly at a loss to respond to it, so I didn't.

"What do you think of your niece, Ginger?"

"Good looking kid," he said. "Little stuck up, maybe. But as I say, I didn't see that much of her."

"Were you at her wedding?"

"Yeah."

"What did you think?"

"Lot of bucks represented there."

"The guests?"

"That too. I'm talking about the cost of the shindig."

"Did you talk to the bride and groom?"

"Yeah, I went through the receiving line, that was about it. The fella married her, they don't come any nicer."

"And Ginger?"

"Little stiffer. If I wanted to think the worst, I'd say she looked down her nose a little, like she was thinking what is a bum like you doing at my wedding. But she was perfectly polite. Maybe it was my imagination."

"What was it like at home when you were growing up?"

"Like? I don't know. It just *was*. Pop was a tyrant. I thought everybody's pop was a tyrant. But he wasn't home much except to sleep. He had two jobs to support all the kids he screwed into the world."

"How many were there?"

"Well, after the miscarriages there were nine live births, but we ended up with five after Sig and Lester and Ruth," he paused as though collecting some afterthought, "and Lucy, of course, the abortion...all died while we were still at home."

"Where are your brothers and sisters now?"

"I'm here. You know the doctor. We have a submarine sailor out west somewhere. He left home at fifteen, lied about his age and never came back. Emory is a truck driver based in Houston. Radishes married an army guy who up and took her to Germany."

"So only two of you still here?"

"That's right."

"The others come back to visit?"

"Not much," he said with a crooked smile. "Would you?"

I didn't answer. I couldn't. "You sure had a lot of tragedy in your family. To lose so many kids," I explained when his face showed no comprehension.

He waved a hand at me. "Ah, no problem. There were a lot more where they came from. Only thing was," he thought on second thought, "I went to a lot of funerals before I was twenty."

"How was it after your sister's funeral?"

"Brutal. Pop wouldn't speak to Stinky—he became a non-person. Sis was the apple of his eye. It was a blow he never got over. And he never forgave Stinky. Didn't go to his high school graduation or college, or med school. He was dead for Ginger's wedding, but I'm sure he wouldn't have gone to that either."

"Rough childhood," I said opening my heart to more sympathy for the doctor.

"Yeah, but Mom compensated. Told Stinky he could be anything he wanted to. Encouraged him all the time."

"Did she tell you that you could be anything...?"

"Nah. Oh, I don't know. If she said that I

wouldn't have believed it. I didn't have the study gene in me. I'm saving my brain for the afterlife. Course," he said, "if it's any consolation I'm a pretty good pinochle player. So Stinky didn't go to Pop's funeral, of course Pop wasn't able to appreciate the snub."

"So there was *no* communication between them after Lucy's funeral?"

"Not much. The off times when Pop was at home Stinky would be studying in our room."

"You *still* call him Stinky."

"Yeah, puts it all in perspective. He may be a filthy rich big shot in the community, but he'll always be Stinky to me."

In my humble opinion, the visage of Stinky was looming larger in my investigation.

Now I turned my attention to locating Christina Wagner.

36

I called the apartment manager, Harley Taggart. Had the report, he told me, but I would have to come back to his office where I could view it on his computer.

"Bring money," he said signing off.

I didn't waste any time getting to the apartment complex. I had a fear that he would change his mind, or attempt to extort more money from me the longer I gave him to think about it.

This time he opened the door right away.

"Your money or you life," was his greeting.

"I'll give that some thought," I said, but laid the extra hundred on his desk. "That's assuming you have it," I said.

"I have it," he said, pausing.

"May I see it?"

"I'll get it on the screen and give you five minutes."

I cocked my head inquisitively.

"I can't give you a copy. I'll be busy here. You may look at it, but it's a one time deal and *no copies.*"

"Well, if you look away and I take a few written notes…?"

"I don't know anything," he said, picking up the money. He turned on his computer, left his desk and went to the file cabinet in the corner where he pulled out the top drawer and pretended to look for something in the files.

I sat at the desk to transcribe what useful information there was on the rental application of Christina Wagner dated five and a half years before.

The first personal reference was Sandy Straus. Straus and Sons Department Store was given as the address and phone number. I wouldn't be able to do much with that.

Next of kin listed her mother out in the hinterlands. Mary Wagner was her name. Ordinarily I would show up at the door in the hope of getting some information, but she was too far away. Probably two hours each way. So I had to call her and hope my sweet talk mechanisms were in working order.

Christina had only one employer in the five years before she made the application: she was an elementary school teacher at The Washington School outside of Muhlenheim.

Her residences in the prior five years listed only one. She was a stable person. I copied it down.

On the back side of the application was a question: Is the combined monthly income of the proposed occupant at least four times the amount of the monthly rent? Yes was checked—on the front page the monthly rent was listed at seventeen hundred and fifty dollars. Times four was seven thousand dollars per month, or an indicated income of more than eighty-four thousand dollars per year. That seemed hefty for an elementary school teacher. Then I noticed an asterisk referring to a cosigner.

I asked the manager if he knew who cosigned and he said that information went directly to the main office.

"Could you get that for me?"

"Eh, no—they'd be suspicious. Why would I need to know that a year after someone moved out?"

"Another fifty?"

"No, no…"

"A hundred?"

"Well," he said, "I'm not making any promises."

"Understood," I said.

I wondered if I had to cough up the hundred dollars—I'd be willing to bet more than that the cosigner was Sandy Straus. But it could have been her mother or father, or even someone else.

When I got out of there I called The Washington School. Christina Wagner had left their employ a year ago, her choice. She was a good teacher and eligible for rehire. The woman was pleasant on the phone, but she wouldn't tell me any more.

I called Jessamyn. "Do you think the paper would have anything on Christina Wagner?"

"What sort of thing?"

"Pictures would be perfect," I said. Any possible biographies. If that doesn't work—or even if it does—can you scare up the photographer at the Kulp/Straus wedding and offer to buy copies of every picture Christina Wagner is in?"

"How will I know what she looks like?"

"How about that facebook thing? Will she have a picture? You know how to work that?"

"Yeah, I'll give that a shot."

"How's your buddy Elwin doing?"

"Making some progress I think," she said.

"You suppose he's willing to talk about it?"

"I'll keep after him. I think he got into Sandy's email, but there are a lot of them. Some don't make sense—they might be in code. I'll keep you posted."

"Appreciate it." As soon as I broke the connection my phone rang.

"Hi Gil, it's Alice," came into my ear with a breathless urgency.

"Hi, Alice."

"When can I see you?" she said.

"What's up?"

"Can't on the phone. I wondered if you had plans for dinner?"

Oh brother, I thought. Here we go again. This had better be good. Well, I thought if it's just a false alarm to get another date with me, I can cut her loose after dinner.

"Okay," I said. "Where can we go—nice and quick?"

There was a silence.

"Oh Gil," she said, "I wasn't thinking quick. I thought we might…make a night of it."

"I'm sure I'd like that, but the Kulps are paying me a lot of money for results and time is walking out on me."

We agreed to meet at my hotel dining room at five. I rehearsed the dialog as soon as I hung up the phone. "Would you like me to see your room?"

"Oh, I'm swamped, I'm afraid—and I need my beauty sleep if I'm going to earn my money."

"All work and no play make Jack a dull boy," that through her battering eyelashes.

"All play and no work make Jack a poor boy."

She would go away disappointed, but she would go away. I hoped.

Then I called Christina Wagner's mother—next of kin on her rental application.

One of the nice things about this neck of the forest was you had a reasonably good chance of finding a person at the same phone number and address that they had five years before—even ten to twenty-five. Not as usual in California—my heavy footsteps grounds.

She answered on the second ring. I like quick pick ups. It curtails the speculation where the person is if they are not in residence and why they're not answering if they are there.

"Hello?"

"Hello, Mrs. Wagner?"

"This is Mary," she said with the guarded voice of a woman who doesn't know the man who is calling her.

"My name is Gil Yates. I've been hired by the Dr. Kulp family to look into the death of their son-in-law." I paused for a reaction. There was none. I mushed on. "I wonder if you could spare a few moments to speak to me?"

"What could I tell you that would be helpful?" she asked. "I suspect you really want to talk to my daughter. She's the one who knew Sandy Straus. I didn't."

"Well, yes, that would be nice. Do you think she would speak with me?"

"I doubt it," she said. "She was torn apart by his death."

"Yes, I imagine. Do you think she feels the Kulps have just cause to question the suicide finding?"

"No, she does not," she said. "She doesn't know why they are prolonging the situation."

"I understand Christina was a long time pal of Sandy's."

"Yes—they go back to grade school."

"I take it you know where she is?"

There was a pause. "Maybe I do, maybe I don't." I thought that meant that she did.

"What might I do to entice you to see me?"

"Why would you want to? Where are you?"

"Downtown Muhlenheim."

"That's not close to me."

"I understand that. But I'd like to solve this thing. I expect Christina would too."

"Yes, but why do you want to come all the way out here to see me?"

"I want to show you that I'm not Jack the Ripper, I have everyone's best interests at heart."

"Including your own?"

"Certainly. But not least, Christina's."

"Well...I don't know," she said. "I just think you'll find out it's a big waste of gas."

"But if I don't see you, I won't know that."

"Well...if you must, but I warn you, I can't think of anything I know that would help you."

"You never know. No rocks not turned over."

"What's that?"

"Just an expression. It means do everything you can."

"Oh, like no *stone* unturned?"

"Yes, well that sounds about right," I said. "So...tomorrow then?"

"Well, okay," she said. "But don't say I didn't

248

warn you, I don't really know anything."

"That's okay," I said. "If you could line me up with your daughter, it would be worth the chance."

"*That* I can*not* promise."

"I understand. But maybe you can talk to her—maybe she'd see me with you present."

"That I doubt."

"If you gave it a try—I'd be forever in your debt."

When the clock approached five I went down to the dining room to wait for Alice. I had a suspicion she might come to my room if I didn't cut her off at the pass.

I got there not a moment too early, for she sashayed in, all smiles.

"Hi," I called out before she could head for the elevator.

"Oh, hi Gil."

She was in one of those blousy get ups that could have been higher at the bosom.

"It's so nice to see you again, Gil," she said with her eyelashes doing the talking.

"Likewise," I said. What would *you* have said?

We eased into the dining room and found we had it all to ourselves. The hostess showed us to a table. I couldn't make a fuss about privacy because there was no one else in the room, unless you count the waitresses who wouldn't be close enough to eavesdrop.

We sat. I had chosen a venue that was the antithesis of romance.

Sterile, beige toned wood—or was it plastic?—with a failed attempt to make it look classy. As I noted before.

I looked at her expectantly. The menus came and I gave it the quick once over. She studied and frowned, her eyes traversing the pages with an intent worthy of the walk up to a final exam.

"Know what you want?" I finally prodded.

"Oh, there are so many good things. I can't make up my mind."

"Want me to order for you?"

"Oh, Gil, you aren't in such a hurry, are you?"

"Well, yes, I am. I have three more days to produce."

"Yes, I know," she said. "I'm here to help you with that."

Then for Freddie's sakes, *help* me, I said to myself.

She finally settled on a tuna salad with some soup to prolong the meeting. After she closed the menu with a self-satisfied clap of the covers, she said, "Watching my weight, you know."

I thought of two responses: 1) Admirable! and 2) Oh, you don't need to watch your weight. After a quick consideration of the ramification of each, I said nothing.

She ladled me small but sweet talk. She flirty, I oblivious until the first course was delivered.

She put a spoon in the runny concoction then examined the contents as though contemplating the pros and cons of moving the implement to her mouth.

She seemed to solve some pertinent equation in the process and she addressed the subject at hand.

"The boys were talking about you," she said, dropping the spoon with a thud.

"The boys?"

"The Straus boys."

"You call them boys?"

"Sure. Anyway…"

"Talking about me? That's very flattering."

"It wasn't flattering."

"Well, what did they say?" I had to prod her—she was reveling in the suspense.

"You were a nuisance."

"But that is flattering," I said. "It shows I'm doing my job."

"I don't think they meant it as a compliment. Anyway, it perked up my ears for the rest of the conversation. They were in Hank's office with the door open. I tried to look busy."

"Was that difficult?"

She blushed. "No, no—of course not."

"Remember how we wondered why the Kulps would go to this trouble and expense over this case that was put to bed over a year ago?"

"I do."

"Well, the boys were discussing your presence here and the fact that the Kulps didn't seem to want to give up. Well, it turns out that Dr. Kulp took out a five million dollar insurance policy on Ginger's husband, Sandy."

Five million! I thought. The exact amount of his contribution to the Catholic church. Surely just a coincidence.

"So," she said, "there's your motive to spare no expense to prove he didn't commit suicide."

"Why?"

"The policy had an exclusion. It didn't pay off in the case of suicide."

"Really?" I said. "So you think Sandy knew about

the policy?"

"Could he not?"

"I don't know. I expect it could be kept from him," I said.

"How? Wouldn't he need to pass a physical exam before they insured him for that amount?"

That gave me something to chew on besides the steak which had just arrived and was tough as screws.

So *there* was the incentive of five million dollars to establish it was not suicide, I thought. If I could produce proof he was murdered or even died accidentally, the five million pay off would make my paltry one-hundred thousand dollar fee pistachios.

"Do you think he jumped so they *wouldn't* get the money?" I asked.

"I don't think so."

"Maybe he had a fatal disease and didn't want to die of natural—read insurance pay out—causes."

"A stretch, Gil."

"Yes."

She wanted dessert, and how could I deny her? There went the calories she saved on the tuna salad— shot to the hot place.

I passed on the dessert. I was afraid it would be as tough as the steak. The Michelin restaurant raters could give this place a pass and consider it a service to mankind.

Alice took her time polishing off the concoction buried in redi-whip. It seemed she thought drawing this process out would endear me to her so I would invite her up to my room.

Instead we went through the routine pretty much as I had imagined it before she showed up.

"Well, okay," she finally pouted, "but I'm still holding you to our agreement for your last night in town." Then she threw me one of her little girly flirty looks—"You might even stay longer if I please you…"

I didn't comment. How could I? But I finally got her out of the hotel by agreeing to walk her to her car.

When I escaped another lunge and finally made it back to my room, I dropped on the bed and exhaled all the air my body had taken in at our tête à tête. But I had to admit (reluctantly) she had given me a giant piece of the puzzle.

Of course it would mean nothing to the Kulps—I'm sure they would rather I didn't have that information. They hired me to find out if he jumped or fell or was pushed, or, more preposterously, was lured to his death after hours when the store was closed; and this I doubted. In light of the insurance policy news I had just received, why did he do it?

Granted the answer to this is more important to me than to the Kulps.

Tomorrow it was to the hinterlands and Mary Wagner, Christina's mother. I had roughly a day to convince her I was a straight quiver in the hopes she would put me in touch with the elusive, disappearing Christina.

And I would be spending half a normal workday commuting to and from her abode.

37

$70,000

Before I left for Christina Wagner's mother, Mary, up country, my cell phone rang. It was Jessamyn with a report on Elwin's progress.

"Okay, Elwin thinks he has retrieved all the stuff, and it's all pretty dull except for one batch of mail that seems to be in some kind of code."

"Any leads?"

"Not yet," she said. "You know what a water closet is?"

"A toilet?"

"That's what we think, but it makes no sense."

"Are there any emails to Christina Wagner?"

"Yes, but they stop around the time of his marriage. I'll keep you posted," she said. "Gotta run."

I, too, had to run to my car for my two hour trek to meet Mary Wagner—and dare I hope?—her daughter Christina.

I know people who got a kick out of driving a car…racing down the highway at speeds homo sapiens were never meant to travel, and as a punishment the gods knocked off more than forty-thousand of those auto jockeys as well as a passel of innocents per year. But we keep on driving like it will never happen to us and while we can still talk about it, it hasn't.

I'm not sure the source of my aversion to driving—perhaps it was the numerous car trips of my youth which distilled to a breeding ground for parental warfare. The car was an acid crucible with all sucked into its vortex, not at all mitigated by my father's alcohol infused system. Our dear mother was not exempt from nagging, needling and ridicule of the faux macho driver. Being seated alone in a car behind the wheel didn't seem to make driving any more pleasurable. But there were a lot of nifty trees along the way on my two-hour plus trek.

What can I tell you about Mary? Does anyone ever look like their phone voice? She was pleasant looking woman, alright, but not quite the movie star I had envisioned. And why do I always envision beauty—or my take on it—when most of us are just people sturdy enough to get by but not beautiful enough to sell cinema tickets?

She greeted me at the door of her neat, modest cottage-y looking place as a short lost friend.

"Mary?" I said. "I'm Gil." Nothing terribly creative about that, but it did the trickster. She had a roundish, open face with hair that sat on her head like a well padded cap with no attempt made to disguise the gray which had pushed its way beyond the fifty percent mark.

The front door opened to the living room, a neat but tiny space with a window on the front that let in enough light so you were not liable to stub your toe on the furniture.

"May I get you some coffee?" she asked. "You've had a long trip."

"Oh, no thanks. Perhaps a little water."

She left for the kitchen and I kept hoping Christina would pop in and surprise me. I did everything but follow Mary to the kitchen, straining my eyes and ears.

When she returned with the water and what looked like coffee for her, her eyes showed her amusement with me.

"She's not here, you know."

"She?"

"My daughter."

"Oh, yes, no—no, yes, no—you didn't say she would be, did you?"

She shook her head, "But sometimes hope springs eternal, doesn't it Mr. Yates?"

I frowned, "No, no, you made it quite clear."

"Even so, you are disappointed."

"Well, yes I am. I have no right to be."

"Well, she isn't here, so unless you want to turn around and head back, why don't you sit down a minute."

We sat facing each other. I on a small chair, she on a love seat. "So," she said, "what do you want from me?"

"Oh, I don't know," I said as though I had never considered it. "I sure would like to talk to your daughter, Christina."

"Yes, you said."

"So I guess whatever you could tell me about her relationship with Sandy Straus, or anything that might have some bearing on the case."

"What exactly *is* the case?" she asked. "I thought the police were satisfied there was no case. It was simply a suicide. Do you have cause to disagree with that?"

"No," I had to admit, "I don't. But you may be willing to admit your daughter's dropping out of her life here could offer vittles for thought."

"But what?" she said. "Christina was distraught. There's no denying that. Beside herself. She felt she was his best friend—maybe the only girl friend he had."

"Not his wife?"

"Well, there was something strange there. I'm not sure what it was."

"Do you think Christina wanted to marry him?"

"Think?" she said surprised at my question. "I'm sure of it."

"Did they ever discuss it?"

"Christina and Sandy? I don't know. I wouldn't be surprised either way. She didn't discuss much with me. The older a girl gets the less she wants romantic advice—especially from her mother."

"How about a father?" I asked. "Is there a Mr. Wagner?"

"Was."

"Oh."

"He went to greener pastures," she said.

"I'm sorry," I said. "The cemetery?"

She laughed. "We're not *that* old. The cradle."

"Cradle?"

"You know the expression—he's robbing the cradle."

"No…sorry…I don't."

"He ran off with a younger woman."

"Oh…sorry."

"It's okay. When I want to rise above the emotional hurt, I realize I wasn't that crazy about him anyway."

"Why do you suppose Christina dropped out and went into hiding? Did she tell you?"

"She didn't have to. It happened the day Sandy was discovered in the alley behind the store. She just literally dropped out."

"Did you think it could have been related?"

"Well, certainly," she said. "Christina was devastated."

"No, but I mean, could his...act...have been related to Christina? Could there have been...something between them that...ended his life?" I don't know why I was so loathe to say suicide.

"I'm afraid you'd have to ask her."

"Do you think she'd tell me?"

"I doubt it."

We schmoozed away, all my conversation calculated to assure her I was not Jack the Ripper. I don't remember exactly which bit of dialog led into my question: "So, can you tell me where Christina is hanging out?"

"My father bought this cabin in the woods years ago. It has no electricity and no running water. The outhouse is indoors. You get your water from a communal well a block away, bring back to the house whatever you can carry.

"It was a summer place—no heat—she's up there in the dead of winter." Her mother shivered in the telling. "Rather her than me."

"Would you mind if I went up there?"

"Mind?" she said as though that was foreign. "I

wouldn't mind. Do her some good to see another human being. It's a ghost town up there in the winter. Course I don't expect she will answer the door."

"Hmmm," I mused. "Can you think of anything I could take to her that might ingratiate me?"

"Chocolate!" she said clapping her hands once. "She *loves* chocolate, and I don't imagine she gets the good stuff there."

"And what's the good stuff in these parts?"

She told me of a place in Muhlenheim that "makes the best in the world."

"Oh, geez, it sounds like I should have brought you some."

"Oh, that's okay," she said. "I get enough to eat."

I made a mental note to send her a pound.

"What kinds do you both favor?"

"Any and all," she said. "There isn't a bad chocolate made."

"That's the spirit!"

"You'll need directions," she said.

"Yes," I said. Then wondered aloud, "why are you doing this for me?"

"Not for you," she said. "I love my daughter and ordinarily simply accede to her wishes. What she's doing is not good for her. She must know it. I expect she'll tell you she doesn't care to live without Sandy which you may contrast to Ginger who *had* him. I honestly believe Christina has stayed alive because she was able to drop out. You may be the one to return her to her life. I like you—your motives are pure—I think—if they aren't, please don't disillusion me."

I didn't. I hugged her goodbye after she parted

with the directions to the cabin in the woods. Alas, a different direction than the course I was already on.

I climbed back into the car and pointed it in the direction from which I came. I had enough daylight left to stop into the Josh Lately Candy Emporium to purchase a two pound assortment to take to Christina Wagner and while I was at it, have the same shipped to her mother Mary with a card expressing my gratitude for her graciousness, etc. Oh, yes, and while I was at it I picked up a box for myself.

My cell phone flashed a message from Harley Taggart. "Gil, this is Harley," his recorded voice said. "The cosigner in question was Edward Straus," then he paused. "You know where to find me." He was speaking of his payoff. He exhibited a lot of confidence in me— to pay him. It was a confidence I rewarded forthwith with a trip to Harley's apartment office.

Then I checked in with Jessamyn and Elwin to see what progress had been made in decoding emails.

38

Progress had been made in the decoding department. Elwin said it was all very simple—water closet initials W.C. reversed were C.W. It was all downhill after that.

Elwin was, alas, the worse for being worn. Encamped in Jessamyn's living room he seemed the poster boy for sleep deprivation. His spirits, however, glowed with a sense of accomplishment.

"I'm getting it," he said with what might pass for a smile in a mental hospital. Whatever it was, it was a huge improvement on his "buzz off" hanging up the phone.

There was evidence that Elwin had slept somewhere, but it was scant.

"Where's Jessamyn?" I asked looking around.

"Went to the paper," he said without looking up.

"So, what did you discover?" I asked boldly, banking on his recent humor turn for the better.

He began spewing a barrage of technical jargon which was Roman to me. But convinced of his temperamental frailties I didn't tell him I had no idea what he was talking about. I rested in the hope that he would come around to the layman's language sooner or later. When he took a deep breath, I said, "So what does it all mean for our case?"

He looked at me as though I had just told him I didn't understand English. But then he began using words I could understand. He spoke in snatches doubtless a reflection of his thought process.

"From what I can decipher to date, there's some secret between them. A lot of the mystery talk refers to it without spelling it out."

"What kind of secret?"

"I don't know. I assume it has to be something neither of them wants known."

"An affair?"

"That's the first thing that comes to mind. Though somehow I don't think so."

"Why?"

"The spacing of these emails for one thing."

"What about it?"

"It's sporadic. Consistent yet sporadic. And why not just use the telephone? Email is easier to hack into than the telephone."

"But that can be done—the phone I mean?"

"Sure, everything can be done. But for the phone you need special equipment and access to the property or phone lines. Possible, but given we have his computer this is easier."

"So what are you saying?"

"I'm saying I think this stuff is the tip of the iceberg. The substantive was probably via telephone."

"Any idea how often those phone conversations took place?"

"No," he said.

"But don't you run the risk of being overheard with a phone?"

"If there's someone around."

"How far back do the emails go?"

"To the dawn of the internet practically."

"Do the emails stop with the marriage to Ginger?"

"No, there is an initial slowing. There seems an undercurrent of desperation around that time. Then a while later the messages from him become morose and hers are more upbeat."

"Than his?" I asked, "Or than before?"

"Both," Elwin said.

"How about his last message?"

"It's a muddle," he said, shaking his head. "I can give you my decoding of the words, but I don't know what it means."

It was then we heard a car door slam and moments later Jessamyn burst into the room with a bulging envelope pressed to her breast.

"Woohoo," she said waving the envelope. "I got 'em!"

She was referring to the wedding pictures which she laid out on the battered coffee table in front of the couch.

At first glance of Christina shaking Sandy's hand in the receiving line, it looked like Sandy was inordinately pleased to see her, so engulfing is his smile. That is until you look at the other pictures shaking hands with the other guests. Sandy has the same all encompassing display of pleasure in seeing each guest.

Christina, on the other hand, looks almost morose shaking the bride's hand and seems not to have perked up with her hand in the groom's. Introspective is the kindest word I can ascribe to her expression.

The countenance stays with her throughout the event, up until the venerable tossing of the rice at the bride and groom as they make their exit from the church—the self same institution so generously endowed by the father of the bride, Chester Aloysius Kulp, MD.

Wistful was what I would call her expression in the rice throwing picture. With one hand, her right, she was making one of those self-conscious half-hearted waves of one who knows the intended wavee was not seeing the waver's wave. In her left hand, as though in a death grip, was clutched the wedding planner's lacy-clothed sack of raw rice—no doubt of the highest quality—the Kulps would never shirk their responsibilities as pillars of the community—Christina's rice remained in the unopened pouch.

I wondered if Christina Wagner had thought, however briefly and with what degree of seriousness, of pitching the sack of rice, opened or not, at the face of the bride as she passed. Either way it could hardly help but smart, and either way she was bound to be noticed in this sea of anonymous faces—just another woman left spinster-like outside the church doors.

She must have wondered if Sandy could be happy having converted to Catholicism.

Is beauty a burden? You can make a strong case that it is, and you could see it on these wedding pictures in the face of Ginger Kulp Straus.

Perhaps what Ginger had more trouble admitting to herself was that because of her staggering beauty she was lax about developing those characteristics she deemed important and was, horror of horrors, able to coast on her looks.

The coding of the language in the emails was still a mystery, but we were getting there. We all agreed to put our macaronis to the task. I promised to check back before I headed to search for Christina Wagner in the hinterlands on the morrow.

39

Three days left. I was satisfied that Sandy Straus had jumped off the roof of his family's department store. But I also realized my intuition would hardly swim with the Kulps. I supposed I could have put in my ten days and legitimately earned my money, a hundred-thousand oysters to be precise. But, you may believe it or not, I would not be satisfied I had earned the money.

Sandy's wife may have been acting strangely, but in this day of easy divorce it would stretch my credulity to believe that would not have been a preferable option to jumping off a roof, head first no less. The magnitude of the pain leading up to the jump must have been so intense that the pain of smashing your skull on the concrete seemed preferable. So....

Why?

This girl I was endeavoring to see on the morrow was not a new heartthrob—they'd been pals almost all their lives. And from all accounts, never lovers. Yet could you call her reaction to his death anything other than abnormal?

I didn't hear from my resident code breaker

before bedtime so I called him.

He was more cordial than before. He admitted to making more progress. "Getting the words," he said. "It's slow, but better than a kick in the pants as my grandfather used to say."

"What words?"

"Oh, Romeo, Juliet, music, swans. You understand this code stuff only started at the precise time of the wedding."

"Whose idea was it?"

"Near as I can tell, his."

"It would make sense, he was the *married* one," I said. "How did they communicate the code?"

"Don't know."

"Any evidence of them seeing each other, outside of these little messages?"

"They did, before the code, and the marriage. After that I don't know. Isn't any evidence I can see that they did."

"And yet the code—it couldn't have come from the tooth fairy," I said.

"Maybe snail mail."

"Wouldn't someone be suspicious?" I asked. "His wife, his secretary?"

"Maybe not one way—he sent the code, he didn't receive it."

"And she acknowledged by coded email?"

"Why not?" he said.

"Okay," I said. "Learn anything else?"

"Nothing certain, only hints."

"Like?"

"Like papa Kulp was the third marriage partner."

"How so?"

"Don't know. He always seems around, using his influence, his weight," Elwin said. "Then the end. That's confusing," he said.

"How so?"

"Well, there are snatches of erratic thoughts—my decoding leaves nonsense. I can't figure it out. It's like there are fixes on a conclusion that would wrap it all up, but..."

"But what?"

"I can't make sense of it."

"Can you speculate?"

"I don't know what good it would do."

"Let me decide."

"Well, towards the end, Christina's messages get longer and more frequent, while Sandy's get shorter and less frequent."

"Like what kind of time are we talking about? Every week, day, hour?"

"Roughly, say in the days leading up to the end there is a long message from her every day, then twice a day, then three times."

"How many in response from him?"

"That's just it. He answers hers, but with one sent to her six to ten, then she gets more frequent and more voluminous, but he doesn't. He never writes more than once a day—then not even that. His last message is two words."

"What are they?"

"Not sure. My speculation at this point is, 'No, sorry.'"

"Anything else?" I asked. "Anything at all?"

"Not that I have concrete answers for. There are mysterious allusions to philosophy, there's the Romeo and Juliet—we know what happened to them."

"Yes."

"And you know, Sandy seemed so happy, so upbeat in the beginning."

"Before the marriage?"

"Yes, but also in its earliest days. Then the messages seemed to turn glum. All speculation of course—just really a gut feeling."

"Anything else? Just gut feelings are fine."

"I'm seeing some patterns. The repetition takes it out of the realm of the trivial."

"Such as?"

"I get the feeling Sandy wasn't fooling around with Ginger *or* Christina. I think he was pretty religious which might have been how he won Ginger. I can imagine every guy she got near wanted to put his paws all over her. My feeling is they weren't doing it, but she didn't have to sell Sandy on it before the marriage."

"And after?"

"There's the rub—there's the dilemma."

"Your gut…?"

"There's some evidence in the emails she parceled out her favors stingily, then stopped altogether."

"Christina knew this?"

"Oh, yes and she offered to take some of the pressure off."

"Did he accept?"

"Not that I can see."

"Any evidence he wanted to have a child?"

"With who—Ginger or Christina?"

"Well, Ginger—but either?"

"That's not clear. There are words—allusions,

philosophy—nothing I can put my finger on."

"You think Christina could have had a baby? That would explain her dropping out."

"No mention, but not impossible."

"Pregnant?"

"Less likely," he said.

"That comes first, you know," I said.

"Wow," he said, "you are a real savvy guy."

"Thanks. Anything else?"

"All I can speculate so far."

"I really appreciate this."

"No problem. I'm having a good time."

I said I'd keep in touch. "How early may I call you?" I asked.

"Anytime," he said. "If I'm asleep I won't answer."

I asked the desk to call me at 4:00 a.m. on the morrow.

40

$80,000

I would earn my money today. I got out of bed at 4:00 a.m. My goal was to get to Christina Wagner's cabin in the woods before daylight to forestall the possibility of her escaping my grasp—like if her mother warned her I was coming and she flew the chicken coop. There was a good moon for my trip to the cabin in the woods where Christina Wagner was reportedly in hiding. It pointed up the difference between Pennsylvania's woods and the shoulder of the woods I come from—which is really no woods at all—asphalt reigns.

But I didn't know why so many of these trees couldn't hang onto their leaves. Gave the place a ghostly look.

I left the giant highway and made my way through thicker forests—bare trunks as far as the eye could see—on both sides of the road. There had to be a metaphor in there somewhere, I just couldn't find it.

I arrived in Marine Lake before daylight as I had hoped. No challenge was presented in locating the house. Not too far from the county road I had been traveling I saw a derelict sign by the side of the road. It said Marine Lake and doddered on some precarious wooden legs that seemed to have been planted there shortly before the Boer War.

Should I call Marine Lake a village? That seemed too grandiose for what I was faced with with—essentially three or four streets—all leading to the lake. Town was out of the question, burg perhaps, connoting a collection of two or more people. I was here. Christina Wagner was reportedly here and if that was true, that made two.

There was no evidence that this was anything more than a summer burg. Though in spite of appearances to the contrary, there had to be more than two of us in this place—deity forsaken, you might say. Another Boer War sign at the end of the road which led into the heart of Marine Lake pointed its arrow to the left and said simply

The Lake

I turned right and went to the end of the street or block up the hill and there on the left corner stood the subject cabin. It would be a mistake to picture some rustic idyll with walls of logs and windows carved therein. It looked rather like a careless structure assembled from the leftovers of a grander construction project.

The street rose to the cross street on which sat the front of the one-story house. But the drop off behind it was significant enough to make it appear two stories from behind. It was lattice work painted white in its prime. Covered as nearly as I could tell, empty space. A small, unpretentious car was parked down the hill from the lattice work. Chances were, Christina Wagner was in residence.

My plan was to station myself where I might hear sounds from within without being seen.

I parked my car out of sight of the house and stole back to the house, the two-pound box of Lately candy under my arm. There was some ice on the street and I almost fell, teaching me to tread more lightly.

I didn't have a plan of the cabin and chastised myself for not asking Christina's mother for a layout. I assumed the front door led into the living room. After that it was an uptoss where the rest of it was. It looked tiny from the outside, like it couldn't have had more than one bedroom. I decided my goal was best served by trying to burrow under the house in back through some compromise in the integrity of the shaky lattice work— then I might hear her footsteps overhead—and be close by her car in case she opted for a hasty exit. Not that I had an inkling how to stop her. I couldn't see myself laying down in front of the wheels.

Getting under the house was easier than I imagined. There were plenty of loose boards which looked like I wasn't the first with this idea.

Staying there was the problem. It was cold and damp and offered few opportunities for comfy repose.

I must have lived the life of a mole for twenty years or so before I heard footsteps above. It had long since become light outside with a glimmer of what passes for sun in these parts.

Would my increased heart rate help me in this unprecedented endeavor? I told myself Christina Wagner was just a person—and a special one at that— which I based on Sandy Straus's apparent esteem for her.

Instead of rushing to the front door with my two pounds of chocolate candy, I decided to give her time to dress and settle into her daily routine—whatever that was—perhaps a breakfast, before I proffered the candy as an undisguised bribe.

I tried to monitor her footsteps above and ascribe specific actions and locations to them. I imagined bedroom, bathroom, kitchen even a dining area, realizing I could have had them all torqued up.

I heard sounds that seemed to connote her preparing and consuming breakfast. Perhaps the candy would not be as enticing so quickly on the arches of the first meal of the day. That gave me yet another consideration to ruminate about.

It was perhaps the inhospitality of my environment that encouraged me to act—moving my stiff body out of this hole and into the daylight like any other human being.

I walked carefully because there was still ice on the ground and it was uphill from my dungeon to the front (and only) door.

The front porch had a roof over it so you could swing on the hanging porch swing in the summertime without getting sunburned.

The front door had a screen door which also came in handy in the summertime.

I knocked gently on the front door.

It was answered only with a dead silence.

I knocked again. A little louder than before. I thought I heard steps approaching, then nothing. The silence that greeted me from inside was excruciating. I was plotting my next move.

I tried one more time with a louder, almost

menacing pounding. "Christina?" I said.

Her voice came from what seemed the other side of the door, indicating she had been next to the door all the time. It was a thin, almost frightened voice. "Who are you?"

"Gil Yates."

"What do you want?"

"I'm delivering two pounds of Josh Lately's finest."

"Josh Lately?"

"Yes."

I could feel her salivate through the door. Finally the still small voice peeped, "*Two* pounds?"

"Yes."

It was becoming clear she had conquered the pacing of life—and it was slowing. I could steer a battleship through her silences.

"How did you know Lately candy?"

"A little bird told me."

Silence.

"Was it a vulture?" she ventured.

I laughed. "Could you please open the door—it's a little cold out here."

She was mastering the silences now.

"Thank you for bringing me chocolate. You can leave it at the door."

I got a chuckle out of that.

"If you leave your address I'll send a thank you note."

She was showing herself a live wire in spite of all the silences.

"Sorry," I rejoindered, "no can do. Admission to your inner sanctum is the price of the chocolate."

Pause.

"What will you do with it?"

"Eat it," I said. "I love Josh Lately's chocolate."

Silence.

There were faintly receding footsteps, then some rummaging around inside—like she left the door to get something, perhaps her purse to offer to pay me for the candy. Or a gun—I hoped it wasn't a gun—but now that I thought of it, wouldn't a woman alone in the woods have gun?

Suddenly, I thought if she confronted me with a gun and said, 'The candy or your life,' I wouldn't hesitate to give her the candy. That was the easy part, but if she wanted both the candy and my life, I would be in the sauerkraut. How easy it would be these days to say she'd shot an intruder—a potential rapist who scared her to death in the wee hours of the morning before she was properly dressed. They check me out, find out I was using a fake name. Good luck getting the Kulps to go to baseball for me when they found out my real name was Malvin Stark.

The only side up of this scenario was if she shot me, I wouldn't live to experience the humiliation.

More stillness from within, then the small voice through the door.

"If I let you in, will you give me the chocolate and leave?"

"Well, certainly I'll leave eventually," I said. "But I didn't come all this way from California by way of Muhlenheim just to deliver candy to this remote outpost."

"So what do you want?"

"To talk to you."

"What about?"

Breathe, I told myself, breathe. This silence was sponsored by yours truly. I guess I thought she might want to fill the silence with volunteer speculations that might help my quest.

No such luck. I took in more air. What were my options after all? She would speak to me or not. She would tell me something that made the trip worthwhile or not.

"I've been hired," I began tentatively, "to look into the...the demise of Dr. Kulp's son-in-law." I thought that was a clever sliding into the subject without rubbing her face in it. Of course, she knew what I was talking about. But I could pretend for a while longer that I didn't realize her relationship to the deceased.

"What makes you think I know anything about it?"

"Call it a hunch," I said. "Talk to me and we'll see."

"Why should I?" she asked.

"Maybe like so many others you are tired of having this tragedy continually dredged up."

"Yes," she said. "Why do they do it?"

"I think I have an answer."

"What is it?"

"Let me come in," I said. "I'll tell you."

She thought a moment. "Well...show me the candy," she said.

"Open the door," I said. "It's right in my hand."

That wasn't good enough. "Go over to the

window on your left."

I did as instructed and held up the box of Josh Lately.

She must have been satisfied because I heard the latch lifted and saw the door open.

41

Christina Wagner was not glamorous—not dowdy—but calling her plain would be an injustice. She had not made any apparent effort to spruce up her appearance in this hideaway, but I could imagine in happier circumstances she had a spark to her. I could see Sandy treating her like the sister he didn't have. Beyond that I couldn't speculate.

She had a bowl of hair that showed evidence of self-immolation. It was a nest no mouse would be ashamed of. She wore beaten jeans and a maroon sweater that had seen happier times.

Christina held her hand out for the candy. I obliged.

While she opened the box, I was no longer a presence. She sat on the blanket-covered couch with the box of chocolate on her lap. I had two choices—next to her on the couch or on a similarly adorned chair facing a coffee table between. I chose the chair.

The coffee table would seem an ideal venue for the box of chocolate. Christina held it instead on her lap, studying its architecture but picking the pieces off like a hummingbird who had to eat many times her weight every day to survive. I soon began to wonder if two pounds had been enough. Had she been living here, as I began to suspect, the life of a cloistered nun? If so, and the flood gates were rupturing, it could be a good sign for me.

A low winter morning sun was oozing across the plank wood floors. Of all the subtle approaches I had considered leading to this confrontation, after seeing Christina I opted for no subtlety at all.

"How long have you been living in this..." I almost said shack, "cabin?"

"Thirteen months, one week, three days and thirteen hours."

"Approximately," I said with a smile.

"Yeah," she said, a small barely discernible smile breaking her lips, "more like precisely."

"Get any pleasure from it?" I asked.

"Pleasure? I wasn't after pleasure. Relief maybe— I was looking for peace and I guess I more or less found it," she said. "Or more accurately it overcame me by default—a byproduct of inactivity."

Christina was a down to the ground kind of girl. What you saw was what you got. I felt quickly this girl would not lie to me—or even attempt to mislead, which is what I had feared.

Another chocolate popped into her mouth. It seemed like the sugar and theobromine was working as a drug releasing her inhibitions, or at least neutralizing her normal reserve. I bore in.

"How much longer do you plan to stay in this," I looked around, "what would you call it? Rustic? place?"

"No plans," she said without emotion.

"So what do you have here? I mean, it isn't exactly a five star—no plumbing, no water, no electricity. It's just back to nature, isn't it?"

"I suppose."

"And you've hacked it more than thirteen months. How?"

She wasn't answering obvious questions. "I mean, how do you pass the time here?"

She didn't answer at first. Then she said, "Contemplation."

"That's a lot of contemplation," I offered more in wonder than in judgment. "You could be in a nunnery," I said.

"Yes," she said. "It is sort of that, I guess."

She guesses, I thought. After thirteen months there shouldn't be any guesswork left.

"So it's all reverie?" I pressed.

"Pretty much," she said, still studying her sugar stash.

I was putting patience to the test—I didn't force anything—or salt her with questions as though with a machine gun, and time—and the chocolate—seemed to relax her. Time to test the air with more substance, but work up to it.

"Does something happen around here?"

"In the summer."

"The lake?"

"Yes, and a pavilion. Music, rental boats, swimming, fishing."

"You do any of that?"

"When I was a kid."

"Was it fun?"

"Oh, yeah."

"So what did you give up to come here?"

"Teaching," she said. "I was a teacher."

"What grade?"

"First."

"I'll bet you were a good teacher."

"Pretty good," she said.

I suspected she was being modest. "Like it?"

"Oh, yeah," she said, seeming to brighten for the first time. "I loved the kids."

I let it sink in before I segued to the obvious. "Ever want kids of your own?"

The long contemplation in the woods seemed to slow Christina's metabolism—she didn't cry right away—it was rather a slow build up to a gentle heaving, intermittent at first with some heroic attempt made to stifle the outbursts, but finally she gave way to the emotion. The chocolates were trembling on her lap along with the rest of her body. They had become part of her—those she had eaten and those she hadn't.

I thought I should make some attempt to sooth her nerves but I couldn't think how to go about it. I just blundered into asking her more questions in the hope answering would blunt the self-pity.

"How close did you come to having children?"

"Close," she said, but that was all.

"When? How? How long ago?"

"A year, year and a half."

I admit to being a slow learner, but I got the picture.

"Were you…pregnant?"

"No."

"Were you…trying to get…"

"No," she said with a heavy sigh. "Thought about it. Wish I had."

"With Sandy?"

"Yes," she said. "Who else?"

"Did you discuss it with him?"

"Yes."

"Offer?"

"Yes."

"How did it come up?"

"I brought it up…"

"But hadn't he just been married?"

"Not just—going on two years."

"Wasn't happy?"

"Miserable."

"Why?"

She looked at me as though trying to determine how much I needed to know.

"Well," I said, "was…didn't she…satisfy him?"

"No."

"Did they want children…but couldn't…?"

"He wanted children."

"She didn't?"

"Near as I could tell, she didn't mind having kids—not initially anyway—she just didn't like doing what you had to do to get them."

"So…they…didn't…"

She shook her head. "She was willing to do it to reproduce—her church encouraged it, she said. But then it only seemed to Ginger to be okay if you wanted kids."

"But she *did?*"

She shook her head again. "She had a miscarriage. She got pregnant with the first attempt and that was fine with her but not with him. She let him know her religion (to which he had converted) did not condone sex not geared to procreation. So once she was preggers that was it."

"But they had no children."

"No," Christina said. "The miscarriage was a sign from God that she wasn't meant to have children—or engage in the act that caused them."

"Oh my..."

"Exactly," she said. "I've heard it said that celibacy was the worst sexual perversity and I believe it."

I nodded.

She began slow tears again. "So Sandy had one experience in his life. One!" she sobbed. "And it killed him."

"The experience?"

"No, the abstinence."

"So...you...offered to...grant him more experience?"

"We talked about it," she said, then stopped.

"And?" I encouraged her.

She sighed heavily. "Sandy said all the right things. The *moral* things. You'd have to understand Sandy," she said. "And not many did."

"You did?"

She nodded.

"So you offered to have a child with him?"

"*Yes*! As many as he wanted."

"But wouldn't that be a scandal in this small community?"

"Of course. That's why I offered to move."

"And?"

"He agonized," she said. "He wanted to, I could

really tell."

"But he didn't?"

She didn't trust herself to talk—she just shook her head.

"Had you ever done anything with him that could have led to a...child?"

"No," she said shortly. "I *told* you, he had only one experience in his life. He was an old fashioned boy—prominent family—he took saving it and marriage seriously—he saved it a long time all right, there just wasn't *any* payoff."

"How about you?"

"Me?"

"Yes," I said. "Were you...active?"

"Active?"

"Did *you* have any experience?"

She shook her head slowly. "You see, Sandy was the only boy that ever interested me that way, and I was too uptight to let him know. We'd settled into this brother, sister thing and I swear I thought it would be like incest."

"Did you ever discuss that with Sandy?"

"Oh no, we didn't talk about it. We just had a silent understanding. We didn't talk about it...until it was too late."

"But *why* was it too late? I mean, divorce is commonplace these days."

She shook her head. "Not so commonplace in this community—God fearing Catholics to boot. No, no, no. The Kulps were pillars of moral rectitude. The Strauses perhaps less so. Nevertheless, they were pillars of the community and while Sandy might have acquiesced to divorce, instigated it even when he was a protestant, after he broke the mold and took Catholic vows for the woman he thought he loved, he thought it was impossible."

She got that faraway look in her eyes again—like she wasn't really there any longer.

"It was that vow," she said and shuddered.

"What vow?" I asked.

"Till death do us part—the marriage ceremony. To Sandy that was a solemn oath and he took his oaths very seriously. I tried to tell him that Ginger had not lived up to her oath of love, honor and obeying, and that should mitigate his responsibility. But to him 'till death do us part' was the only honorable solution. He was only responsible for his oath, not for Ginger's. She of course could die and relieve him of his promise, he thought, but she showed no sign of that happening." Her voice dropped, "Oh, how I wish she had. I even considered killing Ginger myself to save Sandy. I couldn't do it. I think Sandy had some fear I would and it hastened his...act."

"Oh," I grunted at his fate. "Would you call that religious tyranny?"

"That's the nicest thing I'd call it."

"What else?"

"You don't want to know."

She had been startlingly forthcoming so I didn't press for this morsel of opinion.

"Did you know he was going to...jump?"

"Not certainly," she said in her reverie. "Part of me was afraid, part of me was sunk in deep denial. So..." she trailed off.

"So?"

"So when he did it...I snapped. I couldn't face

anything anymore—not my mother, not my job, not...life. Running away was all I was capable of." She sat there spent with her rendition—obviously the longest communication she'd had on a subject in thirteen months. The box of candy sat lifeless on her lap—perhaps it drew the life from her for she was suddenly exceedingly pale.

We sat in silence. I don't know what she was thinking. I hoped it was some relief. My thoughts were gratitude mixed with sympathy—and wonder at what I might do to save her from the same fate. Had she read my mind?

"Of course my first thought when this happened was I should follow him. Romeo and Juliet."

"Why didn't you?"

"Oh, a bunch of reasons. Cowardice—I couldn't see myself crashing my head on the street. But I changed..."

"How?"

"First I thought following him to the great beyond would honor his memory," she said. "Was I, I wondered being the real Christina or a robotic substitute? Then I realized I would not only be stepping on his act—his memory—horning in on his statement with no more reason than I was too weak to live without him. But I guess the overriding factor was—and this hiatus from real life afforded me the opportunity to realize it—what we had—what made it special was...it was a secret. His and mine. Oh, you might not think secrecy was required since we didn't really do anything that called for anonymity—still, I felt if I jumped—or found an easier way, I would be dishonoring his memory. Trivializing his pain, his suffering. Why is it people have such a capacity for perversity?"

"Ginger?" I muttered.

She nodded. "The whole chastity thing," she said. "Perverse."

We considered that in the peaceful silence this milieu offered. I broke it first, quietly, tentatively. "Were there any more...perversions in the relationships? Yours and...Ginger's...with Sandy?"

"Perversions?" she said. "I suppose it depends on your definition."

"What is yours?" I asked.

"Low."

"Low?"

"My threshold is low. I don't see perversions under every rock. We are just people taking in what we can. Processing it as we can," she said. "For instance, do you think pornography is perverse?"

"A lot of people do," I said. "I'm no expert."

"Well, Sandy was—an expert I mean." She took another piece of candy on her lap and set the box on the table between us. I could see she had done yeoman service at the task. There were ten to fifteen empty paper cups.

"What's a porn expert?" I asked.

"He started watching it out of frustration and then it grew to what I'd call an obsession. He found himself falling in love with one of the women. He watched her performance again and again. He told me what attracted him was not only her physical appearance, but what she did so willingly that his wife wouldn't do. How she even seemed to enjoy it. Took it in stride. Like it was not some bugaboo but a fact of life.

"It was a ten minute film. Sometimes he watched

288

it three times a day. She became a substitute for his distant, cold, unavailable, real, church-blessed wife."

The recital had taken something out of her. It was as though, just at that moment she realized letting me, a stranger in on that confidence might not have been acceptable etiquette.

"He told you all that?" I asked, not bothering to, or unable to hide my surprise.

"He did," she said. "The closer he got to the end of his rope, the more that spilled out of him. I could write his complete biography."

"Will you?"

"Of course…not. That was between us—it was special—I wouldn't dilute that special confidence before the world. Not for the world."

And there you have it. She solved my case. I didn't kid myself that it was a solution that would go down well with the Kulps. But the way I felt now, I was almost as drained in the hearing as Christina was in the telling. She was far more important to me than the Kulps.

In the eerie silence that followed between two of the seven odd billion of the human race (with the emphasis on 'odd') I experienced an out of body episode—one of those paranormal things that people talk about and about which I have always been skeptical: my arm shot out in front of me and without realizing (I swear) my hand dropped to the box of chocolates, my fingers spreading then closing on a piece of candy like one of those excavating machines you see leaking trash at the junkyard. Before Christina or I knew what happened, I had popped the chocolate into my mouth.

"Hey!" she exclaimed, and after a beat we both

dissolved into a puddle of laughter.

The proverbial frozen stuff was broken. It wasn't long thereafter that I proffered the thought that this might be a good time to quit this venue for the real world of refrigeration and flush toilets.

She didn't fight me. It was as though all it ever took was someone to listen to her story. But the time was right. Sure there were practical considerations like how would she live? She could substitute teach until the beginning of the next school year when she could claim her old job back. Sandy had subsidized her fancy apartment. Now she would have to live more simply, but that was okay.

Suddenly I had an inspiration: I would introduce her to Alice. I'd take Christina to our farewell dinner—Alice would be angry as blazes—but some good might come of it. There are worse things than introducing lonely people to each other.

"Let's go," I said.

"Go?"

"Yeah, you've spent your last night here. Pack up—we'll go to lunch on the way out."

She didn't move, but neither did she argue.

"Come on. How long will it take to gather your things?"

She laughed, "Oh, three or four...minutes."

"I'll help," I said.

Two minutes was more like it—but she *did* have help.

42

I drove behind Christina in her car to lunch at one of those roadside places with integrity—code for not making any discernible profit.

It was time to talk the basics with Christina.

Did the food have integrity? I was in no position to judge. It was just as well because I can't remember tasting anything—my focus was on Christina Wagner. She seemed a little unsure as you might expect of one who had dropped out for thirteen months.

I offered to sport her to a couple months living expenses until she got back on the soles of her shoes. She seemed to think she couldn't accept that kind of charity.

"No charity," I said. "You solved this case for me. My payoff will be handsome. You are entitled to a chunk of it."

"Oh, no! I didn't do anything."

"Well, we can argue about that later. In the meantime you should be comforted that I won't let you starve."

"You are very kind," she said.

"Oh, no," I said, "just grateful." She almost seemed a different person away from her exile. The peace had descended.

"Tell me, Christina," I asked, "what was it like to live so alone for so long?"

"I have lived alone for all my adult life. What I missed was my contact with Sandy. I was alone, but he was with me in spirit. Maybe that's trite, I don't know—or care, I might add. But now...he's gone and I am really alone."

"How about making new friends?"

"Yeah, right," she said. "Know any?"

"Matter of fact—I do. Not a fella, but a start—get you in circulation."

"Who?"

"Someone who was as crazy about Sandy as you were."

"Oh no..."

"Not what you think. It was totally unrequited. She was his secretary. Maybe if I got you together you might hit it off, starting as you would be with Sandy in common."

"I don't know," she said. "I've been out of it for so long. I might not even know how to act."

"Act yourself," I said. "You are a charming, sensitive, wonderful person with so much to give."

She dropped her eyes. "Thank you," she said softly trying not to let on how pleased she was.

"What do you say?" I asked her. "I promised to take her to dinner on my last night here—that would be the day after tomorrow. I'd love to have you along—be good for both of you."

"But...but wouldn't I be intruding?"

"Not at all," I allowed. "Good for me too."

"I mean, wasn't it supposed to be a date?"

"Oh, gosh no," I said. "I'm leaving the next day—wouldn't be a big percentage in starting anything. Besides, I'm married." I didn't add that I never was so glad to use that condition to insulate me from Alice.

She didn't respond.

"Well, think about it," I said. "You have time."

We parked our cars in the hotel garage and at the desk I gave the clerk my credit card with my pseudonym on it and told her to put Christina's room on my bill—as well as any ancillary expenses she incurred.

After she was checked in I told her I was going to check in with my computer guru and Jessamyn. Would she like to come along?

"Oh, thanks very much," she said, "but I think I should just take some time to adjust—maybe I'll take a walk—drop into Ness's—or just crash. I just don't want you worrying about me."

"You'll be okay?"

"I'll be okay."

I saw her to her room and even carried the backpack in which reposed all her current worldly goods.

I left her at her door when I was satisfied the room pleased her.

"Are you kidding?" she asked after my inquiry. "You saw where I spent the last thirteen months and change."

I drove without incident to Jessamyn's apartment. There I found Elwin in the same position I left him—I swear it looked like he hadn't moved an inch. I told him as much. I don't think he heard me. The best he could do was give me one of his "Oh, it's you" looks—more like an "Oh, it's *only* you" look.

"If I'm reading this right," he said without taking his eyes from the screen, "it seems like Sandy might have been talking about suicide and the other—Christina was it?—was trying to talk him out of it. That would explain the Romeo and Juliet thing."

"Excellent!" I said. "I think you solved it."

He looked perplexed. "I have?" he said.

"Yes, you're a champ. I put it all together and with Christina Wagner—well, you—solved it."

Okay, maybe I was laying on the credit a little on the heavy side, but I didn't see another way of tearing him from his infernal machine.

"So if you could do me one more favor, it will be pay day."

He looked inquisitively.

"Could you copy everything that's on this machine on two CDs, that is, two separate copies? Give them to me, then erase them from the machine."

"Yeah, I can do that."

"How long will it take?"

"Well, I have to get the CDs—and—I don't know—a couple hours."

"Good. How about if we have a dinner celebration? You can bring the computer and CDs. My treat." Jessamyn and he thought that would be a fun idea. We agreed to meet at Jessamyn's favorite—with the pasta-sauce-hiding tablecloths.

I drove back to my hotel and called Christina. She didn't answer.

Then I called Priscilla.

"Priscilla, this is Gil Yates."

"Oh, *hi* Gil. Nice to hear from you."

"Same here," I said. "I'm winding down."

"Do you have news we'd like to hear?"

I'd thought Priscilla was my most sympathetic Pennsylvania patron. Now it sounded as though she slipped with an edge to join the adversary.

"Well, that depends on what you want to hear," I said. "I think I can explain everything logically and follow it up with whatever evidence you require."

She didn't say anything. What, I wondered, was she thinking?

"So, I wondered if we could get together tomorrow. I'll give you my report and save you all ten grand."

"Save us ten thousand dollars? But why?" She was genuinely confused. "We said we'd pay for ten days."

"Yes, I know. I was just thinking to give you a discount."

"But why?" she asked. "Surely it's worth ten-thousand dollars to you to stay one more day."

"Essentially my work is done and I—well, let's talk about it tomorrow. If you want me to stay the extra day, I will."

"Okay," she said.

"When shall we meet?"

"Why don't you come here around eleven. We can talk—and have lunch at the club."

"Fair enough," I said. If she wanted to pay me the extra ten G's I decided not to fight it. "See you then," I said.

I called Christina again. This time she answered. She was back in her room and I invited myself to visit. After a pause, she said okay.

It might have been my imagination, but after she opened the door I had an immediate impression that she was already happier than she was in the woods.

"Want to come in?" she asked as though the answer might be a surprise.

"If I could," I said, and she stood back from the door. I looked around for a place to sit as though this were not a room identical to mine. There were the two choices—the desk chair and the padded one. I took the desk chair, it being the more modest. I said, "Not a huge furniture selection, is there?"

"It's a palace next to where I've been."

"So you're glad, or at least content, to be back in the world?"

"I will be," she said. "I took a little walk down Adams Street and I was so overwhelmed with the hubbub I had to come back."

"Well, good for you for braving it," I said. "I'm here with another exercise in back-to-normal."

She didn't ask, only looked at me quizzically.

"Two people in town helped immeasurably in bringing the case to a conclusion. I'm taking them to a gratitude dinner and I'd like you to come with me."

"Oh," she said as though I'd taken the wind out of her.

"You may think about it," I said. "We won't leave for a couple hours. I'd like you to go, I'm only going to be in town two more days. On my last night I'd like you to meet Sandy's secretary. This will give you a practice run."

"And you think I should do it?"

"I'd be pleased if you did," I said.

"Would you understand if I didn't?"

"I would," I said, "but I'd be disappointed."

"Well," she said, "you've done so much to help me, I'd be ungracious if I disappointed you. But...I don't have anything to wear."

"Neither do the two we're going to meet. It's the starving student fashion that prevails. If anything, you might be overdressed."

She didn't seem to believe that so I said, "I'll call you when I head for the lobby. Tomorrow we can shop at Ness's across the street before my lunch with Priscilla Kulp."

She didn't argue.

Back in my room I began working on the report I would submit to Priscilla on the morrow—or hold it for her husband the next day as the case may be.

I also had to figure how much to pay Jessamyn and Elwin.

In just over two hours, I called Christina and she answered.

"I'll see you down in the lobby," I said. "I'm going now." I didn't wait for her to argue but hung up gently. I wasn't sure she would comply. I waited just a few minutes and when I arrived downstairs Christina was there.

She seemed a little nervous in the car. She admitted it in response to my question.

"These people we're meeting are both real people and you'll see they are nothing to be nervous about."

La Trattoria didn't disappoint. The time-worn musty atmosphere didn't magically disappear. The red and white tablecloths still looked slightly used.

Jessamyn and Elwin were already seated at a four

top and it looked like Jessamyn was valiantly pumping a reluctant Elwin for conversation that didn't interest her in the slightest. She looked relieved to see us. I'm sure she looked up at the door as soon as she heard a sound from that direction.

I introduced Christina who immediately saw her clothes were not a problem. I just didn't tell what her connection was to the case. I thought that would make for more interesting conversation.

I looked at Jessamyn and Elwin, "Did you bring the stuff?"

"It's in the car. We'll give it to you on the way out."

Small talk got us into the menus and ordering.

Jessamyn asked me what the outcome of my investigation was. I begged off. "I'll tell you, but first I'd like you to speculate as though you had to solve it with the information you had."

"Well," Jessamyn said, "no one pushed him, did they?"

"No."

"So he jumped—or was it an accident?"

"What do you think?"

"Jumped."

"Okay," I said, "why?"

"He was unhappy." Jessamyn said to the silence—then sputtered a laugh.

"Makes sense," Elwin said.

"What about the Romeo and Juliet business?" I asked.

"Well, was there a double suicide?" Elwin asked.

"No."

"An attempt?" he asked.

"Well," I said sheepishly, "I'll let Juliet tell it," and I turned to Christina who naturally blushed. But she told her story—somewhat truncated in deference to her audience and the lateness of the hour. I was proud of her—she got through her story, albeit in a Reader's Digest version, with only reasonable choking up and tears.

Jessamyn and Elwin were a good audience. The food came somewhere during the recital and it was given short shrift. The individual consumption of each dish was a mirror into the personality of the eater: Elwin ate like he worked: with his head down, not brooking any distraction. Jessamyn ate with happy, darting movements that miraculously directed the food to her mouth. Christina ate slowly and thoughtfully, considering every motion of the process.

Me? I couldn't be objective.

After dinner we shared some cannoli (again) I don't know why I participated. It wasn't that good the first time. Then we got to the basics—payday. I had decided not to put them on the spot asking what they thought they should get. I figured their approximate hours, then the value of what they produced as well as how much time it would have taken me. I would not have made the ten-day deadline without them.

Then I scandalously overpaid them—as Dr. Kulp thought I was being scandalously overpaid. Figuring the hours they devoted (Elwin seemed to devote all his waking hours with little deducted for sleep) and the value of their findings, I decided to split a ten-thousand dollar day's pay between them.

Three-quarters to Elwin, one-quarter to Jessamyn to be paid on receipt from the Kulps.

They were overjoyed and showed their appreciation by Jessamyn giving me a huge hug and kiss then Elwin awkwardly following suit—mercifully without a kiss.

Christina and I walked Jessamyn and Elwin to their car where we transferred the computer—which Elwin assured me had been wiped clean—and two CDs, each identical with the total content from the computer.

43

$90,000

In most of my cases, my fee is earned when I bag the culprit.

This case was different. Just as in the other cases I had to be sure I would be paid. My fees were so high it was not unusual for some of my clients to try to do me out of some, or all, of the agreed on sum. Certain steps can be taken to ensure payment but there are no steel-clad guarantees.

One of my favorite insurance methods is the escrow account. The money is put in before I begin work. If I achieve the contracted condition, the money is released to me. This is all in writing so ideally there can be no misunderstandings. That's the perfect world scenario. Real world results sometimes vary ("check with your physician…").

The biggest variant is the requirement of the escrow that both parties agree in writing to release the funds to one or another. Absent this written instruction the money remains in the escrow account. So while it's not released to me, it's also not returned to the depositor.

Most people are not sophisticated about these loopholes. Some may think all they have to do to get their money back is ask for it. That's my advantage. My disadvantage would be in a case where the client put the money in the escrow, and I achieved the agreed upon conditions to earn the money, but the client was so angry with me he refused to release the money for spite, even though he couldn't get it back himself without my approval, which I was of course, not about to give. The next ploy is to bargain with me to reduce the fee. I also would refuse to do that—especially in this case.

In my favor, Priscilla Kulp was custodian of the money. I had insisted on that because I feared the doctor might pull the no-release of money stunt. He might still attempt to influence his wife, Priscilla, in that direction.

Hence my preference to meet Priscilla alone today—offer her the ten-thousand dollar discount so I wouldn't have to face the doctor and suffer the shenanigans he was perfectly capable of pulling.

Besides, he was so unpleasant I thought it would be well worth ten grand not to have to see him again.

In this racket one notices that solving the puzzle is a part of the war—communicating the result can be more challenging. But just because you expect difficulty doesn't make it any easier. For my meeting with Mrs. Kulp I tucked Sandy's computer and one of the two CDs in the trunk of my rental car. If she accepted my proposed compromise, I'd give them to her today. If not, I'd save them for tomorrow's foray with the big shotguns.

The second CD, my keeper, I put in the safe in my hotel room.

I gathered Priscilla at her house for the short drive to her country club. In these parts the club was your sign of arrival. In my observation Priscilla took this status boost with less gravitas than her husband. She was warm and genuinely friendly with the help. He seemed never able to forget his exalted status in the world as the healer and savior of men.

I tried to orchestrate my pitch. I had convinced myself that I would so much prefer to give the ten thousand dollar discount and skedaddle a day early, rather than unload my tale on old Dr. Sourpuss. So much, I realized, he already knew and would be mucho angry I knew. He was obviously a man of some considerable brain power, and yet he had his sacred blind spots—making him a master of denial. I trembled when I envisioned our confrontation with me laying out the bad stuff which we both knew would cost the troops five million buckaroos. I realized he could reject my findings as mere conjecture and fight on to the death (probably his), but I would have done my bit.

Priscilla and I passed the less than two miles to her club with agitation-free smallish talk. At the club, she worked her charm on all the employees we encountered until we were seated at the best window table in the house, looking out on the swimming pool and the woods beyond.

We settled in with the menus and I ordered a Cobb salad in keeping with the ladies lunch this seemed to portend. Priscilla had something similar—perhaps a caesar salad—but how important can that be?

My preference was to procrastinate the flesh of the matter until after lunch. I thought it would be kinder to our digestions. Alas, Priscilla pressed:

"So, what did you find out?"

"Find out?" I asked, not even fooling myself that I was being cagey.

Her look left no doubt she knew that I knew that I knew and she knew.

"This is, if I'm not mistaken," she said, "yet another ten thousand dollar day. Is that correct?"

"Yes, but I'm offering to cut ten off my one hundred price."

"So you said," she said with a smile and nod. "And I said that proposal does not excite me."

"Well, it's worth thinking about," I said. "Another ten thousand dollar day will not change my findings. You can tell the doctor what I found and he should be pleased to have saved ten grand in the process. He should be happy not to have to see me again."

The shaking of her head was ladylike, and yet undeniably firm. "Sorry, Gil," she said. "I perfectly understand—but after what we have all been through, I'm not compromising on half gestures. So give it to me straight—what did you find?"

"I, ah, was hoping we might eat discussing less...agitating matters..." I said. "Our digestion and all..."

"Oh, nonsense," she said. "We've both had enough meals so if this one ends with a vomiting session over the toilet we will survive until the next meal."

You had to admire her attitude and quaint perspective. But I wondered, she was in such good shape, especially for this locale, could she be bulimic where most meals ended in the aforementioned vomiting session? I didn't inquire.

Instead I sighed a sigh worthy of one of

Shakespeare's better tragedies. "Okay, you're the boss," I said. "Did you know about the insurance policy?"

"What insurance policy?"

"The one on Sandy Straus."

"No…what…?"

"Your husband took out a five million dollar policy…"

"Five million?"

"Yes."

"Did he collect?"

"No," I said. "There's the massage."

"Massage? Someone got a massage? What has that to do with anything? Oh," she said, the light going on in her cerebellum or one of those places. "Rub, there's the rub. That's how that one goes, Gil."

"Glad to hear it."

"So what are you talking about?" she pressed. She wasn't going to let me off the fish hook gladly. "Why didn't he collect? Wait a minute," she stopped herself, "you aren't saying Sandy isn't dead?"

"No, he's dead all right. But the policy had a restriction. They didn't pay in the event of suicide."

"Oh," it was slowly sinking in—all the details and ramifications of the whole drama.

"There was a three-year limitation."

"What's that mean?"

"If he had waited three years—Sandy, I mean, to jump—the doctor would have collected."

"But—oh, no—but he doesn't need the money."

"I expect he did it for Ginger. So she would be taken care of if her husband could no longer bring home the sausage."

"Five million you say?"

I nodded with imagined solemnity.

"But that's a mere fifty operations, three to four weeks work, for him," she said. "We don't spend a lot of money. His expenses aren't that high—as a percentage—so why would he go to all this trouble?"

"I don't have the answer," I said. "But in my experience money is a complex motivator, so many elusive factors involved."

"Like what?"

"Oh, pride, his childhood—his sister's death from the abortion he arranged. The sleeping arrangements when he grew up. The hiding from his father as a result of the...tragedy. I expect you could add to the list with things I don't know about."

She didn't answer, instead getting one of those long distance looks. But she didn't deny it either.

It was during the faraway look that the food came. Somehow it was consumed, though I don't remember how. Since neither of us did much but pick at the food before us, we declined dessert, but while we sat inert, I think the insurance news was taking root inside Priscilla, I eased into the other bomb casing.

"Did you ever get any feeling about Ginger's marriage to Sandy? Perhaps something out of the ordinary?"

"I don't know," she said. "Why?"

"Well, we uncovered some...things."

"Uncovered?" she said. "How?"

"Sandy left behind his computer."

"Behind? Where?"

"At the store—in the storeroom."

"How did you find it?"

"Long story—short story—that's my job. That's

what you pay me through the ears for."

"Nose," she mumbled. "What did you find out?"

This was the hardest part. I took a deep breath. "Did you know Ginger had a miscarriage?"

"Yes," she said. I didn't say anything. She stepped in, "That's not uncommon."

"No," I agreed. "What is perhaps more uncommon is having that end...all..." it was not that easy for me to verbalize this, "...intimacy."

Priscilla stared at me. A deep, blank stare. I couldn't read her expression. Was it just shock at the news, or was it something...else?

I stepped into the void. "As you know, Sandy converted to your religion to marry Ginger."

She nodded.

"The strictures of which Ginger took to heart."

"Yes, she was conscientious about her religion. All that training from the nuns, I suppose."

"So there was nothing...premarital."

She nodded; that didn't surprise her.

"What may be more surprising," I said picking up on her reaction, "was there was only one...occurrence of...intimacy and that resulted in the pregnancy— and that was all Ginger would allow. It was clear the church only sanctioned that sort of behavior if the end result was a prolonging of the species. A child. And when the miscarriage resulted Ginger decided God didn't want her to have children—so she shut down the baby-making apparatus."

Priscilla's jaw dropped.

"In essence," I continued, "Sandy Straus was blessed with one experience in his life. That apparently was not enough for him. And since he took his marriage vow more seriously than most, I'd say, the death do us part part hit home. He knew he had to part with Ginger and death appeared to him the only option."

There was a devastating silence, which I thought I should break. But for the life of me, I couldn't think of an appropriate thing to say. There was nothing I saw to further illuminate the message, nothing to alleviate the shock, no suitable subject to switch to. I was, in essence, a blank.

So, apparently, was Priscilla. Without a word she rose from the table and made her way out of the room. I saw no alternative than to follow.

She got in the car.

I got in the car.

She said nothing.

I said nothing.

At her curb, I made one last plea.

"Something has bothered you—significantly, I'd say. So what do you say we call off tomorrow—I'll take the ninety and run."

She looked at me with a kind of severity in her eyes—hatred, I hoped, was too strong a description— she tightened her lips and shook her head. She reached for the door handle, pulled it open, then under her breath as though any more exertion might let the demons out of the bottle of her insides, "Like father...like daughter," she muttered.

Then she got out and without turning back said so softly I was not sure I heard it right: "Ten tomorrow—my house," and she shuffled up the path to her front door a woman who had just piled another twenty years on her life.

44

$100,000!?

It was snowing again. Lightly, but it was cold. This corner of the world had not yet gotten the message the planet was warming.

I always got palpitations when I drove up to the Kulp manse. It made it no easier that it was likely my last visit.

Another Cadillac was parked out front—likely Ginger's. It was a three-Cadillac family. Had they ever heard of Lexus, Mercedes, BMW and imports of that ilk? Or was it simply an expression of patriotism: "Buy American?"

Eager to get it over, I repressed my inclination to procrastination and presented myself at the front door at precisely ten a.m.

The lady of the house opened the door (always a relief to not be confronted with the man of the house cold chicken). She appeared to have rebounded from yesterday's blows and she managed a warm smile, doing her small bit to help warm the planet.

The dramatis personae were not so casually assembled.

The seating was as before, except this time Priscilla joined her family opposite (though I hoped not *necessarily* opposing). The time of reckoning was nigh. We all sat as if we were letting the air out of the plastic shells that passed for our bodies.

One thing was clear to me: Dr. Kulp was angry and impatient for the results of his one-hundred grand investment and I expect he knew already the findings had not gone his way. I set the computer on the coffee table between us.

"Alright, Yates," he began, chasing right to the cut, "what have you got?" He looked at the computer on the table. "What's this?" he asked.

"A computer."

He shot me one of his atomic bomb glances.

"I know that," he said ever the iceman. "What's on it?"

"Nothing now."

"Nothing?"

"I transferred Sandy's mail to a CD."

"Where's that?"

"I have it."

"Where?"

"In a safe place."

"Look, here, Yates, don't get cute with me."

"No, indeed," I said. "You're the last person anyone in the world would want to get cute with."

"Don't smartmouth me," the doctor said. "I want that CD."

I took a breath and sank back in the chair—demonstrating once again, I was not above cheap dramatic gestures. I looked up at length at my audience.

The doctor was a master of the vituperative face. Priscilla, his wife, sat impassive, her mind seemingly elsewhere. Ginger was unreadable. She had the expression of a stoic about to be exposed as a fraud at which time I expected her to dissolve into a puddle of tears.

"Well, Doctor," I began slowly with deliberate understatement, "I don't know what claim you would have on it. I expect if Sandy wanted you to have it, he would have given it to you."

"Sandy is *gone!*" Dr. Kulp verily shouted.

"Yes," I said, "Yes. Isn't he."

"What's that supposed to mean?"

"Nothing very elusive," I said. "This entire case was about Sandy being gone and why."

"Yes, and if you did your job you'd be here with news of who pushed him."

I stared at the doctor. Did he really believe what he was saying—in the shadow of the facts I had uncovered? I had trouble believing that, but the mind of man is malleable and can be convinced of almost anything.

"I am here with the news," I said—it was a sudden, whacky, reactive inspiration that in retrospect I might have been better off not having. For the good doctor's face mutated into a glowing almost religiously inspired vision of peace, hope if not exactly love.

"Who?" he said in simple wonder.

"Who?" I said stretching it out unmercifully.

"Yes, *who?*" he pressed.

"Why—*all of you*," I said sweeping my hand across my facing audience.

Dr. Kulp sank back from the edge of his chair and the edge of his patience.

"Don't be ridiculous, Yates. What are you talking about?"

Did he really want to know? Did he *not* know? Did I really want to tell him? Did I really want him to know?

For whatever reason, I told him. In my own way to be sure—some might not unreasonably label it devious—but that was not my motive. I didn't want to hurt these people. The only one of the three I even *liked* with enough positive charge to lift the feeling over the horizon was, of course, Priscilla. Even if she turned on me now, as I feared she was doing, I would continue to consider her kindly.

"All right, Yates," the doctor had spoken. "Out with it."

I suppose in his line of work his word was law. I just continued to have trouble adjusting my feeling to his omnipotence. As I look back, I continue to wonder if I wanted to bring him down because I didn't like him. Because I thought he was a pompous bore who needed a bit of grounding, a shot of reality.

"All right," I began trying to not be so obviously mimicking him. "Shall we begin with the insurance?"

"What insurance?" he reacted with the speed of a whiplash.

"The five million policy on Sandy."

The doctor waved a peremptory hand. "You aren't suggesting *we* killed him to collect on the insurance?"

"No indeed," I said. "Because you didn't collect." I paused for a reaction, but it wasn't forthcoming. "But it is the insurance policy that motivated you to insist it was not suicide."

"What are you talking about?" was the weak, unconvincing retort from the doctor.

"Oh, I expect you know," I said, perhaps a little prouder of myself than the standards of modesty might dictate. "The suicide exemption it contains. If he died by suicide before three years were up, the policy didn't pay off. So that might explain why a guy as close with the moola as you would sport me to a hundred grand to get the results you wanted."

"And you failed," the doctor spat, "miserably."

"Perhaps I failed to support your preconceived notions."

"No perhaps about it."

"Yes, okay. I failed," I said, "but I did discover why your son-in-law jumped off the roof."

Doctor Kulp waved another imperial hand roughly in my direction. "We don't *care* why he jumped."

Priscilla spoke up for the first time. "I care," she said. "Perhaps Ginger cares, and I want you to care. Proceed, Mr. Yates." I expect she was teaching her husband some manners with the "Mr." business.

Dr. Kulp shot me a killing glance that let me know if I did continue he would consider it a personal affront. I stole a sidelong glance at Ginger. She looked like she understood what was coming but had no idea how to prevent it.

"Ginger," I began like a loving grandfather—though I was not that much older than she was. "Would you say your sex life with Sandy was satisfactory?"

The doctor blew. "You are way out of line

Yates." Darn. He hadn't picked up the "Mr." from his wife.

"That's all right," Ginger said with equanimity. "It was satisfactory to me."

"To him?"

"I guess you'd have to ask him," she said.

"Well, we can't do that can we," I said. "But I have the next best thing—the email record—and the word of...a friend of his."

"Look here, Yates," the doctor had spoken, "we don't deal in hearsay here."

"Let him tell us," Priscilla said softly.

Dr. Kulp looked to his daughter. She gave a slight nod which I could easily have missed.

"All right," I said. "Here's what I have pieced together. There were no intimate relations before the wedding."

"That's as it should be!" Dr. Kulp declaimed.

"After the wedding ceremony the bride let it be known she only considered these intimate relations to be appropriate in pursuit of offspring. Am I right so far?" I asked looking at Ginger. She nodded.

"A pregnancy was achieved with one attempt." I looked to her again. Again another nod.

"The pregnancy was terminated by a miscarriage, is that correct?"

"Yes," she muttered.

"Then what was the course of your relations after the miscarriage?"

"It was terribly disappointing to me—and to Sandy. I took it as a sign from God. He didn't want us to have children."

"So you stopped all attempts of relations that

could lead to offspring?"

"Yes. My church and my God dictated—relations between a man and a woman were sacred if they led to reproduction."

"If not?"

"They were sinful."

"And you accepted that?"

"I didn't *accept* it Mr. Yates, I lived it. I had been brought up that way."

"By whom?"

"My religious upbringing."

"By your teachers?"

"The nuns, yes—and my..." she turned an uncertain glance tower the doctor, "my father."

Priscilla seemed to be quietly seething. I asked her, "Did you know about that?"

"I did not," she said. "So the five-million dollar insurance policy on poor Sandy's life wasn't the only thing I didn't know about."

"There was no need to upset you, dear," Dr. Kulp said in his best patronizing tone.

"Did he upset you by telling you he called Ginger every night at dinner time so she couldn't have that—even that much intimate time with her husband, Sandy?"

"Yates," the doctor cut in, "you are so far from your job here as to be absolutely insulting. I haven't liked you from the start."

"I noticed that."

"And I'll thank you to keep your smart mouth shut."

"No," Priscilla interjected quietly. "No, we've been silent too long."

"Priscilla!"

"And one of the things I have been silent about is *your* warped sexuality. Nobody takes that edict of the church seriously—but *you* did. But it wasn't from any holiness, it was from fear—fear that the same thing that happened to your dear sister in that alley would happen to Ginger—or you—or *me*. Like father, like daughter. The amazing thing to me is not your warped celibacy, but that you would see to it that your only child followed that demented lead."

"Priscilla!" Kulp shouted. "See what you've wrought, Yates! And by the way, just where did you get this scurrilous info?"

"I got it," I said slowly, carefully, "from a life-long friend of Sandy's."

"Oh—who was that?"

"Her name isn't important," I said.

"*Her!*" Dr. Kulp blasted our eardrums. "I always suspected Sandy was not the paragon of virtue he made out. Had I known he was unfaithful to my little girl he wouldn't have had to jump—I'd have killed him."

"What a quaint construct in this circumstance," I said.

"What circumstance?" the doctor demanded.

"This swirl of celibacy."

"Watch your tongue!"

"You know, it has been said celibacy is the worst sexual perversion."

"Is that so?!" Dr. Kulp said. "I can think of many worse—was Sandy having an affair with that woman?"

"No indeed," I said. "He was not. Perhaps if he had—if he could have escaped the suffocating bonds of his marriage vows he might still be alive."

"Better dead," the doctor said.

"Daddy!" Ginger exclaimed. "That's cruel."

"He's talking blasphemy—'Thou shalt not commit adultery' and he's advocating it!"

"And you think being dead is better?" she asked her father.

"I wouldn't rule it out."

"Oh, Daddy!"

"He resisted all attempts," I put in, "and he married Ginger—not the other friend. She tried to get him to relent—to bear his children. You know what he did instead? 'Greater love hath no man...' How does it go?"

"I want no more of it," the doctor said. "Now get out of here."

"That would be a pleasure," I riposted. "If you would hand me my check, I'll be on my way."

"You'll be on your way without any check. You didn't do what I asked. You didn't earn your ridiculous fee."

I nodded as a man holding all the aces. "Suit yourself," I said. "Just remember it was Priscilla who hired me—and we took the precaution—in anticipation of this day—to put the money in escrow—where it can only be released to me—or not at all."

"Then it will be not at all!" he hurled at me while Priscilla shook her head at that thought. "No, dear, Mr. Yates earned his fee. He didn't provide the answer you wanted because it didn't exist. Perhaps if we're very nice to him he'll give us the CD and we can read it till kingdom come. I don't know, but I'm fairly certain without his fee we won't get the CD. And who knows, with your celebrity around here he might be able to sell it for more than the hundred-thousand dollars."

The doctor was a deer in the headlights until Ginger cooed, "I want the CD Daddy. Maybe I'll learn something about my husband that I didn't know."

"No, damn it!" he shouted. "I'm in charge here. I'm the breadwinner. Always have been. I don't knuckle under to blackmail. You girls just don't get it. This shyster has you hypnotized. He is working for *us*—or was—not the other way around. That CD is *our* property, not his."

"But Daddy, we would never have found it if Gil hadn't."

"*Shut up!*" he was turning blue. "I'm in charge here—you're just a kid—one who made a serious mistake marrying a *convert*," his emphasis bespoke his disdain, "who didn't...who couldn't understand the doctrines of the church. Those are not manmade, they come directly from God. If the boy had been brought up in the church he might have understood that."

"As you did, dear?" it was a quiet jab from the distaff.

"Yes, damn it, *yes!* As I did—and you didn't die in the same alley—how would you know how *lethal* sex could be?"

"If I may interject a different view," I said. "Isn't it supposed to be joyous, and not scary and fear inducing?"

"What would you know," the doctor said, "you're not a Catholic."

"Do Catholics have a lock on all knowledge?"

"In spiritual matters we think so…"

"Have you talked it over with the Muslims or even the Protestants?"

"I've had all of your smartmouth I can take for the rest of my life, thank you. Now just take your irreverence and *get out of here!*"

"Chester!" Priscilla raised her voice to match her husband's, "That's enough. Gil has worked tirelessly and effectively for ten days. We aren't going to throw him out like some old sock. You may not like his results, but he has done what we asked him to do. I am in charge of his hiring and I say I am going to pay him. The CD is a bonus. I would be pleased if he gave it to us, but in any case, he's earned his money."

"Oh, Priscilla, really," he turned to Ginger, "Ginger," he said, "talk some sense to your mother."

Ginger held him in her gaze, steely, penetrating. At last she said, "You're the one who needs the sense beat into him."

"Ginger!"

"Yes, you—I know—don't I know—who would know better? I've lived all my life under your muscular thumb—God knows how often I heard about your talented fingers creating this unbelievable living for us. Sometimes I think your belief in God is so firm because you think you are God! God—to think I left my husband alone to his dinner because that was when you chose to call. Speaking of unbelievable!" She broke down, buried her head in her hands and sobbed. "What a fool I was." She came up for air through the silence. "I *loved* him," she cried. "He was the only one—I'll never replace him."

"Don't say that dear," Priscilla said.

"I'm not just saying it. I'm living it. He was so good. So pure. None of us could match him—and you, Daddy knew it—that's why you were so intent on my not getting too close to him—and just as though a few dinners would compromise my bond to you, you even ruined that."

"You didn't have to talk to me," he said, rather weakly.

"No," she said. "I know that now. But I loved you too. I didn't want to hurt you. And oh, God, that insurance policy. I didn't even want that five-million, but the thought that Sandy felt he had to jump to do us out of the money..." she shuddered, "the thought—the mere possibility makes me physically ill. I want to throw up every time I think of it. And yes, I think he really was faithful and true to his marriage vows till death do us part. Not divorce—merely divorce but the church demanded death and he obliged."

She hung her head and her hands rose again to her ears, "I was *so stupid!*"

"No, dear..." her father attempted some comfort.

She rejected it with more force than might have been necessary. "No! Don't patronize me. No! You don't think I know? You don't think I see through it all finally?"

"Some day you'll understand."

"Understand? What more is there to understand? If you mean see your view, I can only hope I never do."

Priscilla rose.

"Where are you going?" the doctor demanded.

"I'll be back," she said. It seemed to mollify him. Quiet seething was the order of things while she was gone. She returned with a sheet of paper and a pen. She wrote on the paper while all eyes were on her. She signed it with a flourish and handed it to me.

To Whom it May Concern
Muhlenheim National Bank

Please release the funds in escrow to Gil Yates. He has completed the required work.

Priscilla Kulp

45

I picked up my check with all the zeros at the bank and drove to Jessamyn's place to give her and Elwin their portions. They were well pleased and overly grateful.

My fear was if I told Alice I was bringing Christina to our farewell dinner, she would throw a tantrum. I further thought if I surprised her with Christina she might be even angrier—but that she would sublimate her anger in deference to the stranger in our midst, Christina Wagner.

Funny how wrong you can be. Though Christina seemed reserved and held back because of what I shared with her—she thought Alice would consider it a date with an intruder.

But she did nothing of the kind. When I told her who Christina was, and a lifelong friend of Sandy Straus, she lit up like one of those seasonal trees covered with tiny lights for one of the big winter holidays. Easter was in the spring—so the other one. When she learned they had Sandy in common, rather than be jealous, suspicious or angry, Alice embraced Christina like a lost beloved sister and they hit the home run immediately and just as quickly I became superfluous. I realized my only function was to pay the bill—or I could have slipped out of there without being missed.

Both girls (or women if you're semantically sensitive) kept in touch with me, sending mail to my dummy mailbox in the door of my dummy office—and calling me from time to time. Oh, and I was finally starting to catch on to email so we utilized that wizardry. Getting them together turned out to be one of my better achievements. They kept me a chest of the local Muhlenheim news and before long moved in together to economize on rent.

It is from them that I learned what follows after I risked my life on an airplane to fly back home to the solar kingdom of Southern California.

For her part, Ginger went to work at the Straus department store in the jewelry department. After all, she could wear the standard issue breast plate sign with the name Straus on it. Diamonds in the criminal vernacular were sometimes known as ice; it was the perfect fit for the ice maiden.

She thrived on it and sold a record number of necklaces and bracelets and was the only department to compete with the Ness store up the street.

Ironies came by cheaply but one could not help but savor the fact that a record number of her jewel sales were to men. But the role of the woman in a man's fantasy did not require any personal participation.

When a man asked her out, she would flash a bittersweet smile, which quickly faded to a thoughtful, sad quasi-grimace, before she would say, "That's awfully sweet of you and I really appreciate it, but I hope you'll forgive me for still mourning my late husband. I know I should get over it and perhaps someday I will, but for now I have to be content in my loving thoughts of him. Let's just say when I become myself again, I would be privileged to go out with you. Might you give me a card or a phone number where I might reach you in that event?"

They were only too eager to oblige. Pushing forty and beyond, Ginger was still knockout gorgeous, and she had a drawer full of wishful suitors' cards and bits of paper with names and phone numbers. A tribute to her convincing theatrics was that some of the phone numbers appeared without names—as though they and they alone had impressed the pretty jewelry clerk to the point of asking for a phone number.

The news of Ginger Kulp at his competitor's jewelry counter bemused Manny Ness. His own jewelry clerk had forty-two years in the saddle. Her picture was near the top of his yearly full-page newspaper ad featuring all his employees by years of service—sixty-one being the prize winner (Effrim Schwartz of the custodial staff). Manny could easily have put these high number workers (he called them not employees, but co-workers—less feudal I suppose) out to pasture, but it was a point of pride to Manny that he didn't lay off anyone who still wanted to work. A lot of people just up and die when they have no routine to go to.

Of course, with his jewelry clerk, Mildred Kuss, the ravages of time and country fried potatoes had taken their toll. She had a candle which she couldn't hold from Ginger Kulp Straus in the looks department. Manny could have hired a dozen raving beauties to compete with Ginger at Straus and Sons. He could have slashed his prices more severely but he let Straus and Sons have that territory. Chalk it to sentiment. Most of the fellows who went to Ginger's jewelry counter to buy necklaces, bracelets, rings, pins bought nothing else in the store. Ginger was, after all, only in the one department.

One morning after her daddy died, Ginger stole into the house while her mother was out and packed up her wedding dolls and took them straight away to the Catholic charities' gift shop where they became a hot item—the volunteer clerks being at no pains to conceal their origin.

Ginger had become a quasi-celebrity.

It would be gratifying for me to report that Ginger was working to get out of the house—inculcating a ploy to keep her mind active—a relief from her maudlin thoughts and the twinge of guilt that was bound to taint them.

If Dr. Kulp thought of writing a new will to include Ginger, he never got around to it. More likely since she was so beautiful, the doctor thought she could fend for herself.

(To hear her tell it, she tired of being called beautiful. Though how anyone could tire of that, I don't know. What else would she have liked to be known for—compassion, a warm, loving nature? Intelligence, wit? Those attributes took effort, an effort you didn't have to expend if you were as beautiful as Ginger. All she had to do was comb her hair and brush her teeth.)

So the death of her father, the venerable Dr. Chester Aloysius Kulp left her bereft—not so much emotionally as financially. The good doctor had no insurance. While no one talked about suicide, the insurance company would not have been so circumspect. It was as though he wanted to rub their noses in the brutal fact that all manna came not from heaven but from *him*. And now that there was no more him, there was no more manna, and heaven was also in doubt. In keeping with his religious passions—the narrowest, most restricting aspects—the doctor bequeathed another five million to his local Catholic church where his daughter, Ginger, had developed her ideas about love and marriage.

Timing being what it was, the doc's stocks had bottomed out, which after paying the tax gatherers, left a manageable but not excessive stipend for his beloved Priscilla. It was enough to see her through whatever travails might lie ahead without becoming a ward of the county, but far from being as she otherwise should have, the richest widow in the valley.

Did Priscilla suspect he might end his life? Did suspicion increase as the hours ticked by and he didn't come home? Did she simply think it was the best solution all around? She had become so weary of his self-centered rants; his thoughts, words and deeds she found demented.

Though I gave Priscilla the CD of Christina Wagner's correspondence with Sandy, she never opened it and decided not to share it with Ginger who could only, she thought, be hurt by it.

After a short mourning period—some thought it was *too* short—Priscilla got back in circulation. It was not an easy step, for all those forty some years she had devoted her being to the great doctor Kulp. She was there for him, at his beck and call, but over the years the becks and calls were less frequent.

Now, in her late sixties, she had to begin over. She began taking adult education courses ("very adult" she joked pleasantly), subjects she had always been curious about, but except for occasional cursory reading, she had no truck with them.

She had played some bridge with Dr. Kulp when he thought that socialization would aid his trade. But as he became more successful, the need to curry favor faded.

She was such an equitable and pleasing person. She had no trouble connecting with women of her creeping age. Men were another matter. Even at her age they seemed to be interested in one main thing and she had so little experience the thought of it spooked her.

But she was an indisputably attractive woman and as soon as those stray and straying men got it into their heads that the twenty and thirty year olds were not interested in taking on another parent, those who craved companionship began cruising for the obtainable.

Long story longer, she met a man at the bridge table (he wasn't a half bad bridge player). He was a sweet soul, pleasant, courtly with a passable sense of humor and he adored her.

He had a decent pension and told her his firm belief that two could live as cheaply as one (if you were each satisfied with half rations) and especially if they lived in her free and clear house in the country club estates. They could sell his house and even manage to belong to the club which had a nice senior single status for those whose breadwinners were out of the dough as a consequence of being out of this world.

But the biggest surprise of all was his attitude toward intimacy. He brought her along as though he taught the introductory course. At her age she was long past any fear of pregnancy, abortion or the wrath of her church. She lost all fear that the procedure was sinful or dirty. She actually enjoyed it.

So for the years left to her, her patience, forbearance and conscientious attention to duty as she saw it were rewarded. Proving, I suppose once again, that in matters of the heart one never knew when lightning would strike.

Other Critically Acclaimed
Gil Yates Private Investigator Novels
By Alistair Boyle

The Missing Link (1st in the series)
A desperate and ruthless father demands that Gil bring him his missing daughter. The game quickly turns deadly with each unburied secret, until Gil's own life hangs by a thread. The debut of the Gil Yates series. (Also available as an e-book.) "Inventive, quirky…charm oozes from his pages."
    —Publishers Weekly

The Con (2)
Gil Yates backs into the high-stakes art forgery world, bringing the danger, romance and humor that Boyle's fans love. "This book is an easy read and just quirky enough to hold the reader's interest."
    —Books of the Southwest

The Unlucky Seven (3)
Do seven people rule the world? Someone thinks so and is systematically sending bombs to kill each of these seven wealthy and influential men. Three are dead already by the time Yates arrives on the scene. "Another lighthearted and amusing romp…Yates' fantasy life is geared just right for mystery fans."
    —Publishers Weekly

Bluebeard's Last Stand (4)
Mega-priced, contingency private investigator Gil Yates' latest adventure combines a rich widow, a gold-digging boyfriend and a luxury cruise to New Zealand, with all the charm and humor Boyle's fans have come to expect. "Boyle's off-the-wall humor and unadorned, concise prose is refreshing…the book moves along swiftly as a good mystery should, and should satisfy those who enjoy Alfred Hitchcock or Ellery Queen anthologies."
    —ForeWord magazine

Ship Shapely (5)
A shapely all-female crew sails the Pacific with the salty skipper who ends up dead, an alleged accident. "Boyle offers a wonderfully comic, mixed metaphor-spouting hero who combines awkward charm with cunning instinct. Fun reading."
—*Booklist*

What Now, King Lear? (6)
An obscenely wealthy entrepreneur is murdered and the prime suspects are his three daughters—with the division of a billion dollars at stake. "Hilarious adventures. Gil, with his quirky sense of humor, tendency to mangle the English language, and innate intelligence, manages to finally unravel a mystery with a surprising solution."
—*Mystery Scene*

The Unholy Ghost (7)
An offensive movie mogul hires Yates to track down his wife and daughter, who are caught in the tentacles of the mysterious Techsci cult.
"A nicely worked plot and slick dialogue complement the characters in this offbeat P.I. novel."
-          —*Mystery Scene*

They Fall Hard (8)
Gil Yates, amateur P.I., tackles the twenty-five year old case of the mysterious death of a prize fighting world champion. "Boyle remains true to his peculiar form (think Carl Hiaasen in Southern California); in fact, the banter is so much fun one wishes Boyle would give Gil another 100 pages or so per outing."
—*Booklist*

Individuals: We encourage you to order any of these titles from your local bookseller, library, online, or contact us.
Collectors: Selected signed first editions available.
Bookstores and Libraries: Available through Baker & Taylor, Ingram, Brodart and other distributors.
Our ISBN prefixes are 1-888310 and 0-9627297
Reviewers/bookstores: Review/reading copies for any title available.
Please contact us to be added to our mailing list for upcoming books.
www.knollpublishers.com

ALLEN A. KNOLL, PUBLISHERS

Established 1989
We are a small press located in Santa Barbara, Ca,
specializing in books for intelligent people who read for fun.
Please visit our website at www.knollpublishers.com
for a complete catalog, scintillating sample chapters,
in depth interviews, and thought-provoking reading guides.
Call (800) 777-7623 or email bookinfo@knollpublishers.com to receive
a catalog and/or be kept informed of new releases.